FIGHTING HEARTS

A friends-to-lovers steamy sports romance

ANNABETH SARYU

ANNABETH SARYU
Heat. Heart. Happy Endings

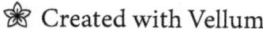

AUTHOR'S NOTE:

This book was written by an American author using an American-English dictionary and style guide. Spelling and grammar usage may vary from your local practice.

ACKNOWLEDGMENTS

Every debut author has a long list of people to thank, and I'm no exception.

To my writing peeps, Ellanor Kelsey, Cheryl Etchison and the guys at Red Horn who let us write all day.

Jan Whitson, KC Crouch, Terri Harlow and especially Jeanell Bolton for their support, sage advice, and sense of humor. The Austin RWA for their camaraderie, courage and generosity of spirit. Rock stars, every one of you.

Holly Atkinson at Evil Eye Editing, for working her magic on my manuscript. Syneca Featherstone at Original Syn the beautiful cover.

Last but not least, to my beloved Akshay and darling Cece, whose supporting roles lasted longer than they expected.

To Grandma Mary, the original family storyteller.
Thank you for keeping my dream alive.

CHAPTER ONE

"Goddamn it, what the hell was that?" Coach Rodgers rants from ringside.

Lucky Mike, my hotheaded sparring partner, lies pinned on the ground, locked in my brutal Americana. He writhes in pain and frustration as his wrist rotates hard into the mat while his elbow twists up and I torque his shoulder. To no one's surprise, Mike taps out.

"Let him up, Usalv," Rodgers barks at me.

I release Mike and slap his arm. He sits up and looks ringside.

Rodgers leans over the top rope and bounces up and down while his feet remain on the floor. It's a posture anyone he trains knows all too well.

Poor Mike.

I pace along the far side of the ring, pretending to catch my breath.

"Mike, you cannot go to his good side when he's ready like that." Rodgers' voice carries like a church bell during a funeral.

"His good side? Um, which side is his weak one again?" Mike's frustration fills the air like a balloon about to burst.

"Exactly. You're not going to catch him off guard and you'll eat shit every time."

Around the gym, uninitiated newbies shift their attention to the ring.

"Well, goddamn, Coach." Mike shakes out his sore arm. "With that reach of his I shouldn't fight him standing and now you tell me not to fight him on the ground? What the hell am I supposed to do?"

"Good question." Rodgers smiles and nods in approval.

"You got a good answer?" Mike fires back.

Rodgers' bouncing stops as his normal demeanor returns. "Kicks and quick strikes."

"Sure, Coach." Mike sounds calm but unconvinced.

"You've got to be more patient, Mike," Rodgers insists. "Usalv is a fine boxer and one hell of a wrestler. Do not let him get you on the ground."

Lucky Mike responds with a curt nod, then glances over at me. I walk over to him, extend my hand, and let Mike pull himself up.

"Don't worry, Mike," I try and assure him. "It's

coming along. Slowly. But it's going in the right direction."

"Tell that to Coach," Mike grumbles and casts his eyes ringside.

"Rodgers knows his shit. Never doubt it." My eyes meet Mike's until he nods. "But I'm the guy taking the hits. And it is harder to take you down."

"I wish Coach saw it that way."

At ringside, Rodgers checks his phone while another trainer talks to him. He's been my coach for seven years, and he's as proud of himself as he is of me.

"He does," I assure him.

"I doubt it."

"You've got some mad Muay Thai skills. Why do you think you're still one of my sparring partners?" I ask.

"Thanks, Usalv."

"Your ground game needs work. Hell, you know that. It's the reason I need to keep peeling your sorry ass off the mat." I smile but keep my voice sober.

"Bastard," he replies, returning my smile.

"Never doubt it."

Mike claps me on the shoulder while we wait for Rodgers to finish up his conversation.

He finally waves us over to him. "Good work today, guys."

"Thanks Coach," Mike and I reply together.

"We need to keep this up. With luck and a good trainer"—Rodgers flat palms his chest—"the Madman will have another title by year's end."

"Yeah, about that…" I lean over the ropes next to Rodgers and lower my voice. "I want to talk about the payday for these fights."

Rodgers stands straight up. "What do you want to know?"

"That all the perks are nailed down. That's where the real money is and I expect every penny of it."

"Sure, sure." Rodgers points to my hand. I rest it on the rope, and he turns it over to untape me. Money discussions can be difficult for Rodgers, an honest man who feels second guessed when it comes up. "Let's go over it again."

"I want to double check how much they're worth. And when they're payable."

Rodgers looks up at my unwavering gaze. Discussing money comes easy to me. Since my twelfth birthday, I've been paid by the job.

"I'm twenty-eight years old." My voice is a calm whisper. "I need to know how much is coming with me when it's time to check out."

Rodgers hand stills on my wrist. "I get it." He smiles. "But if you ask me, you haven't peaked yet."

"In this line of work, it's never too early for an exit plan."

He pats my tape-free wrist. "You want to do this now?"

The wall clock says six-thirty. I'm tired. I want dinner and a shower. "Can we do it tomorrow after training?"

"Not tomorrow." Rodgers shakes his head. "Got a new guy coming to check the place out."

"Another fighter?"

"An instructor. Need him to take over some of the regular classes."

"Which ones?" Rodgers had never mentioned a new hire before.

"Depends on the guy. Hope he'll do both the taekwondo and kick boxing."

"Slowing down in your old age?" I ask.

"Shit." His voice is tinged with disgust. "Nothing like that. I need to keep the lights on while we're on the road."

"Where's he from?"

"Chong Kim's. Earned his black belt at nine from a retired Korean Olympic coach in Indiana. Been training ever since. Seems like a pretty good guy."

"What's his name?"

"His name is Becker. Lou Becker."

"Never heard of him." I shake my head.

"He doesn't fight on the circuit. Which can be a good thing if he's the right guy."

"Guess you'll know soon enough."

"Yeah." Rodgers looks over at Lucky Mike, who's pacing a discrete distance away.

"I don't want to put you off." Rodgers shakes his

head. "Get your other glove off and then meet me in the office."

"Sounds good."

"Mike!" Rodgers yells. "The Muay Thai guy will be here tomorrow at four."

"Sure Coach," Mike replies.

"Remember, for tomorrow it's kicks and quick strikes. Kicks and quick strikes."

"Right," Mike replies.

"I'll see you upstairs, Usalv." Rodgers hops down off the ring and heads toward the main corridor. He stops at the stairs and turns back around. "Hey, Madman. Let's see how your new diet's working out. Weigh yourself before you come up."

"Sure, Coach." I roll my eyes at his retreating frame. "Shit."

Beside me, Mike snickers. I shoot him a death glare, which makes him laugh louder.

"I hate this fucking diet he's got me on," I grumble at Mike.

Mike extends his hand, and I start to unwind the tape. "What are you eating?" he asks.

"Bland, whole roasted chicken. Christ, I'm so hungry right now, even that sounds good."

"What else?"

"Not much really."

Mike shrugs. "It's lonely at the top."

"How the hell would you know?" I snap, then pull the end of his tape hard. It unspools like a ribbon and the rapid unwinding forces Mike's fingers together.

"Christ. Take it easy, Madman." Mike yanks the tape out of my hand. "What the hell's wrong with you?" He tries to turn it into a joke, but I know he's pissed. So am I.

Damn. Mike's not the fighter he should be, and the reasons are a source of jealousy and admiration. It makes for a tight friendship tinged with resentment.

"It's funny that I've got to lose weight?" My voice becomes quieter, my tone even. "It's my job, Mike. Sometimes I don't understand what the hell you're doing here."

Mike's eyebrows purse together. "The same thing you are."

"Me?" I grunt in disgust. "Oh hell no. You finished college. Your family's loaded. *Really* loaded, and they're praying you'll take over their business." I shake my head. "Our motivations couldn't be more different. Sometimes, it bites."

He takes the time to slowly roll the tape up. "I thought you wrestled in college."

"I did. For two years."

"What happened?"

I shrug. "Started doing smoker fights the summer of my sophomore year. Four months later, my record was six and zip, and I was ten grand richer. A manager signed me and when the school bell rang in September, I was long gone."

"So you left school for the money?"

"No. I left for the freedom." I was a teenage immigrant, sent to live with my uncle in Chicago during the Macedonian War. I earned my keep helping with his construction business after school.

"The freedom?" Mike's question intrudes on my memories.

"I worked in a family business. My uncle always took good care of me, but I never had any money of my own. The same in college. I got an athletic scholarship to wrestle, which is basically a job. But I never got any money or control over the outcome of my success. I was always working for someone else's goals. Until I started doing paid fights."

"What about your parents?"

"Fickle," I explain. "They didn't like me wrestling in high school, until they heard the word *scholarship*." In fact, I remember they were so happy that they decided I should stay in the States after the war ended. "Then when I quit school, they were pissed off about my fighting again."

"Really?" Mike's disbelief burns my ears. "But you've been a title holder in last three years and never ranked lower than fourth for the past five years. They've got to be okay with it now...don't they?"

"The fact that I never finished college somehow

creeps into every conversation between me and my father. Despite sending money home to support both my parents and sisters, who I love and miss very much." I feel the bitterness seethe. "We're not close."

There's an awkward pause, and Mike gestures for my still taped hand. I extend it palm up, and he begins untaping. "I'm sorry, Madman. I was only fucking around."

"It's my bad, Lucky Mike. But...don't waste your life, okay?"

"Waste my life? Because I want to be a fighter?"

"No. Because you want to *try* and be a fighter. Decide what you want to be and get it done. Cut out the booze, quit hitting the chicks, start doing five-mile evening runs instead. If you can't do that, then forget about it." I pause to take the rolled-up tape from him and stretch my free fingers.

"So we good, Madman?" Mike asks.

I shake my head and smile. His fighting careers sucks, but everything else in his life is great. My fighting career is solid, but it's the only thing that has ever gone right for me.

"We're good."

CHAPTER TWO

"Is this it?" Macy asks. "Louise!" she shouts from the driver's seat.

"Sorry." I look up from my phone's map app. "Yeah, turn here."

Macy brakes and swings wide, then turns onto the narrow driveway wedged between two parked cars. Snow mixed with broken concrete softens the impact of the potholes on her tiny Subaru as it inches its way up to the gym's entrance.

"Thanks for the ride." I peer out at the foul weather separating me from the industrial dark metal door. "Especially today."

"It's on my way, so no worries. Besides, you'd have froze your ass off in those." Macy looks down at my taekwondo pants.

"You're right about that." I push the passenger door open and its hinges groan as the wind catches it like a sail. A cold blast of sleet rips through me as I step onto the pavement. Shit.

"Anytime, Lou. And relax. You got this."

"I hope so. See you tonight?"

"Yeah." My roommate waves and then adjusts her rearview mirror.

I slam the door and shuffle across the snowy pavement, determined not to land on my ass.

My pace slows inside the main gym. It's a serious overwhelmingly masculine place, with an energetic intensity that's palpable. Devoid of laughter or pleasant chit chat, the occasional curt praise or profane outburst are the only things audible over the slap of canvas against flesh that emanates from every corner of the room.

Top-of-the-line cardio machines, punching bags, and weight lifting equipment line the long walls, while octagon-shaped cages occupy the far corners of the long rectangular room. The center of the gym provides plenty of room for mat work and two boxing rings.

Humid air mixes with polar blasts from a large open window. When a wave of cold air reaches me, my eyes close as it elicits a pleasant shudder. When I open them, a fiftyish looking man with steel gray hair and a wrestlers' barrel shaped body watches me with a puzzled expression. I recognize him from his website bio.

Terence Rodgers. The man I'm here to see.

Proficient in several fighting styles, he holds the rank of grandmaster in my own discipline of taekwondo. A former Olympic wrestler who taught combat skills to law enforcement and private security, Rodgers currently owns this gym, where he trains and manages professional fighters.

He's the Real Deal.

I raise my hand to wave at him and his head jerks back. What gives? His email said to meet him at six. The clock on the far wall says I'm right on time. We approach each other from opposite corners of the room and meet in the matted floor area centered in the long narrow gym.

"Grandmaster Rodgers?" I ask.

"That's right." He gives me a peculiar look. "Can I help you with something?"

"I'm Lou Becker," I announce and extend my hand. "You asked to meet at six tonight?"

Rodgers recoils from my outstretched hand and looks at me with a stunned expression.

"Lou Becker?" His astonished tone startles me. "*You're* Lou Becker?"

"Ye-es," I reply. "Lou or Louise. I answer to both." My smile goes unreturned and I withdraw my outstretched hand.

His jaw drops while he gives me an assessing look. At five-foot ten and some change, I'm slightly taller than him, so he tips his head up before his gaze descends. It skates down my body, and he shakes his head until his eyes reach my ankles. He fixates on my sparring shoes, which I put on in Macy's car. The long black stadium coat I'm wearing coat covers most of my uniform, but my pants are recognizable for what they are.

When he's finished, Rodgers looks quickly around the gym, and several men cast curious glances in our direction.

"I was expecting a man." His granite voice brims with disapproval.

"Really?" I try to check my cynicism, but can't tell if it's working. "Who told you I was man?"

"No one." He pauses and becomes super conscious of his words. "No one... I assumed that a fourth degree black belt named Lou would be a man."

"Oh." I give him a patient smile. "So you didn't bother to ask?"

"No," he admits.

"I see." I meet his eyes for several seconds without looking away.

"Damn," he finally speaks. "This could be a big problem, you know."

"Not for me." I speak with assurance.

He glances around. "Are you sure about that?" The corners of his mouth turn up, ever so slightly.

My gaze follows his around the gym. There's no

shortage of slick sculpted male muscle in here, and this gym has a different vibe than other places I've worked. But I need this job and a place to train.

"Yes." I try to project confidence.

Rodgers shakes his head and sighs. "Let's continue this conversation in private."

He gestures toward a staircase and we walk together silently. I take a seat on the step he indicates, while he remains standing and props his large elbow along the metal railing.

"This interview got off on the wrong foot." He leans over the rail and down toward me. "You come highly recommended, and it would be foolish for me to ignore that."

"Thank you." My instincts tell me the less I say, the better.

"I was told you're leaving Chong Kim's because of a schedule change?"

"Yes." Even now, the old *danjo* is a hike for me. With school, it's way too much.

Rodgers nods. "Tell me about your experience as an instructor."

"I've taught taekwondo, kick boxing, self-defense. Families, children. Junior competitors. On and off for about nine years."

"Excellent." Rodgers nods. "Do you compete yourself?"

"Only as needed to advance my rank and if time

permits." I hesitate, then continue, "I have a physically demanding day job that I need to keep."

His eyes leave my face and a pensive look settles over him. "Let's head up," he tells me.

I suppress a sigh of relief as we climb the stairs together. Two adjacent workout rooms lie on each side of the staircase, with a row of sturdy equipment lockers between their entrances. Murmurs of conversation flow out from the room nearest the staircase. Rodgers halts our progress at the top of the stairs and continues our conversation in the hall.

"Last month, I got rid of the tenant from hell." His voice is a mixture of relief and disgust. "I'm not doing that again, so I need to revamp my taekwondo and kickboxing programs. I'm losing too many students and without a tenant, I can't afford to anymore."

"Why do they leave and where do they go?" I ask.

"They leave because I train pro fighters, and not everyone can or even wants to train at that level." He snorts in disgust. "I have a good reputation. It brings in clients. But many don't stay, and I lose a lot to yoga studios and mega chains."

"I see." Now I understand why he hadn't changed his mind on the spot when he saw me. My old *danjo* had an after-school program that was at capacity five days a week. In the evenings at seven adult classes began. Taekwondo, self-defense, recreational kickboxing, even master classes for serious practitioners. Everyone was on a contract, which provided substantial cash flow.

"So you want me to teach the less competitive classes?" I'm relieved to find myself in familiar territory.

"Yes. Taekwondo and kickboxing, Thursday evenings and Saturday mornings. You're welcome to use the weights and bags. If you want to train in one of the master classes, let me know."

"Thanks."

"As I said in the email, I'd like to observe you teaching tonight's taekwondo class." Rodgers gestures toward the occupied room. "I see you're dressed for it. Ready?"

"Sure."

He waves me inside the mat room, where I walk alone to the front corner. My coat and backpack slide off together and land in a crumpled heap on the floor. Tightening my belt with its four golden notches, I move to the front of the room.

"Hi, everyone. My name is Louise and I'll be teaching this class tonight."

The students line up in rows across the room as they take their places on the mats. Relief settles over me as I recognize the familiar types that populate multi-level martial arts classes. That's a good thing, because right now I've never felt so out of place in a gym before.

Awkward teenage boys, looking for ways to deal with bullies besides getting their asses kicked. A bunch of young practical women, interested in learning self-defense but hoping to never apply it. A few urban professionals who know that nothing beats stress like striking a bag, pad, or person. There're even a few mid-lifers and a grannie or two, trying to keep fit without getting bored.

"Since you all have different reasons for being here, please break out into groups according to your goals. Introduce yourselves if you don't already know each other." For each goal, I point to different sections of the room. "Fitness, self-defense, competitive ambitions. If you have more than one goal, go to the group of your most important goal."

After the students find their groups, we begin the warm-up, calling out exercises while I wander through to learn names, skill levels, goals and to correct form when needed.

"Nice job everyone." My announcement ends the warm up. "Let's work on basic forms. I'll lead them up through the advanced forms."

Facing my reflection on the large mirrored wall, we begin with the first form. I love forms. They are almost like yoga. They appear deceptively simple at first and then your mind becomes engaged to get them right. Then, before you know it, that mind-body synthesis is doing wonders for your well-being. Thanks to my forms, I'm able to forget why I'm here and that Rodgers is watching me from the back of the room. At least for a little while.

"Nice job on the forms." A pleasant exhaustion permeates the room and I've broken out into a slight sweat. "Everyone should be practicing those at home. Let's use our last twenty minutes for contact drills. Get the equipment out and break up into goal groups again."

My announcement results in quiet murmurs. I glance back at Rodgers, who leans against the wall with an inscrutable expression. Well, if he doesn't hire me, it will be because of my teaching style rather than a poor imitation of someone else's. How the hell do you train people if you don't watch them move?

"Really?" a lanky young man with a yellow belt asks after raising his hands. "Even the lower belts?"

"What's your name?" I ask.

"Lucas."

"Lucas, taekwondo is a combat sport." I make my announcement for both Rodgers and the class. "You must spar with others or you won't improve."

When everyone is suited up in their protective pads, including myself, I pull the lanky young man to the front with me. Holding a large striking pad firmly away from my body I brace myself.

"Front snap kick. Right here. Go," I tell him.

"Are you sure?" he asks.

"*Go!*"

My voice startles him, and he throws an off-balance kick that glides past the bottom corner of the pad.

It takes another four tries before he's able to land his kick in the center. "Make sure you're balanced and close enough before you throw your kick, otherwise you'll get clocked with a counter attack."

The lanky kid nods and his demeanor changes. He goes from being scared and embarrassed to pissed off and determined all in the space of a minute.

"Keep it up. As many as you can in the next two minutes."

A surprised look crosses his face, and he ends up kicking the hell out the pad for a solid two minutes. At the end, he's exhausted with a satisfied smile on his face.

"Lucas, right?"

"Yes, ma'am." He smiles between breaths.

"Good work."

"Thank you, ma'am."

"Everyone, get with your partner. Same as Lucas, two minutes fast as you can with perfect form. Alternate legs and then switch."

The class ends on an energetic note. Rapid breathing and sweaty faces indicate most have had enough. I gather my things from the front corner of the room, where several students approach me.

"Zumba's got nothing on these speed drills," a middle age woman tells me as sweat rolls of her brow. "Will you be here next week?"

"It's Kate, right? I'm not sure yet. But if you like the speed drills, consider a kick boxing class."

"Thanks," she says and wanders off with a good looking middle-aged man.

"I'm Alison. I love the kicking drills," a young woman tells me. "They do a lot for balance. I never hit my target until I was aiming for someone. Hope you're here next week."

"Thanks, me too."

Rodgers stands at the back of the room, arms crossed around his barrel chest. Several people greet him as they leave. I feel him watching and waiting for me to be done so he can deliver his verdict.

He approaches me from the door and we meet in the middle of the mat room. Standing in front of him at my full height, he's forced to look up at me, but gives no indication he's uncomfortable doing so.

"Louise, you're obviously a good instructor. Very patient and knowledgeable. I'd like to offer you the job."

"Thank you, Grandmaster." I give him a relieved smile. "I would like that very much."

He smiles back and extends his hand to me. I reach out and shake it.

"Just Rodgers, please. I believe in respect. Formality, not so much."

He leads me out of the training room and as we reach the stairs, he turns to me and stops. "I find teaching mixed level classes very frustrating," he admits.

His confession catches me by surprise. Appearing to give him advice on the subject would be impolite, even if it seems like that's what he wants.

"Yes, it can be frustrating," I agree. "But that's because everyone's goals are different. Sometimes we aren't even sure what we want." I smile at him. "Mostly, I think we're all fighting our own demons."

"Are you fighting demons, Louise?"

"Every single day."

"Maybe that's why I've always enjoyed working with pros." Rodgers grunts and ushers me down the stairs. "They know what they want. The rest is easy."

"Makes sense," I reply.

"All right, Louise. See you back here, Saturday morning at nine?" he asks at the bottom of the stairs.

"Of course I'll be here," I assure him. "Thank you again."

"Do you know your way to the locker room?" he asks.

"Is it this way?" I turn and point toward the corridor where I entered.

"No," Rodgers corrects me. "It's the other way."

I turn to see where he's pointing as his arm swings down.

"Thanks." I take one final look around and then walk briskly down the corridor.

CHAPTER THREE

"**D**amn… While I hate like hell to say it, you're in the wrong locker room," a masculine voice with a faint accent declares.

"A-h-h!" My indrawn breath echoes off the tile into a wordless scream. Mortification sends me diving behind a nearby locker door, where I place as much distance as possible between that voice and my naked body.

"Easy, sweetheart." His deep voice conveys reassurance. "I don't bite. Not unless I'm asked."

"Yeah, I'll pass. Thanks." With my back pressed against the locker door, I peer around the side to look at him.

My hot rush of embarrassment turns to a hot, inconvenient rush of something else.

A Riace Warrior statue has come to life, and it's

standing at the far end of the lockers. His Bad Boys, slung low on lean muscular hips, encase an impressive pair of sculpted thighs. Each hand holds the end of a crumpled black T-shirt draped around his neck, while the shredded chest it adorns glistens with sweat.

"Sorry. It wasn't an offer." Concerned cobalt eyes meet mine around the edge of the locker door. "More like an assurance."

A scar extends through the arch of his jet-black eyebrow, a jagged white streak that runs the length of his almond-shaped eye. The contrast between the scar and deep cobalt color make him look more alert, more predatory.

"Lucky me." My twisted hip begins to ache against the locker door. As I shift to find a less painful stance, a substantial portion of my inner thigh peeks out from behind the locker.

"Hey, are you...?" He waves up and down at the awkward arch of my back and the bent leg.

"Um, yeah. Another minute and we'd have met in the shower."

"Oh Christ." His head snaps back. "You do know what kind of gym this is, right?"

"I am aware." My voice is filled with irritation as he retreats toward the entrance, granting me a glimpse of his powerful back. "Thanks."

"This could have been a lot worse, you know," he warns as his muscular form disappears from view.

"Please tell me you're joking." My gaze follows him before I snatch my clothes from the nearby bench.

"Joking?" Annoyance seeps out in a single word. "Look around and take a deep breath. How the hell could you mistake this for the woman's locker room?"

"Locker rooms get converted from one gender to another all the time. Besides, there weren't any guys in here, and that's usually the big giveaway." Of course, I clearly misunderstood Coach Rodgers—a fact I withhold from him.

"And the smell?" His voice booms past the lockers.

He does have a point. Locker room funk tends to give away the occupying gender. I inhale deeply and the odor of strong industrial cleaner burns my nostrils.

"This place reeks of Pine-Sol," I answer.

"Sure smells like the boys' room to me," he replies.

"What do you think they clean the ladies' room with? Lavender water?" I snap. "And yes, this is a fight gym. I wasn't expecting fresh cut flowers and free hairspray, okay?"

Between his potent presence and my predicament, it's difficult to focus. I want to get dressed but I can't find my underwear, and hiding behind the locker door doesn't make it easy.

I sort through my clothes, until only a pair of periwinkle sports panties remain in my hand. I slide them up my legs, but the sticky sheen of sweat on my skin makes it slow going. A badly needed shower is out of the question and a disgusted groan escapes from me.

"And what about the urinals?" he asks.

My fingers cease their tugging. "What urinals?"

When he doesn't answer, I turn toward him and see the back of a long sinewy arm pointing at a neat cluster sitting loud and proud by the shower entrance.

Shit. "I didn't see them."

"Clearly."

"Damn. How did this happen?" I wonder aloud, trying to remember where Rodgers had stood and pointed when he'd told me to go the other way.

"The locker rooms are diagonal from each other, on the opposite sides of the main gym." His words echo off the tile. "If you come in from the parking lot, you're by the women's. If you come in the front—"

"—you're by the men's. Damn." I thought Rodgers had pointed to the other side of the corridor, not the other side of the gym. "Well, thanks for the tip."

"You're welcome," he replies.

At first his remark strikes me as snide, but his tone remains calm and certain, as it has been throughout our conversation. Sometimes fighters can be over the top and in your face, but many elite ones possess a calm quiet confidence that can permeate a room.

They know their skill, their power, and confrontations don't rattle them. His certainty of presence—and monstrous physique—tells me a great deal about him.

"This is my fault. Obviously. And I'm sorry. You have no idea how sorry." Rodgers hadn't wanted to hire a female at all. What will he think about all this locker room commotion? Is it possible to be hired and canned on the same day?

"I'll bet," he replies.

"Listen, I know I'm in the wrong locker room, but would you mind leaving so that I can get dressed?" I try to sound calm and reasonable, but it's hard to tell if I've succeeded. "Please?"

He gives a short laugh. "Only stayed so this didn't happen again with someone else."

"Thank you."

"You're welcome," he replies. "And I'm Usalv."

"I'm Lou. Or Louise. Either one works."

"Sweet Lou?" he asks.

"I get that too. Sometimes." I start to relax a bit. "Mostly from men who have trouble calling me by a guy's name."

"Well, you sure as hell aren't a guy."

"Nope."

"Well. I am. And believe it or not, I'm a pretty good one, most days." His relaxed tone becomes serious. "In about two minutes, there's going to be about ten guys in here, and I won't vouch for any of them. You need to hurry."

"Oh my God, that's all I need. It will be weeks before I can show my face again. If that soon."

"I'll go stand by the door," he promises. "But the sooner you're out of here, the better for everyone." His feet scuff gently against the tile. A few seconds later, I hear wood slide across the tile floor as he kicks the door jamb away. A loud *whoosh* follows and the door slams shut.

Good Lord.

I collapse on the bench, panties halfway up my thighs and take a long deep breath. I gather myself together and give them a good yank up over my hips, wedgies be damned. I retrieve my sports bra from the heap on the locker floor and pack the girls in quickly.

"Are you done?" Usalv calls from the doorway.

"Almost," I reply.

Since no one was here, I'd taken the liberty of spreading out the entire contents of my bag along the bench. Nursing scrubs, make-up case and street clothes are all being shoved into my bag when I hear Usalv's voice.

"Hey, Drew, give us a minute," says Usalv.

"What's the problem, Madman?"

"No problem," he replies. "But...there's a woman in here. Give her a minute, eh guys?"

"A woman?" another voice bellows.

"Yeah." Usalv's reply is calm.

"Is she naked?" a third voice asks.

"No," Usalv tells him.

"Hey, are *you* naked?" the second voice asks.

"Fuck off," Usalv replies.

As the door slams shut, there's an eruption of male laughter mixed with curses in the hallway. Moments later, I reach the entrance, wearing my workout camisole and taekwondo pants. Along the way, I struggle to stuff items into my backpack.

Usalv stands with his back against the locker door. As I get closer to him, I see he's even more striking up close. At least six feet-four, with blue-black hair styled in a geometric undercut. Long and wavy on the top, short on the sides and back, fading to a close-trimmed beard that frames full lips and a strong square jaw. His nose is perfectly shaped except for a high bump on the bridge where it's been broken. I don't wonder how.

The backpack zipper is almost closed when a final good yank sends the contents of the front pocket spilling out onto the floor. I bend to retrieve my make-up case and keys, then look up to find Usalv standing above me, his hand extended.

"You're a black belt?" He holds my belt out in

front me, the four golden notches exposed on top of the coiled cotton belt.

"Actually, I'm a new instructor." I stand slowly and retrieve my belt from his outstretched hand. "Thank you."

His brows arch in surprise. "Rodgers hired...*you?*"

He's been pretty decent to me all things considered, but his comment makes me bristle. "Of course he did. After all, he's a very knowledgeable guy."

Usalv responds with an impassive look. I give him a patient smile and then reach for the door handle.

"Sweet Lou...wait." He reaches out to stop me and his hand touches mine for a split second. I feel a rush of electricity before he withdraws it.

"What is it?"

"When I came in and found you here...well... You weren't scared of me, were you?" He's so motionless, I wonder if he's holding his breath.

"Scared of you? That's strange question, Usalv."

"Yeah... You didn't scream, or curse, or accuse me of being a predator or a pervert."

"You've got a lot presence. It's hard not to notice." I shrug. "But no. The minute you backed away I wasn't scared. Only really...embarrassed."

"You shouldn't be," he replies.

"Yeah, sure."

"Well, okay maybe a little." He pauses. "But I

didn't see anything. Only lots of long, curly hair. On your head—I mean, hanging down your back." He flushes, then turns his gaze to my tangled sweaty hair. "I knew right away you weren't one of the guys."

"Why are you telling me this?" I ask.

"Because I don't want you to hold it against me."

"Against you? I wouldn't do that. That wouldn't be fair."

He smiles. "I hope you still feel that way when I see you again."

I can't help myself. I smile back.

"Hey, come on, hurry up in there!" an impatient voice calls from the corridor.

"Thank you, Usalv," I tell him, then reach for the door handle.

As I face the men huddled in the corridor, their conversations cease. When I step into the hall, the man nearest to me takes a half step back.

"Sorry, guys." My voice carries. "It was an honest, G-rated mistake. It will not happen again. Thanks for not being jerks about it."

Without another word, I walk down the corridor while the men move out of my path, and I refuse to glance back.

CHAPTER FOUR

"Tell me there's beer in the house." The front door slams and I hear Macy's bag hit the tile floor of the foyer. Tonight is Thursday, when we partake in our weekly slumfest of beer and tasty, gut-busting food.

"It's covered," I announce from our kitchen.

"You goddess." Her clogs clip-clop over to the living room table, where she drops a plastic takeout bag. "What did you get?"

"Dark chocolate stout." The nose-ring attired beer snob at the liquor store had dispensed quite a bit of advice on the subject, so I feel very accomplished tonight.

"Atwater or Sexual Chocolate?" she asks.

"What?" My beer prowess flags.

"The beer." She laughs. "I bet it's the Atwater."

"Probably. I'd remember, 'would you like to try some sexual chocolate?'"

"I hope so. Although with you—" Macy starts a familiar dig.

"—and what did you pick up from the deli?" I cut her off.

"A Sherm and a Schwartzy."

"Extra fries and pickles? Please say yes."

"Of course."

"Yay! I'll take the express train to hell. Give me the Schwartzy."

Macy pulls a takeout container from the bag and the smell of smoked beef brisket makes my stomach growl. I emerge from the kitchen and place the six pack on the table.

"Let's eat. I'm starving." Macy grabs a bottle from the cardboard holder and yanks the cap off with the opener on her keychain. "And I want one of these."

It's her last twelve-hour shift of the week, and my weekend started at seven thirty this morning. After I get a good day's sleep, I teach taekwondo and kickboxing then get home about the same time as Macy.

Tonight was my third time teaching classes, and it went well. Very well. In fact, tonight I stopped waiting for the axe to fall over my locker room disaster. Instead, Rodgers said hello, asked how the classes were going, and told me to check in with him as needed.

"Go ahead. I want to change out of my sweaty gym clothes."

My bedroom is the smaller of the two, but I don't mind. Macy and her husband Paul share the larger one when he's not deployed overseas. I toss my workout clothes on the daybed that doubles as a sofa, and grab a clean pair of leggings and Chicago Bulls sweatshirt out of my mission style dresser.

Dad had refinished it for me himself. He was the kind of man who never had time to do anything, because he had some project he needed to finish. But when I'd managed to get a partial academic scholarship to nursing school, he'd made the time.

This dresser means a lot to me. I run a long, loving finger over the smooth tiger wood finish before joining Macy.

"I've got one for you." Macy nods to an open bottle on the coffee table.

"Thanks." I dump my fries and brisket sandwich onto a plate from the kitchen and head toward my usual spot on the couch.

We'd met four years ago, one year after a big city ER job brought me to Chicago. The dumpy studio I'd rented made me miserable, the same way Macy felt about Paul's first deployment overseas. Macy wanted to keep her job and their nearby apartment, so she'd posted an ad for a roommate.

When we realized that we worked in the same ER but just hadn't met yet, the rest was history.

"How did it go tonight?" She's perched on her favorite chair, roast beef sandwich and fries spilled onto a stoneware plate resting in her lap. Her half empty beer sits by the Betty Boop clock on the end table.

"Better than I hoped, actually." I reach for my beer and take a long, curious gulp.

"Really? Why?"

"This is pretty good stuff." I raise the dark bottle to study it.

"Yes, it is," she compliments me. "Now answer the question."

"Well, at first the boss was kind of pissed that I was a woman. He didn't want to hire me because of it."

"What a load of shit," Macy replies.

We've been roommates for far longer than either of us planned, and in that time, we've become close friends. I can always count on Macy for an unvarnished opinion, just like anyone else in her close circle.

"Yeah, but he needs someone to teach classes, and he gave me a shot. So far so good."

"Still sounds like a real jerk. You should find another gym."

"That's not a good idea right now." The image of a living Greek statue enters my mind, but I force it away. Something tells me he got the guys to keep the whole debacle on the down low. I'm grateful and relieved, but puzzled as well. Why didn't he just sit back and enjoy the joke with the rest of them?

"Why the hell not?" Macy asks.

I hesitate, then take another long, slow gulp of stout. I'm not a beer drinker, but this stuff is pretty tasty. That's a good thing, because it's time to share my news with Macy.

"I was accepted to graduate nursing school for the spring term. Classes start in six weeks." Another slow gulp of beer flows down my throat while the news sinks in. "And this gym is close to the university."

"Congratulations. I guess." Surprise gives way to a mask of irritation on Macy's elf-like features. "When you didn't say anything earlier, I thought you either got cut or changed your mind."

I shake my head and there's a long, awkward pause.

"What program?" she asks after a short, painful eternity.

This chocolate stout gets tastier by the minute. "Nurse anesthetist."

"Holy shit, Louise." Macy glares at me. "What the hell's wrong with you? I thought you were happy in Trauma-ICU?"

"I am happy there." I'd transferred almost three years ago to gain the ICU experience required for this program. And because of Tim. "But if I want to go back to school, now's a good time. No debt. No kids."

Macy replies with a loud snort of disgust. "Have you lost your damn mind? I know you did well in undergrad, but that program is brutal."

"But for me, that's part of the appeal," I explain. "I'm a good trauma nurse who likes managing trauma cases. I'll be a good anesthetist. There's nothing crazy about that."

"Not at all," she replies in a sad voice. "Except that it won't make you happy."

Happy? "Macy, happiness requires optimism that I lack at the moment."

"Is that the way you're looking at this?" She leans forward in her chair, ready to argue. "Get over it. You dodged a bullet with Dr. Dumbass." Her voice is filled with familiar hostility.

"You were right." I raise my hands in a defensive gesture. "I wish I'd listened to you."

Macy had loathed Tim almost from the start and warned me not to trust him. But I just couldn't see it. When we crashed and I burned, Macy put up with my melancholy numbness for over a year. In the greater scheme of things, the amount of shit she's dishing out right now barely registers on the IOU-meter.

Her voice softens. "It's been over a year since you two broke up. It's well past time to get over him and move on."

I shake my head and give her a tired smile. "I'm over Tim. I have been for a while."

"Then what's the problem?"

I twist a thick strand of hair around my finger until my scalp tingles. "It's hard to explain. I don't like being alone. And dating sucks too." I shrug. "So I don't want to be alone, but I don't want to date. Does that make sense?"

"Um...not really..." she replies.

I sigh in exasperation. "It's okay, hon. I really don't expect you to understand. You and Paul are high school sweethearts who got married out of college." I twist my hair again. "But it doesn't work out that way for everyone."

"Fair enough." A tiny 'w' appears between her eyebrows. "But how will going to nursing school fix that?"

"It won't. That's not why I'm doing this."

"Then why are you doing it? You like trauma-ICU and you don't have to deal with that asshole at work anymore."

"Because I'm resigned. I need to focus on something that doesn't make me feel like a constant failure."

"But is that what you really want? Being married to your job, not being done with school until your thirties?" From the waist up, Macy's body syncs with the vigorous back and forth motion of her shaking head. "I thought you wanted kids."

Ouch. "I do. But I don't want to be a single mom, or go to a sperm bank and there's no one on the radar right now."

An image of a nearly naked Usalv flashes through my mind, but I force it away. After all, it's just a primal thing. It must be, because I've never seen a guy that looked so good without clothes on.

"Whew." Macy folds her arms. "Then I really don't understand why you're doing this. You do realize there are nuns who live less cloistered lives than you will be when school starts?"

"What can I say? We all deal with our shit in different ways. I work myself to the point of exhaustion. If nothing else, it leaves me with a sense of accomplishment."

"Let me tell you something." Her voice quiets, like it does when she discusses something deeply personal. "More work won't fix your relationship problems. It just makes you too overwhelmed to deal with them. I know, I've tried. It just adds tiredness to the loneliness and depression."

"When was this?" I ask. Macy's never told me this before.

"During Paul's first deployment." She pauses and shuts her eyes tightly. "I was on antidepressants for the first six months, but I didn't like the side effects. So I started taking more shifts, even extra jobs."

"I had no idea." Macy and Paul are both Jefferson Park natives who had met in kindergarten. They'd grown up in the city surrounded by a large circle of family and friends. With her support network, I would never have guessed she'd struggled so much.

"By the time you moved in, I had my shit together."

"What happened?"

"Paul came home. He was on leave and neither of us liked what I'd become. But while he was here, we ended up spending a lot of time with family and friends that I'd given up with all the extra work." She gives me a gentle smile. "That's what really helps. Spending every minute I can with family and friends. Not double shifts. Or second jobs...or school."

"Macy... I don't have those options. My family lives in Indiana. As much as I love them, I'm not going back. My life's here in Chicago now. I've got a great job, great friends, lots of things to keep me busy. But those distractions don't work anymore. I need a new one."

Macy's response is a sad shake of her head.

"It's okay. You and Paul got lucky. This is what life looks like for the rest of us."

"Lucky? You call this lucky?" She makes an open-handed gesture toward the apartment that's empty without Paul.

"No. This sucks." I mimic her gesture. "Like life does sometimes. But he's the guy you want to be with. You both do. And far from being a douche, he's a great guy."

"I know we'll be fine." She wipes a tear from her cheek. "It's you I'm worried about. You are a bright kind woman, worthy of all the love and happiness you crave. Right now. No self-improvement plan required."

"I haven't given up hope." I smile at her. "Just put it on the shelf for a while."

CHAPTER FIVE

Acid heat courses through my muscles from that last set of bench presses when I overhear two guys five minutes past high school work themselves up into a froth.

"Check that out," the guy on the Smith machine tells his spotter.

"Damn. Wouldn't mind tapping that." The spotter leans onto the metal frame and looks toward the main aisle.

"For sure," the first guy agrees.

Ah, the good old days, when the smell of perfume or a glimpse of lacy underwear could get you sprung. I shake off their comments and power through my reps, promising to check this goddess out between sets. But it's not a 9-1-1 for me. At seven thirty on a Saturday morning, my expectations aren't high.

"Fuck," the spotter complains, "she's coming this way."

Christ. I bang the barbell back on the rack with an annoyed clang. I snatch the white towel from my waistband, wipe the sweat away from face, head, and hands, then scope out the main aisle of the gym just as Sweet Lou struts into my field of vision.

"God*damn*," the first voice announces, echoing my own thoughts.

Looks like the hot mess from the locker room is running just plain hot today.

That curly caramel hair, no longer weighed down with sweat, rests in a messy bun on top of her head, except for loose wisps that fall from her neck and temples.

While her face is pretty enough, with a small nose and a sweet mouth and full lips, it's those round amber-colored eyes that catch my attention. They remind me of an exotic cat, luminous and alert. I find myself hoping like hell they aren't colored contact lenses.

"Look at those pins," the spotter gawks.

"Fuck. Boobs you can buy, but those..."

The dick-headed duo has a point. Those cropped pants emphasize every ripple of her toned legs, and that powder blue tank top doesn't hide her athletic shoulders and lithe arms. Though there's nothing bold about her clothes—that body aches to be watched.

"Say something," the first guy urges his friend.

For some reason, the thought of these guys giving her shit pisses me off. I stand from the bench with my back to the main aisle and take some weights from the nearby stacks.

"Careful with her," I warn them from the stacks by the Smith machine. "You don't want to mess with that."

"Yeah, why's that, Madman?" the spotter asks.

I sigh and look over my shoulder as she approaches. Since sophomore year in high school, females have noticed me. Lately though, it's gotten monotonous, although it's hard to explain why.

"Because she's way out of your league, kid," I reply.

He snorts with contempt. "Hey, Madman, sure you're not just trying to save that all up for yourself?"

My body shakes with laughter. The pair on this guy...

Even if I weren't a pro athlete, which amounts to a special brand of sexual crack for all types of women, these two don't worry me. Not. At. All. Sure, I'd try and get with Sweet Lou, but my size, strength, and libido come with issues of their own, and not every woman is up for it.

"Piss her off and she'll have you constantly doing a ball check." My teeth clench as I spit out the words. "Because on of top everything else, she really can kick your ass."

"That's bullshit," he replies.

"Now you're starting to piss *me* off. And you *really* don't wanna go there." I turn my back and restack the weights from the barbell.

Louise reaches the cluster of machines with a distant expression on her face. Thank God she's not paying attention to us. Damned if I want to get accused of trash talking her.

"Morning, gorgeous," the second guy standing on the other side of the machine calls out.

Jesus fucking Christ.

Sweet Lou doesn't answer and I wonder if she realizes he's talking to her. She's nearly past us when all-balls-and-no-sense tries again.

"Nice, bitch!" he yells.

Sweet Lou stops as if someone threw cold water on her face. She looks up and glares at him with a raised caramel eyebrow.

"Are you talking to me?" She doesn't shout, but her tone speaks volumes. Around the free weight area, people look up and take notice of the exchange.

"Looking tight there. That's all." Ballsy sounds confident, but he leans in behind the machine and crosses his legs. Yeah, he might want to keep those closed.

"So now what?" Her hands rest on her hips. "Am

I supposed to leap in your lap and celebrate the fact you think I'm stacked?"

The son-of-a-bitch grins at her. "Sure."

"Hmm, so you want just go for it, right now? Here, in front of everyone trying to train?" Sweet Lou lowers her head and glares at him through her long dark eyelashes. "After all, there's not a snow-ball's chance in hell anyone would believe it otherwise."

Faint laughter erupts among the free weights.

"Hey, easy babe—"

"Easy babe?" she cuts him off in a hostile voice. "That's the last thing I am. Don't confuse me with your right hand again."

A collective "oohh" breaks out among a few of the bystanders. Sweet Lou looks around the stacks and silences them with her death stare.

"Anything else?" she asks him.

"Nope. We're good." Ballsy doesn't sound so sprung anymore.

"That's what you think. And my name's not *bitch*. Don't ever call me that again."

A shit-eating grin spreads across my face, and I do my best to appear preoccupied with restacking the weights.

"Hey, Madman. You sure as hell were right about her. She's a-l-l yours," the loser on the bench calls out to me as I pass the Smith machine.

My eyes shift from them to Sweet Lou, who

spins back around just in time to see us together by the stacks. Shit. Now I'm busted for something I didn't do. Our eyes meet and she stares for a moment before a look a recognition flashes across her face.

Fuck.

"Are you part of this loser-fest?" she asks.

"Hell no," I tell her.

"Mmmhmm," she replies. "Madman? That's you?"

"That's me. But it's not what you think."

She watches me for a long time then shakes her head. "Good to know." Then Sweet Lou turns and walks away. Just like that.

A wave of heat rushes to the back of my neck and my glare hones in on Dumb and Dumber. "Hey, assholes. The only thing getting a workout around here today are your big mouths. Don't ever drag me into your bullshit again."

The stunned looks on their faces tell me they get it.

I finish off a few sets of shoulder presses to give us both a chance to calm down before heading upstairs to the mat room to find her.

"Louise, can I talk to you a minute? Please?" Her brutal warm up made me reluctant to interrupt, but somewhere in the last few minutes, I started to feel like a voyeur.

"Now's not really a good time," Louise's speaks

with closed eyes. She's balanced entirely on her forearms, with those impossibly long legs arched gracefully over her back. The soles of her feet rest on either side of that messy nest of curly hair as she takes a controlled breath.

"Take your time, I'll wait."

Shit. I hope that didn't sound as sleazy as it felt. Not only is that body fit, she's more flexible than a rubber band.

These rooms used to be for CrossFit and most people don't realize it's okay to use them when there aren't classes going on. Sweet Lou shouldn't feel entitled to privacy, but damn if she's doesn't make me feel like I'm watching something naughty and nasty.

There's an awkward pause as she holds her position. Heat rushes up the back of my neck while I count ceiling tiles. Then her feet slam to the ground and she stands to face me.

"My classes start at nine. I need to hurry and finish my workout." She turns her back and walks away from me.

"Didn't know you taught on Saturdays." I remain by the door, watching as she strides toward the far wall.

"Surprise." Her sarcasm sounds almost cheerful.

Impatience makes me groan and follow behind her. "Louise, you're a little pissed off about downstairs. I get that."

She tilts her head and looks at me. "A little? Is that what I am?"

"Those guys were assholes and I didn't have anything to do with it." I gesture toward the ceiling in frustration. "That's all I've got to say."

Louise studies my face. "What were you right about?" Her voice is a fluid mix of caution and curiosity.

"What?"

"That douche downstairs said you were right about me." Louise's hand flies to her hip. "What were you right about?"

"That they should leave you the hell alone," I reply.

"Truth?" Her voice sounds skeptical.

"Yeah." I give her an intense, no bullshit look. "Truth."

"Thanks." She's got a pretty smile when she uses it.

Louise turns toward the human dummy stored in the corner and tilts it onto its base. Quietly, I walk up and lift the dummy by the chin out of her grasp.

"Where do you want this?"

She's ready to protest, but I'm stronger and taller, and it's halfway across the room before she can come up with some clever objection.

"Center right please," she answers.

I push it into position and the base rocks to the

floor with a dull thud. When I turn around she's watching me.

"Thank you again," she tells me.

"You're welcome. Again."

"Yeah, about that...thing in the locker room." She glances around the room and approaches me. Or rather, the human dummy. "I appreciate what you did for me. With the other guys and all."

"Forget it. It was a simple mistake that could happen to anyone." Although I'm glad that no one else got to spend time with naked Louise.

An uncomfortable silence settles between us, then Louise twists the dummy by the shoulders, trying to place it at some imaginary perfect angle. After it's in place, she gives it a few kicks to the lower torso, then stops again to speak.

"When those guys were trash talking me and they said you were right..." Her voice trails off as she pauses to turn the dummy's back to me. "Well, I thought you were talking about something in the locker room. When we met the first time."

"Oh hell, not this again." While the view was hard to forget, I knew it would come back to bite me in the ass. "You've got to stop holding that against me. Forget the whole thing. Please."

"Against you?" Her brow furrows, marring her features with a worried look. I don't like it. "But I'm not. It's my screw up and everyone knows it."

I reach back and impulsively start to pull the

short hairs at my crown. "Who cares who's to blame? I got to see more than you wanted me to see. Or anyone else here, for that matter. And you're upset about it. But now it's time for you to get over it."

She moves in front of the dummy so it's between us, and talks to me over its shoulder.

"I'll try. And I am over it now. Mostly. I just keep wondering when the other shoe will drop." Louise adjusts the dummy's shoulder so she can see me better.

"Other shoe?" I move to stand in between her and the dummy. "What the hell are you talking about?"

She snatches a strand of hair hanging from her temple and twists it tightly. "Rodgers. He was in a bind or he wouldn't have hired me. He was afraid I'd be disruptive. If he finds out—"

"He won't. Trust me."

"Well, maybe not from you, but one of the other guys might—"

"Louise." I put my hands on her shoulders. "Relax. He's not going to hear about it." My eyes lock onto hers. "I got this. Trust me."

"You...got this?" Her voice is hopeful.

"Yeah." I smile.

It's true. After she left, all the usual locker room talk started. I told the guys they could give me all the shit they wanted over it, but Rodgers better not give me any, because not a goddamned thing happened.

Then what the hell took so long? They'd wanted to know.

How the hell should I know why it takes a woman so long to get ready? One of the great mysteries of the universe, I'd told them. *Hell, she had her girl stuff scattered everywhere, and it all had to go back exactly in those sacred purses and packs they carry. What the fuck is all that, anyway? It's a major pain in the ass, that's what.*

I got a hell of a laugh out of it and that was that.

"What a relief." She lets out a deep breath and I feel the tension leave her shoulders. "I work nights and this fits my schedule."

"Nights?" That surprises me. "Are you a stripper or something?"

Just like that, the look on her face goes from grateful to hostile.

"A stripper?" She steps out from under my hands. "What the hell makes you think that?"

Fuck. Am I in trouble here?

"No reason really." I clear my throat. "Just thought of a job that a gorgeous, super fit woman would have at night." My voice stays calm.

"You've got to be kidding me." She turns and squares her body in front of the dummy. "That's the first thing you thought of? Really?"

"Well, you've sure as hell got the body for it." I gesture up and down the length of her frame.

She gives a loud screechy groan as she strikes the dummy with an axe kick to the side of its head that nearly topples it.

"Okay, my mistake. But I make a good living from my body, so you can't blame me for going there."

Louise loses focus on the dummy. She turns to me, her sexy mouth formed in a perfect oval that takes me places I shouldn't go right now. She responds to my nervous smile by resuming her assault on the dummy.

This isn't going very well.

So I stand there and watch her beat the hell out the dummy for the next few minutes, counting all the ways she can hurt a man. Ouch.

"I'm not a stripper." Her quiet voice is calm, her breathing heavy and rapid when she speaks. "I'm a trauma nurse."

And I'm screwed.

"Listen, I got it wrong. Sorry." What the hell else can I say?

"What happened downstairs put me in a bad mood." She gives me a genuine smile. "But you have been nice to me. Can we just forget the whole thing?"

"Sure. I'd like that too." A heated rush of smug satisfaction surges through me. Females like me.

"Good. Because I'd like to ask you a question, if you don't mind?"

"Go for it." I'll be honest—I'm expecting her to ask me out. Because damn it, I have been nice to her and when all is said and done, women find me attractive.

"It's about your accent," she tells me.

I pause for second, certain I've misunderstood.

"My *accent?*"

"Yes." She nods. "I noticed it in the locker room, and just now when you asked me if I was a stripper. I can't place it." Her head shakes. "Where are you from?"

What the hell? I moved to Chicago as a teen. My accent is long gone. Except maybe when I'm drunk or angry or nervous or...

Oh, fuck.

"It's Macedonian," I hear myself answer. Shit, has anyone else noticed that I talk different around her?

"Where's that?" she asks.

"The Balkans," I reply.

She gives me a satisfied nod. "How long have you lived here?"

"Since I was a kid. Why? You got a problem with guys who have accents?"

"Not at all." She laughs. "I'm just trying to understand you better."

"Is it really that difficult to understand me?" This can't be happening.

"Sometimes," she admits. "It's not so much your words as it is what you're trying to say."

"I don't understand," I tell her.

"Don't worry about it. It's my fault," she tells me before a quick glance at the clock. "If you don't mind, I'd like to finish my workout. There's not much time before classes start." She stands with her arms crossed low on her torso, waiting for me to leave.

Whoa.

Did I just get turned into a nice guy who talks funny and doesn't make much sense, so now she'd like me to leave her the fuck alone?

Hell no.

"Actually, you've got quite a bit of time." I nod at the clock. "And I've got an idea. Stay right here."

"What?" she asks.

"I'll be back in a few minutes," I promise. "Don't go anywhere."

I'm out the door and headed for the equipment closet before she can object.

CHAPTER SIX

"Louise," Usalv calls from the doorway of the mat room.

His voice brings a flush of heat to my nape, like it had the first time I heard it.

Damn, I wish that would stop.

"I'm almost done, Usalv." I took a job here for the free gym time and extra income. The free gym part is an epic fail.

"Take a break from that," he insists. "You need a real target."

"A what?" I turn around to face the door and come to a sudden stop.

I gasp in surprise as Usalv enters the mat room wearing full protective gear from head to toe, complete with extended focus mitts. He stops in front me and I look up at his massive well-padded frame.

"Take a break from that," he repeats. "Come on. You and me."

"Um...what are you doing?" He's got my full attention. Although I'm not a small woman by anyone's standards, he makes me feel pint-sized.

"I thought since you were new, you might not know anyone to spar with." He shrugs, then folds his arms." I thought I could help you out with that."

"You look like the Michelin Man," I tell him after an awkward pause.

"Thanks," he replies as if I've given him a sincere compliment. "But you can't really blame me, though. Given what I have in mind."

"Sparring?" A mix of worry and excitement wash over me. "With you?"

"Don't worry, Sweet Lou." His voice ripples with throaty laughter. "You'll be fine."

"Wait a minute... *I'll* be fine? I take it you see yourself as the more skilled participant in this scenario?"

His eyebrows arch upward and he shoots me an assessing look, which makes me wonder if we're still talking about combat sports.

"Well, yeah," he admits in an isn't-that-obvious-tone.

Many reputable fight gyms have beginners start out sparring with experienced fighters, the rationale being that they can defend themselves without being hurt or losing their tempers, which spares the newbies a potentially serious beat down.

I'm new to this gym but far from being an inexperienced fighter. And Usalv knows that, which makes his assumption a disappointment.

"Thanks, but I don't think that's a good idea." I turn back around and focus my irritation on the human dummy, and mentally will Usalv to leave.

"Louise," he calls in a calm tone that's become too familiar. "I would never hurt you."

"Hurt me?" I turn around, startled to find him inches from me. "What if I hurt you?"

He laughs aloud. "No offense, but I do this for a living. If you hurt me, I'll deserve it."

"You fight for a living?" That doesn't surprise me. "What kind of fighting?"

He shoots me a puzzled smile and shakes his head. "MMA."

Mixed martial arts. Hearing him say it out loud, it doesn't surprise me at all. The man looks completely dangerous, and every encounter with him makes my heart race and sends a hot rush of blood to my temples.

Like now.

"Our fighting styles aren't compatible," I tell him.

It's the truth. Of all the martial arts styles, taekwondo is considered the least useful for MMA fighters. While strikes to the face and overpowering an opponent on the ground are key components of MMA matches, taekwondo relies on kicks, which are of limited use in a ground fight. Besides, hand strikes to the face and head are hardly used in taekwondo matches, even in the Olympics.

"You could just drill," he offers. "I'm not going to fight you, which is why I'm padded up. Something I normally don't do. And I have worked with taekwondo guys before."

"You mean you've worked with guys who've studied taekwondo and incorporated it into other fighting styles for MMA. I need to warn you, I'm a purist who's never been in a street brawl or a non-refereed fight."

That's not entirely true, but I don't think ninth grade girls count.

"Fair enough, I've been warned." Usalv raises his padded hands. "So you want to do this, or what?" His question contains an easy but pointed challenge.

"You know I can't reciprocate," I tell him. "A guy your size would put me across the room if I just stood there like a padded target."

"No problem." He's confident, assured.

"Are you sure?" It would be nice. I haven't sparred with anyone in weeks.

"Positive."

"Okay then." I smile at him. "Let's give it a try."

Usalv nods and walks over to the front of the room, where the mats run parallel to the long, mirrored walls. Worry creeps over me as I approach him.

"How tall are you?" I ask. "It's hard to tell with all that gear on and I want to gauge my kicks."

"Six foot-five." His voice is calm, certain and unapologetic.

Unlike most men, he's not exaggerating. I tilt my head upward to look at him, something I rarely need to do. I don't encounter many taller men, never mind ones that tower over me. In other circumstances, that would be nice.

"And how much do you weigh, Usalv?" Wearing heavy pads make it impossible to guess.

"Right now, about two fifty-five."

Wow. And from my memories of him shirtless in the locker room, most of it is muscle. "You're pretty solid, aren't you?"

"I sure the hell hope so." He pauses. "What about you? And don't get pissed at me for asking. I never fight women, so I'd like to know what I'm dealing with, too."

"I'm not pissed." Fair's fair. After all I'm bigger than most women—a fact that's hard to hide.

"Good. And please don't lie. Because you've got nothing you need to lie about."

"Thanks. I'm five-ten, one fifty-five." It's an odd thing to discuss with a man, but nice to be honest about it.

He gives me a nod just before his demeanor

changes. Now he reminds me of a feral cat in that split second between spotting its prey and pursuing it.

"I'd like to start with hand strikes, go to hand and kick combos, then end with kicks. Okay?" Even though I'll be the one attacking, the feeling that this real-life warrior has the advantage is unshakeable.

He acknowledges me with a single nod, and my hands touch his focus mitts before he pushes them away.

I'm timid at first, so I start with basic hand strikes that are met with solid resistance. My God, he's strong. He braces himself but his hands don't move when I strike them. It's a little intense to hit someone with so much physical strength, even when you know they won't hit you back.

As we progress, I start to throw more kicks at his legs then move on to his torso as I inch my way up his gigantic frame. Usalv starts to push back on my contact, which forces me to work on my balance. I respond with quicker strikes.

Through the face pads of his helmet, sweat starts to bead across his forehead, and I suppress a smile. Two MMA style fighters would be on the ground by now. I give him lots of credit, using his arms this aerobically must be unusual for him.

But no one can say he wasn't warned.

"You okay?" My voice is breathless.

"I'm good," he replies.

Shit. His breathing sounds almost normal and his resistance is still solid. His strength and skill make him a wonderful partner, and as my feelings change from cautious to confident, my strikes become more complex.

Until a single mistake changes everything.

Usalv misreads my high round kick. An MMA fighter expects hand strikes to the face rather than kicks, especially a man that size. He's tall, but so am I, and my heel heads straight for his jaw. When I realize his block is too low, I check my kick.

Too late.

Usalv's natural fight instincts take over. He steps toward me and blocks my leg with a solid muscular forearm, which smashes into the side of my quick-moving knee. He grabs my extended leg and takes me to the ground like any well-trained wrestler. My back hits the mat. Hard.

Ow. Damn, that hurt.

I'm on autopilot and try to roll, but he's got my leg in an unbreakable hold. I grab his right shoulder, and try to steer his two hundred fifty pound frame away from my face and throat as our momentum thrusts him toward me.

I'm in big trouble.

I gasp in anticipation of our collision. Somehow he manages not to land on me, and the side of his right hip slams into the mat with a loud thud. Usalv grunts at the impact before his shoulder pivots out of my grasp. But he retains hold of my left leg, the knee firmly pinned against his hip. I scramble to stand on my other leg, but his hand snakes out, trapping my ankle in his huge hand.

A primal panic swells inside me. With my legs restrained, I hurl my open palm at his face, but he turns and braces for it. The gesture checks my visceral fears and the strike aimed at his chin lands beside his ear on the mat instead.

Usalv gives a large sigh of relief, but I'm panting from a mixture of exertion and something else. My breathing normalizes slowly, then comes to sudden stop when I realize I'm sitting spread eagle.

On his cup.

Neither of us move. My inner thigh, resting low and motionless on his muscular abdomen, tells me he's not breathing either. Perversely, I wonder how long he can hold it. My eyes dart from his eyes to his chest, waiting for it to move again. Usalv's fingers straighten, releasing their grip with a long slow breath.

"Your move, Louise." His cobalt eyes radiate heat.

My heavy breathing renders me speechless, thank God, because my natural tendency to joke this off would result in further disaster. Common sense screams at me to leap off with all due speed, but I can't. My shocked body can't endure anymore heat or friction.

Instead, I nod and remain silent during my slow, tortuous dismount. As I lay next to him in a silent heap on the floor, a flood of emotions overcome me. Anger, embarrassment, and something that remains unnamed.

"You okay?" he asks.

"I think so." My eyes skate down his muscular body, watching his chest rise and fall in a slow rhythm. No fatigue there. Wow.

I prop myself up on my elbows next to him. My own breath resumes its normal rhythm, and a bead of sweat rolls down my forehead between the bridge of my nose and eye.

"That was a mistake." I wipe the sweat away with the edge of my hand.

"Yeah." Usalv stares at the ceiling. "I didn't think you'd be that good."

"Gee, thanks," I reply.

"Well, your hand strikes really are underwhelming. I got a little too laid back, too early." He reflects out loud in a distant voice. "But Christ, those kicks…"

"Hello?" I sigh in frustration. "Like I said before, our fighting styles are different. That's why I was worried."

"You panicked," he accuses. "That never helps."

"I panicked?" I bolt upright, rising with my temper. "Before or after I almost broke your jaw?"

He sits up and brings his face inches from mine. "Were you really going to bitch slap me?"

My heart races at his closeness, but I chalk it up to fury. "Did you really try to dislocate my knee?"

He winces. "I dislocated your knee?"

Troubled cobalt eyes dart to my leg. His large hand touches my knee, gingerly feeling the area around the joint. My skin burns where he touches and I roll away from him.

"Jesus, it hurts that much?"

"Give me a minute." I go into nurse mode, and assess my knee. It's perfectly positioned, and there's no swelling. Curious, I lift my leg into the air and bend it before recoiling in pain. As I do, Usalv leans over me to watch the joint work.

"My inner thigh hurts like a bitch, but the knee's okay." I'm both impressed and irritated that he incapacitated me without inflicting serious injury. The man knows his business.

"Try to walk it off." Usalv rises and extends his right hand down to me. "Let me help."

I want to tell him to shove it, but getting up without help isn't happening anytime soon. Reluctantly, I take his hand, and he hauls me to my feet in a powerful fluid motion.

"Put your arm around me." He coils his arm around my waist.

My shoulder tucks under his arm while the side of my body presses against him. I dig my fingers into his hip and he presses me into his side to support more of my weight.

As he steps forward, I put weight onto my hurt leg. His grip tightens on me and the scent of heat mixed with bergamot rises from his skin. Despite the pain, his closeness distracts me.

"You good?" His deep voice rasps by my ear.

"Yeah." I force myself to focus. "Keep going."

I move forward, but my hurried attempt makes my leg buckle from too much weight. Usalv swings his free arm out to break my fall. He grips me underneath my arm and touches the side of my breast, while my other arm remains hooked under his shoulder.

"Take it easy, Lou. It'll come." He removes his hand from near my breast.

I lean against him. "Damn it," I complain.

We take another dozen steps together before my leg takes the full weight. He continues to hold me, and I'm in no hurry to let go. To fill the awkward silence, I give my curiosity free rein.

"Have you been a pro fighter for very long?" I ask.

"Yeah." He's focused on my hurt leg.

I take a few more steps. "Are you ranked?"

He rolls his eyes. "Yeah."

"I saw that." I wait for him to look at me. "Well… are you going to tell me what it is?"

"Does it matter?" His arm drops from around me.

"After this?" I point to my leg. "Yeah, it matters. Besides, I'm curious."

He steps away from me, and pinches the bridge of his nose. "If you don't know by now, I really doubt it."

"By now?" I rest a hand on my good hip. "Am I supposed to know something about you other than what you've told me?"

He shrugs. "Well, it is a small place and word does get around."

"Sorry, I missed the memo, but so far the only conversations anyone around here tries to have with me are about my girly equipment and where it does and doesn't belong."

"Point taken." His spits through gritted teeth.

"At least tell me your real name. The only thing I've heard anyone call you is Madman."

He sighs. "It's Markovski."

"Usalv Markovski? Madman Markovski? *That* Madman?"

He looks at the floor and nods.

Oh shit.

While I'm far from an MMA junkie, I enjoy an occasional fight night as much as the next girl. Although I've never watched him fight, Madman Markovski is often a topic of past fight results and future match ups.

"Well…I guess you are ranked."

"Yeah."

I stand there, oscillating between feeling like the village idiot and being betrayed. He just expected me to know? Well, maybe I should have, but that's beside the point. This isn't high school.

I start to pace despite the dull ache in my leg. "Why didn't you tell me?"

He shrugs. "You haven't said much about you either before today. Thought maybe that's how you wanted it."

"That's different. I don't expect people to know who I am."

He grins. "Don't worry, Sweet Lou. Every guy here knows who you are."

"What the hell should I do?" My voice fills with disgust. "Paint myself puke green like the locker room walls to blend in better?"

"It's not you. We're guys. In a fight gym. Most of the time, we're either talking about fighting or fucking." He explains in a sober voice.

"Really?" My forward motion screeches to a halt. "Just so I'm clear, which one are we discussing right now?"

A flash of fury crosses his features, but it passes in an instant. He stands there, his eyes assessing me, much the way Rodgers did the first time we met. But Rodgers' expression was one of disbelief and indecision. Usalv's expression remains inscrutable.

"You've got beautiful dangerous kicks. Seductive even." His words are dispassionate. "In most fights, you'll kick the other guy's ass. But if you run into someone who knows what they're doing, they can hurt you."

"You're not most fighters, Usalv. You're a world class one with a monster reach. Trying to outbox someone like you wouldn't go well either."

"I can teach you better hand strikes," he offers.

"Thanks, but no thanks. My class starts in twenty minutes. I need to ice my leg."

He nods. "You want one of the trainers to look at it?"

"No. It's a sparring accident. And I am a nurse. It hurts but it's not serious."

"I'm glad it's not.

"And I'm glad your jaw isn't broken, Madman."

CHAPTER SEVEN

I panicked.

After Louise blew me off, a wave of disbelief hit me like a Mack truck. Women do not dismiss me. It just doesn't happen, especially for being some stunted moronic clown who speaks with an accent.

Then and there I wanted her attention back, any way I could get it. She's into workouts and combat sports, my rock star super-powered area of expertise, so naturally an offer to help her train the way to make that happen.

What could go wrong?

In my haze of outraged egomania, it had never occurred to me that she would be any damn good.

But a few minutes in, she's tapping my A-game. And damn it, Louise was right. It's rare for me to defend my head against high kicks. Now her leg is fucked up and it's my fault. I need to make this up to her but damned if I know how.

I pull the band collar of my jacket up before leaning back against the wall next to the outside door of the gym. A quick check of my phone tells me it's been two hours since she went off in search of ice and to teach her class.

The door to the gym flies open and Sweet Lou emerges. She doesn't notice me—the angle of the open door hides me from view. But I sure notice her.

The wind kicks up and smacks my face with the rush of her scent, a mixture of sweat and sandalwood. Heat races to my groin and I blink hard to get a grip. Her rubber soled shoes crunch against the snow as she moves away.

She favors her kicking leg slightly as she walks, and guilt gnaws at the pit of my stomach. I step toward her and start to speak, but someone beats me to it.

"Be still my heart," a familiar voice says.

Fuck. Not him. Not now.

Louise stops as the tall, fit owner of that voice comes around the corner and into view.

"What's your problem?" she snaps.

I smile and hang back to watch the show. After the day Louise put in, she's sure to shut down Lucky Mike's hit-on parade.

"Louise?" Lucky Mike asks.

Her demeanor does a complete one-eighty. "Michael?"

Michael? Where the hell do they know each other from? Sunday school?

"Damn, gorgeous. It's been a while." Mike flirtatious voice that makes my skin crawl. "Can I get a hug?" he asks.

She looks at him a minute and hesitates.

"Come on, Louise," Mike pleads. "I promise not to cop a feel."

"Just so you know," she warns, "copping a feel comes with a swift kick to the balls."

Yeah, that's my girl. The thought of Lucky Mike on the business end of her kicks makes me smile.

"No worries here." Mike raises his arms in mock defense. "I know all about those lethal kicks."

He does? How?

She smiles and stretches her arms out. Mike steps toward her embrace, clinging to her body like Velcro. Resting his chin on her shoulder, he snatches a good look at her ass.

My blood starts to boil.

Wait until I get that son of a bitch in the ring. And what the fuck is her problem? How could she fall for his horny high school moves?

"Damn, it's good to see you. How the hell are you?" Mike asks.

Fuck dude, stop gushing already.

Sweet Lou pulls away from him. "Good. I'm good, Michael."

It pisses me off that she calls him *Michael*. It smacks of a prior history... Has he slept with Louise?

The thought sends an adrenaline spike through me.

It would give props to his nickname. Mike's known as 'Lucky' because of his prowess with women. I study their body language. Not only has Mike not let go of her arm after that fake-friendly hug, he's leaning in like an abandoned barn eager to keel over.

It makes me seethe.

"Macy was up this weekend," Mike says. "She told us you enrolled in school or some crazy shit like that?"

"Crazy is her word, not mine." Louise shrugs. "Yeah, it's true. I start next week."

"Well, good luck with that." He nods toward the gym without taking his eyes off her. "So what are you doing here?"

"I teach taekwondo and kickboxing," she replies.

Her stance looks pretty neutral toward him. Or is it a little too neutral?

"Nice," Mike replies.

Can't she tell he couldn't care less? Keep your eyes off her breasts, asshole.

"How about you?" she asks.

"Doing MMA," he swaggers. "Trying to go pro."

Trying...well that's the first above-board thing he's said so far.

"I heard something about that." She nods. "What happened? Commercial real estate not your thing?"

"I've got time for that later. MMA comes with a limited window."

His aggressive confidence leaves him. Good.

"That's true," she agrees. "Got a sponsor?"

"Not yet." Mike squirms.

"Got a coach?" Louise presses.

She's not one to be played.

"Terence Rodgers."

"He's a good guy. Very knowledgeable," she says.

"You think?"

Fucking poser. As if Rodgers' reputation is news to Mike.

"That's why I'm here," Louise replies.

Fuck. She's talking shop with Lucky Mike? Hello? Top ranked contender here. I can tell her all she wants to know and then some.

"Go Rodgers." Mike pumps his fist in the air.

"Speaking of going...." Louise nods toward the street and steps away from Mike.

About damn time.

Mike picks up on her cue. "Hey, are you headed to the EL?"

No. Fucking. Way.

I've been out here in the cold for almost an hour

so I could ask to walk her to the EL. Mike is not beating me to it.

They can't see me from where they are on the path that leads to the sidewalk, so I open the door and let it go. It slams back into its jamb with a loud clank. Sweet Lou's head jolts up and she looks back toward me as I make my way down to the street.

"Hey, Madman, how the hell are you?" Lucky Mike calls out, friendly and easy-going. Damn his playa charm.

"Hey, Mike," I reply while looking straight at Louise.

When our eyes meet, Louise shifts away from me, swinging her backpack off the shoulder it's on and switching hands. It hangs suspended just off the ground by the tiny top strap she grasps.

Shit.

My day job makes me an expert at body language. Facial expressions can tell a story, but too many people can fake them. Faking a stance is much harder. Louise just freed up her striking arm while using the backpack to shield the injured leg. I wonder if Sweet Lou even realizes what's she done, or if it's just second nature to her. Whatever the reason, it's hard not to feel like an absolute monster.

My gaze shifts over to Mike, whose eyes dart back and forth between me and Louise as he rapidly transmits silent guy code. *I'm working it, dude —move on.*

I don't budge.

"Oh, hey sorry." Mike glares at me over Louise's shoulder when it's obvious I won't go. "Madman, this is Louise. She lives with my cousin's wife. Louise this is—"

"We've met," I announce.

Mike looks stunned.

"You two know each other?" He glances at Louise for confirmation.

"We do," she admits.

Her admission feels like pulled teeth, involuntary and painful. Louise's eyes lock with mine, and both of us refuse to look away first. Well, I'm the wrong guy for that, because those beautiful amber eyes immobilize me. Hell, I could stare at them all damn day and never get tired.

"Hello, Louise," I say.

"Usalv," she replies.

"How were classes?"

A slight smile plays on her lips. "Today was a lot of do as I say, not as I do... Hope people weren't too let down."

"With you? Never," I promise.

"I hope not." She looks worried and her tension distresses me.

Beside us, Mike takes a step back and his hand releases Louise's elbow. I don't have much time before he diverts her attention back to him.

I hesitate a moment before pointing toward the ground. "How's your leg?"

"Painful." She reaches down and rubs her inner thigh gently. "I've got a huge bruise on my inner thigh. It felt a lot better after kickboxing, but for the first half it was super sore. Don't worry though." Her voice rings with reassurance. "It's much better now."

"What happened to your leg?" Mike interrupts, looking back and forth between us.

"She got hurt it in a sparring accident," I reply.

"Actually it was more like drilling," she corrects me.

"With who?" Mike looks down at her leg.

Louise starts to speak, but I cut her off. "With me."

"What?" Lucky Mike's easy demeanor disappears. "Louise you were sparring with...him?"

"Yeah." She gives Mike a regretful smile.

I don't think Louise wants to discuss this in front of Mike either. But who knows when we'll see each other again, and I couldn't let this to fester for weeks. We had to talk about it.

To hell with Mike. This is none of his fucking business.

"I wanted to apologize again. It was my fault, and I'm very, very sorry."

"You didn't strike me—you blocked with an unpadded elbow. It was an accident." She reaches out and touches her gloved fingertips to my fore-arm. "I'm sorry for not asking sooner, but how's your arm?"

"I'm fine." My God, she's adorable. I hadn't felt a thing.

Mike snorts with disbelief. "Louise, do you know who he is?"

She shrugs. "I do now."

"No way," Mike erupts. "You didn't tell her?" He glares at me like he's going to explode.

While Mike stands here ranting at me on the sidewalk, I try to stifle my guilt. I feel like a total shit about the whole thing, but Lou and I both know the truth. It was an accident.

"That's enough," Louise cuts him off. "Stop it, Michael."

I'm surprised to hear Louise speak.

"He did tell me he was a professional MMA fighter who had experience with taekwondo oppo-nents. The rest of it wouldn't have mattered." She turns to me. "It was an accident."

I nod in agreement. "It was. And I'm sorry."

"Are you fucking crazy?" Mike continues his rant. "How could you?"

"Mike, I owe her an apology. Not you."

"Forget it. Please," she asks.

I nod. "Are you heading to the EL?" I ask her.

"Yes she is," Mike cuts in. "I was about to take her there." He smiles down at her. "We haven't seen each other in ages, and it would be good to catch up."

That easy playa charm returns, cutting through the tension. For a moment, anyway.

"Sure. It would be nice to catch up a bit," Louise replies. "Thanks, Mike."

Mike's face wears a smug grin as he glances back toward me. "Madman, if you see Drew, could you tell him that I'm running late?"

Jerk.

"I'm headed out to get some lunch. You should text him."

Mike looks toward the door and hesitates for a minute. Drew will be pissed, and that's not a pretty sight.

"Thanks, Madman," he sounds irritated.

But my satisfaction is short lived. I watch Mike put his arm around Sweet Lou's shoulders and steer her toward the sidewalk. As they move away, Louise looks down where Mike's arm rests, her expression a mixture of resignation and annoyance. She shifts her backpack to the opposite shoulder and scrapes Mike's hand off with the strap.

She looks down to check her shoulder, then back at me. She gives me a quick apologetic smile then turns back to Mike and nods in response to something he says. I watch them walk down the street together absorbed in their conversation.

Lucky Mike Daughtry. Really, Louise?

His frat boy popularity, good looks, and big fat bank account allow him to avoid success while still attracting plenty of women. Of course, some women don't care how a man makes it, just that he has it.

Truth be told, my bank account is pretty impressive. But I don't want a woman who considers that my best quality. Sweet Lou seemed different. The black belt thing, the trauma nurse thing. Hell, she'd even stood up to Rodgers.

But Mike?

If Louise is the type who lets a guy like Mike insist on being in her life, then she's not the woman I thought she was.

And that's a fucking shame.

CHAPTER EIGHT

"Yabba dabba doo!" The thud of the apartment front door shutting fills me with a sense of relief. It's Wednesday morning and my last twelve-hour shift for the week is history.

"Do you want to get a drink tonight?" I call out to Macy. When she doesn't answer, I slide my Dansko clogs off and plant my backpack on the tile floor.

"Macy?" I call into the kitchen from the doorway. She's usually up by now making coffee.

Macy's not in here. She made the coffee today, but the pot is almost empty. A cough erupts from my now scratchy throat, and that's when I notice the thick cloud of cigarette smoke that hangs in the air, burning my eyes. Macy's a social smoker who's always trying to quit, but we agreed she wouldn't smoke inside.

Something's wrong.

"Macy?" A veil of dread washes over me.

This time, a loud anguished cry erupts from the living room and I race out toward it.

"Oh my God, what's wrong?" I ask.

In the living room, Macy sits with folded legs on her favorite chair. The fingers of one hand drum out a disjointed rhythm on the end table. The other hand holds a cigarette between her delicate fingers.

The foil lid from a yogurt cup rests askew on top of the Betty Boop clock. It serves as a makeshift ashtray that's filled with at least half a dozen butts, some of them still smoldering. Ash drops onto the table, displaced by the vibrations of Macy's tapping fingers.

"Paul's been hurt." Her voice sounds strained and hoarse from stress and cigarettes.

"Hurt?" I struggle to process the word. "He's an engineer that builds roads and bridges. How did he get hurt?"

"The corps of engineers decided to build a new hospital next to where the old one was bombed out." Her eyes are puffy from crying and smoke. "They were scouting the job site when a bomb they hadn't cleared went off."

Macy stops speaking, her words replaced with quiet sobs. I kneel in front of the chair, grasp her cigarette-free hand and rub it gently for several minutes.

"He wasn't close when it went off. Thank God. But he caught a lot of shrapnel on his right side."

I nod silently. "Sweet Christ."

Macy grinds her cigarette out on the makeshift ashtray, spilling a sticky stream of ash over Betty Boop's coy eyes.

"He was treated at Bagram Air Force Base before being taken to Landstuhl in Germany."

I take a deep breath, exhale slowly, and ask the question I already know the answer to. "How is he?"

She grabs her pack of Marlboro Lights from the table and smacks it against her knee, forcing the end of a cigarette out the top. "Not good."

"Yeah." I nod. "So what's the plan?"

"His estimated rehabilitation extends beyond his end of service."

"How long did he have?" I sit back on my knees in front of her. "Like another year?"

"Nine months."

"Damn. Still, that's a lot of rehab."

"They're giving him an early discharge." Macy pulls a cigarette out of the pack, folds her arms and tucks it beside her ribs.

"Then he'll do his therapy close to home." I try hard to sound positive. "That's a good thing."

Macy leans away from me to grab her lighter, which lies on the table next to an ash covered Betty

Boop. "For Paul. For me, maybe." She pauses. "Not so much for you."

"What?" I ask, confused.

"Sometime in the next month, Paul will be home." Macy's voice is tired, sad, and scratchy as she blinks back tears. "Louise… We need you to move out. The sooner, the better."

"Move out?" I repeat, confused and shocked.

"You know the drill. We're going to need to put a hospital bed in the living room, plus other medical equipment." I watch her throat as she swallows hard. "And I'll probably need a home health aide for the times I'm not here."

"But we've talked about this before." I stand up and move away from her. "You told me that you and Paul wanted a bigger place after he was discharged and that I could keep the apartment."

"Our plans are down the shitter right now." Macy lights her cigarette and takes two long drags. "We assumed Paul would be working when he got back, not doing physical therapy. On my salary alone, we can still afford this apartment."

I sit on the edge of the coffee table and stretch out my long legs, trying desperately to quell the acidic wave of nausea that threatens to overwhelm me.

"Things are a little tight at the moment. A big fat tuition payment was just due, and I won't get hospital reimbursement until after grades are

reported." I rock bath and forth to soothe my stomach. "And since we're three weeks in to the
semester, I'll get next to nothing back if I withdraw."

"We can give you your security deposit back.
And we owe you few months rent for breaking the
lease. If you need more to get settled, let us know.
We'll figure it out." Puffy dark circles protrude from
underneath her eyes.

"It's not just the money, Macy. I'm working two
jobs and I've got classes on Fridays, plus two eight
hour shifts to keep me full time for the month." My
knees start to bounce. "I don't have a lot of time to
look, and my crazy schedule hardly makes me the
ideal roommate."

"Louise...I know your name is on the lease and
you could give us a lot of shit about this if you want
to...but I'm asking, I'm *begging*...please don't."

Tiny lines have become etched in the pale skin
around her mouth, and she looks like hell. It makes
me both sad and alarmed. Macy's like a sister to me
and has been for ages. Paul is like the older brother I
wish I'd had. Of course I'll help them, any way that
I can.

"Don't worry, hon." I force my tone to be calm.
"You two have enough on your plate. I'll figure
something out."

CHAPTER NINE

"**L**ouise?" I approach her from the path behind the Tin Man statue. "Is that you?"

Sweet Lou's hands grasp her hips while she leans over in front of the Tin Man, her breathing deep and rapid.

"Usalv? I thought that was you back there." She smiles and stands straight up. "I didn't know you ran in Oz Park."

By unspoken agreement, we've both moved on from our drills disaster a few weeks ago. Neither of us ever mentions it. Ever since that day, our interactions have been friendly but casual.

"My favorite is the zoo. Unless I'm headed to my uncle's." I pause a few seconds more so she can catch her breath. She paces in a circle and stops, then reverses and repeats.

Sweet Lou arrives at the gym about the same

time I leave, but somehow we always manage to run into each other. We chat about how our day went, Rodgers' current mood, and my fight schedule. Once she's out of ball-busting mode, Louise is very sweet in a low-key way.

"That's a fast clip you were running at. It was tough trying to keep up with you."

"Thanks," she replies when her breathing normalizes.

"You're a serious runner." Another discovery that surprises me.

Louise laughs. "Back in the day. During high school, I made it to the state finals in cross-country. Twice." A distant look crosses her face. "I was fast back then."

"You're fast right now."

"Not really. I don't train the way I used to. Hell, I don't even get to run every day."

She's here to train, not to hook up, she's made that very clear to everyone in her no-nonsense, cut-through-the-crap way. Mike hangs around on the nights she's there, but Lou makes short work of blowing him off. I can respect that, even if I think she's too nice about it.

"Do you miss it?" I ask.

"Not so much as I thought." She looks up at the Tin Man and gives him a conspiratorial nod. "My dad loved to run. He loved to run with me. Then he loved to watch me run." Her voice is tinged with pain. "When that ended, I didn't care anymore. After that, running was mostly a fitness crutch and stress management tool."

"What happened?" I ask.

She looks up at the Tin Man statue while she answers. "He died."

"I'm sorry, Sweet Lou." Regret courses through me.

Those big amber eyes swallow me whole. "It's not your fault," she assures me.

"When did it happen?"

"In college."

I nod and change the subject. Or hope to, anyway. "Is Tin Man your favorite? You started and ended your run by him, and you always look up every time you're nearby."

She laughs out loud and blushes scarlet red. Relief courses through me.

"You noticed, huh?"

I notice everything about you, Louise Becker. "Kind of hard not to."

"Yeah, he's my favorite." She glances up toward the polished pile of auto parts at the park entrance. "Whenever that scary witch or hideous monkeys showed up, I'd freak out until the Tin Man arrived."

"So he makes you feel safe?"

"I guess." She shrugs. "He also reminds me of my dad." She looks up again at Tin Man, like she's embarrassed to talk in front of him.

The topic seems to put her in a good mood, so I push it a little. "How's that?"

"He was strong in lots of different ways. And much, much smarter than he got credit for." Her eyes dart from the statue then back to me several times. A pensive look flashes across her face, but it's gone in an instant.

"Yeah. He never seemed to need the crackerjack keychain heart that Oz gave him either." Weird. I don't remember much about it, but I do remember that.

"Not your favorite movie?" she asks.

I laugh. "Uh, no. Saw it my teens. An American rite of passage. I passed."

She shakes her head. "To be fair, most kids here see it when they're smaller. It makes a much bigger impression then." She looks down the paved trail and hesitates. "I need to walk or I'll be sore. Would like to come with me, or do you have more to go?"

"I'm done. Walking's good," I tell her.

"Well, come on then," she orders in a fake bossy voice and gestures for me to stand by her side. I fall in next to her, my pace an easy match for hers.

It's late Saturday afternoon, and neither of us are in a hurry to be any where. My uncle doesn't expect me at any particular time, and Sweet Lou hasn't checked her phone once since we ran into each other.

A dense plop of water hits my shoulder and

diverts my attention to gray waves of layered clouds moving briskly overhead, shedding slow drops of rain as they pass. I glance down at Louise, who wipes a raindrop from the tip of her nose and keeps walking. If she doesn't mind, then I don't either.

"An American rite of passage?" she asks. "Did that go okay for you? It must have been hard, coming here so young."

I look down at Sweet Lou and watch as several drops hit the top of her head, but she doesn't seem to care.

"Things were fine at first. But I wasn't supposed to stay that long."

"You weren't?" She looks up and waits for me to explain.

"No. I was supposed to come back when things settled down after the war." Christ. I've never told anyone about that. And outside of my family no one knows that's why I stayed here.

"The war?" Her voice quivers with distress and astonishment.

"Yeah. My parents sent me to stay with my mother's brother. But then they decided that I should live here." My father informed me of that decision in a five-minute telephone conversation on my fifteenth birthday. No one in my family had spoken about it again. I just...stayed.

"Why?" She frowns, etching deep wrinkles across her forehead.

"My uncle had no sons and needed help with his construction business. And if my younger sisters needed to move here later, then I could support them."

Her forward motion stops and she stares up at me, her amber eyes brimmed with shock and sadness and sympathy. "That's a lot to put on a kid that young."

She grips my forearm with her right hand, while the other strokes the back of my hand and wrist. We continue down the path, but now our pace slows and becomes more casual. We're not cooling down after a run—we're taking a walk together.

It feels nice.

"Was it very difficult for you?" she asks after a few minutes.

"Well, high school sucked. At first anyway." I smirk at the memory. "But it did wonders for my English. And once I started wrestling, things got better overnight."

"Mmm. Were you hell on wheels back then, too?"

"Afraid so." Yeah. I'm bragging. "I went from the guy who didn't know English and being the punch line of jokes to a high school badass. Made things easier with the girls, too."

Sweet Lou groans. "If only the social and emotional problems of high school girls could be solved by varsity sports." Her light strokes cease as she reaches for her hair and wrings her ponytail into a tight twist.

"Please—I bet you had the guys bent over backwards to get your attention."

"Far from it." Her voice is low and haunted. "Trust me, there is no hell like high school for an awkward girl."

"Awkward? Now that's hard to picture." I can't stop myself. "You're the most stunning woman I've ever seen."

"No, I'm not," she insists.

"You've got to be kidding me. Come on, Louise."

"I'm serious." She folds her arms and picks up the pace. "I was the tallest person in my class until junior year. I wore braces, glasses, and was flat as a board. My arms and legs are still way too long. I looked like an ostrich, which became my nickname." I watch a deep breath of air rattle through her ribcage. "God, I hated that."

"So when did all this happen?" I wave at the knockout beside me.

"This?" Louise's hands contort in a gesture of confusion. "There is no this. I grew up, that's all. The braces came off. The extended wear contacts went in. I filled out eventually in college, during clinical rotations when I didn't have much time to work out."

"But you never really got over your awkward phase, did you? Or got comfortable with your looks?" I watch her from the corner of my eye. "Bet you even have a hard time believing compliments are sincere."

Minutes pass as we continue our walk in silence. "It was a long time ago. But it's not so long ago that I can look back and laugh at it." She stops and looks up at me with a troubled expression. "I don't think I ever will. Part of me will always be the Ostrich." Sweet Lou shakes her head.

"That explains a lot."

"Like what?"

"Like why you're such a ballbuster." I tease her with the truth.

"A…wait…what?"

"You take charge in situations that a woman normally wouldn't, and you're indifferent to the commotion that causes, especially with men. You just expect everyone to get over it."

"Thank you. That's the nicest compliment I've had in a while."

"Are you serious?"

"That was a compliment, wasn't it?"

"See what I mean?" It's not really a compliment or a complaint. At least from me.

The number eleven appears above the bridge of her nose. "Not really. Then again, boyfriends were never my major. Maybe that explains it."

A wave of relief and excitement surge through me. "That's not a bad thing, Sweet Lou."

"I suppose not. Since becoming a nurse, I have a lot more women friends now. But I like guys. In many ways, I'm more comfortable around them. Probably because of sports. I had a lot of guy friends in school."

"Bet that pissed off the other girls."

"Sometimes it did. But that never made any sense to me. I didn't date the guys I was friends with. Many of them had girlfriends."

I shrug. "Face time is face time."

"Whatever, I guess. If you don't trust who you're with, then you're with the wrong person."

"It's that simple?" I ask.

"For me it is."

Good to know.

She pauses and after a few minutes, looks back and forth between me and the path we're walking on, then hesitates before she asks, "Hey, I haven't busted your...um, you know, blues brothers, have I?"

I laugh. Just a little. "Not too much. Not yet, anyway."

"That's a relief. Can't have those big boy pants of yours all twisted up with worry."

"You noticed those, huh?"

Sweet Lou's face flushes deep crimson. She looks up and gives me a death glare, then bursts into laughter. She starts to speak but a loud crash of thunder interrupts her. Seconds later, the slow *plop,*

plop of rain transforms into a biting sleet that stings the skin wherever it strikes.

We both look around for shelter, but we're on an open part of the path where there isn't any.

"How'd you get here?" My hand shields the side of her face from the rain.

"I ran."

"My car's parked on Webster," I tell her.

"Webster's on the other side of the park."

"Well, we can't stay here. You want a ride?" I offer.

"Hell yes," she replies.

I extend my hand and she grabs hold of it. Neither of us looks back as we sprint off together under the gray evening sky.

CHAPTER TEN

"It's right here, Louise." Usalv's powerful hand pulls me close as I attempt to run past a metallic plum SUV parked on Webster Avenue.

The electronic purr of the door unlocking fills me with all the jubilation of the Chicago chamber choir at a holiday sing-a-long. The freezing rain causes violent fits of shivering as it soaks me to the skin. Despite the nasty weather, Usalv opens my door and helps me up before he scrambles to the driver's side and jumps in.

"Tha-n-ks." My teeth chatter as he switches the engine on and cranks the heat up.

I lean into the passenger side of the console and soak in the warmth from the heat vent. Wrapping my arms around me, I rub hard to erase the emerging trail of goosebumps along my body. I'm wearing a thermal shirt underneath a light cotton shell and they're both soaked through.

"You're freezing." Usalv removes his baseball cap and waterproof shell before tossing them on the seat behind me.

I nod, shaking uncontrollably. Ice crystals have formed on the collars and cuffs of my soaking wet clothes. The tops of my thighs sting as heat hits where sweat, sleet, and frigid air collided on the surface of my wet cotton-lycra pants.

"Come here." Usalv grabs a wool varsity jacket from the back seat and wraps it around me. He massages my arms and back vigorously through the thick quilted material.

His touch surprises me with its gentle but powerful warmth. Soon my hands recoil from the vents as I lean closer to Usalv, preferring the heat of his hands along my shivering spine.

My eyes are closed when he stops. I look up to discover my face inches from his chest. One hand stills on the small of my back, the other grips my shoulder.

"You good, Lou?" His face hovers inches from my forehead.

"I'm good." I shift back into my seat, avoiding his eyes. "Thanks."

He clears his throat and examines the sleet scratching against the windshield. "Let me take you home. Are you far from here?"

"About a mile North-ish."

He nods and puts his seatbelt on while I do the same.

Usalv checks his mirrors. "Where to?"

"Larabee, then make a right on Fullerton."

We ride in silence for a few minutes. I wrap his jacket around me tightly and inhale the rich scent of bergamot and a woodsy fragrance I can't name. I'm so preoccupied we almost pass my apartment.

"This is me!" I interrupt the sedate atmosphere inside the car. "On the right...up here is me."

Usalv hits the brakes and checks his rearview mirror. We crawl along in search of a space, but end up double parked. The car stops, but I remain motionless, not wanting to leave. Usalv sits in silence, waiting for me.

"Thanks for the save," I tell him.

"Anytime, Sweet Lou." He doesn't smile, but his voice is sincere.

I start to remove his jacket, but notice the nylon lining and shoulders are soaking wet from my drenched hair and clothes.

"Damn, I'm sorry." I pull the jacket back as he reaches out for it.

"No worries. It's fine," he assures me.

"It's not fine. What time is it?"

"About four-thirty."

"Macy doesn't get home until about six. Pull into that driveway." I point out the window. "You can park in her space for a bit. Come up and I'll throw it in the dryer for you."

"It's not that big a deal."

I sigh, irritated. "I'm not sending you out in this with a useless wet jacket."

"You sure?"

"Up here," I point. "I've got a code for the parking lot."

Usalv turns into the narrow driveway, and I lean over him to access the key pad. Somehow we manage to avoid touching, which leaves me inexplicably disappointed.

He navigates over to Macy's empty space in the detached garage. Then we sprint across the narrow driveway to the apartment entrance, where a middle-aged man cradling a frigid Scottish terrier waits for the elevator, and we all ride together up to the fourth floor.

"Please come in," I tell Usalv after opening my front door. "The living room is that way."

"Thanks."

"Would you like something to drink? Something hot?" I ask after he settles onto the sofa next to my favorite spot.

"Like what?"

"I know it's weird, but I'm going to heat up some chicken broth. Otherwise there's coffee, tea—"

"Chicken broth," he answers, amused. "I haven't met anyone else who drinks it."

"Parsley and garlic salt?" I ask.

"More of a ginger-turmeric guy, myself. But sure, why not?"

It's my turn to look amused. "I guess you really do drink it."

"I'm on a diet that would bring most chicks to their knees," he replies.

Whatever he's doing, it sure works for him. "Give me a minute. I'll just throw this in the dryer." I point to his jacket wrapped around my arm.

"Show me where your kitchen is and I'll make it." He gets up and follows me. "You need to go change out of those clothes."

He follows me into the kitchen and waits by the stove as I pull out a carton from the fridge and some spices from the cabinet.

"We've got ginger, but no turmeric. Sorry."

"No worries." He points toward the kitchen entrance. "Now go."

I head toward the closet outside the bathroom where the dryer sits and toss his jacket inside. The closet next to the dryer holds clean towels, and I then grab two of them to take into my bedroom.

I shut the door and strip my wet clothes, which land in a messy pile on the floor. My naked body warms up quickly after being rubbed vigorously with a towel. Several strands of my hair are frozen together at the ends. I'm starting to feel normal again when the loud slam of the front door heralds Macy's early arrival home.

"Some asshole parked in my space. Do you even believe this shit?"

A heated flush creeps up my spine as Macy's bag hits the foyer tiles with a familiar thud. I reach into the top draw of my dresser and pull out a black camisole and pale pink bikini underwear.

"...Of all the damn days," Her angry declaration echoes down the hall. "And it's this large ass luxury SUV. How the hell they even crammed it into that tiny space is beyond me..."

Macy's on a rant, and she probably thinks the person making noise in the kitchen is me. I'm determined to get out there before she says anything else or discovers Usalv, but I can't find my bathrobe.

"Whoa!" Macy exclaims. "And you are?"

Too late.

"I'm Usalv. You must be Macy. Nice to meet you."

"I'm sorry...who?" she asks.

"I'm the asshole parked in your space." Usalv's calmness can be annoying. I wonder if it's natural or if he does that on purpose.

"You are?" Macy replies.

"Sorry about that. Sweet Lou didn't think you'd be back for another couple of hours. Do you want any chicken broth?" he asks.

"Where is Louise?" Macy asks.

"She's in her room getting dressed."

The entire apartment goes stock-still. In the sober silence, I remember my bathrobe in the dirty laundry and dive into the pile to retrieve it.

"Oh." Macy breaks the stillness. "Well. Of course she is. Um…nice meeting you Usa… Us-salv? And don't worry about the parking thing. I…think I'll go get mine washed. Or something."

I open the door, tighten the belt of my robe and dash into the kitchen. Macy and I collide as she's backing out of the doorway.

"Hey, Macy." I'm blocking her exit. "You've met Usalv?"

Macy turns to face me and her eyes bulge as they take in my wet hair and bathrobe. When she looks up at my face, her expression is brimming with shock and questions.

Oh God.

"Sorry about the parking thing," I stammer. "I didn't expect you back so soon."

"Clearly." With her back to Usalv, her bottom jaw drops to her chest.

"Louise got caught in the rain. I gave her a ride home." Usalv pulls two clean mugs off the dish rack. Taking his time, he fills them both from the sauce pan of boiling liquid on the stove. When they're full, he takes two strides toward us and hands me a mug.

"Thank you." As I take it from him, my fingers brush against his hand.

He smiles down at me. "You're welcome."

Macy rolls her eyes at me.

"So… where are you parked?" I blurt out before she speaks again.

"I'm in Scott's spot and he's gone until tonight, so no worries for now. But…" Macy glances over at Usalv, who's retreated to lean against the kitchen sink. He watches us over the rim of his mug. "Are you…going out?"

I peer over Macy's shoulders and fixate on Usalv. He gives me an expectant look, but when I say nothing, it fades as he takes a drink from his cup.

"Um…no." I tell her, breaking eye contact with Usalv. "After a very hot shower, I need to study."

"Good. That's good." She pauses. "Well, if you're going to be home, Mike's coming by a little later."

Not my idea of great news. "Why?"

She hesitates. "Well, I thought he could help us both out."

I glance at Usalv, before nodding toward the kitchen door. He nods back in understanding, and I usher Macy out, following behind her.

"Damn it, Macy, no you didn't." I tell her when we reach the living room.

"Listen… Paul's coming home in the next ten days. Have you got a new place yet?" she pushes.

Ashamed, I answer, "No," then set my mug on the table.

"That's what I thought." She chews her bottom lip.

"I know this sucks for you. And I'm really sorry. But truthfully, you couldn't have asked me to do this at a worse time. My schedule sucks, so it's hard to find a roommate. And now that I've got tuition payments to worry about, finding a decent place by myself hasn't panned out either. I am trying, though."

Damn it, I didn't want to say that to her. Not like this anyway.

"I get it," she replies, placing a gentle hand on my forearm. "That's why I called Mike. He's got a lot of connections in real estate and I think he can help."

My voice conveys a mix of frustration and irritation. "Macy, I don't want his help."

"Are you kidding? Why?"

"Because it's Mike. Hello? We both know he'll think I have ulterior motives for asking him."

Macy removes her hand from my forearm and rubs her temples. "Lou, we're both getting a little desperate here." Her voice rises. "Can't you suck it up and deal with any blowback later?" She pauses, then adds, "You could do a helluva lot worse, by the way."

"Not this again. Please." Her comments force me to recall our uncomfortable argument in the ER.

"What do you think of that guy?" Macy cornered me in a supply room during one crazy St. Patty's Day shift.

"What guy?" I asked.

"The big blond with the arm that needed stitches?" she replied.

"You mean Mister 'I-don't-need-no bottle opener, I'll just bicep-curl the top off? You want my opinion? Seriously?" I asked.

"Be nice, Louise. That's Paul's cousin."

"My condolences."

"He thinks you're smoking hot," said Macy.

"It's the beer goggles. His vision will clear up just before the hangover sets in," I replied.

"Can I give him your number?" she asked.

"Hell no."

"You're missing an opportunity here." Macy bobs her head in encouragement.

"More like dodging a bullet."

"Louise, sometimes you're really harsh."

"Easy for you to say. You didn't treat him."

"Okay, so he got a little out of control on St. Patty's Day. It was stupid, but he's really a good guy. You'd like him."

"You think it's a good idea for me to date someone who's here to be treated for drinking game related injuries? Thanks, but I'll pass."

"Fine," she replied before whooshing past me and out the door. She didn't speak to me for the rest of our shift.

"Mike Daughtry?"

Macy and I turn together to see Usalv propped

against the wall next to the kitchen with his arms folded.

"Yeah." Macy's tone is puzzled. "How do you know Mike?"

"We work out at the same gym," he explains.

"Oh," Macy replies, stunned. "You're a fighter like Mike?"

Usalv rolls his eyes before flashing a wicked smile. "Something like that."

"Oh," she replies.

Damn. There aren't too many people that can leave Macy speechless. It's kind of refreshing.

"Louise, I couldn't help overhear...sorry about that." Usalv tells me with undetectable remorse. "But I own a four-unit duplex with a one bedroom I'm getting ready to rent." He shrugs, glancing over at Macy before looking back at me. "Let me know if you're interested. It'll save me from finding a tenant."

"I'll take it," I blurt out.

"What?" Macy explodes. "Just like that?"

"Not exactly. I've known Usalv for a little while now." Memories of our locker room encounter flash through my mind. "He's a good guy, Macy. Besides, I don't have too many options at the moment."

"Are you sure you don't want to talk with Mike first?" Macy asks.

"She doesn't have a lot of time or leeway," Usalv interjects. "You've made that very clear."

"Take a look around," Macy snaps back. "How the hell are three people and major medical equipment supposed to squeeze in here?"

"They're not. Obviously." Usalv's voice rings with that calm certainty of presence. "But Louise needs to find another place and fast. The reasons why don't make it easier for her to do it, just more critical that it gets done." He shrugs. "Renting from me solves everybody's problems."

The loudness of the dryer buzzer interrupts their verbal sparring.

"Let me get your jacket, Usalv," I interject before leading him back toward the hall where the dryer sits.

The thought of them not getting along horrifies me, and I'm overcome with a mixture of disappointment and frustration as I hurry him out before round two starts.

The dryer door opens with a click, and a rush of hot air hits my face as his jacket tumbles out. The dryer heat only makes the woodsy-bergamot smell stronger. I'd like to slip it on, but resist with Usalv standing next to me.

"Here—it's dry." I extend my arms to hand it to him, but he hesitates for a moment. There's a lot to discuss, but not while Macy's within earshot.

"Thanks." He takes the jacket and starts to turn away, but I grasp his forearm, restraining him gently.

He looks down at me, and I glance behind him before whispering, "Can I move in next weekend?"

"Next weekend?" His voice rises before looking back over his shoulder. "Maybe you should see it first."

"Why? Are you some kind of a slum lord?" I ask.

"Fuck that. Of course not." He sounds offended.

"Perfect. How about next weekend then?"

He blows out a long slow breath. "That's too soon. The plumbing won't be finished." He pauses, then pins me with a direct look. "But you can move into my downstairs bedroom if you want."

"Your downstairs bedroom?" I repeat. "As in your apartment?"

He nods. "It's on the first floor." His eyes watch me. "Mine's upstairs."

"Yours?"

"Bedroom. I sleep upstairs."

"Oh." I'm speechless.

"We'd share the kitchen, laundry, living room, and entry way." His voice is calm and certain. "But you'd have your own bathroom, closet, and some garage storage."

I hesitate. "Um...how long until the one bedroom is ready?"

"Another month. My uncle needs to send a crew over but won't if I'm not there. And I've been busy."

Wow. Living in the same building as Usalv is one thing, but the same apartment? That's unexpected to say the least. But what else can I do? Macy's a wreck over this apartment thing, and my own search hasn't turned up anything.

"Think about it and let me know." His words interrupt my thoughts.

"No."

"No?" He sounds disappointed.

"No, I don't need to think about it. I need to move. Like now." I sigh. "Besides, one month isn't so long. And it does solve all our problems. I get a place, you get a tenant. Macy and Paul get their apartment back, and I don't have to deal with Mike —not in that capacity, anyway." I smile up at him, but he doesn't smile back.

"Louise, I'm just trying to help, not pressure you. If this doesn't feel right, then…"

I squeeze his arm and his stops speaking. "Actually, it does feel like the right thing to do. And it helps me out a lot." With my other hand, I gesture toward the hall and lead him to the tiny foyer.

We turn the corner and stop near the front door.

"Thank you." I smile up at him.

He smiles back. "Let me know what time next weekend. See you at the gym?"

I nod.

"Good." He opens the door and steps into the hall without a backward glance. I leave the door a bit ajar to watch him walk down the hall before shutting it with a gentle click.

When I turn back around, Macy stands in the hallway just outside the kitchen, her face a mixture of shock and amusement.

"What?" I ask.

She gives me a worried smile and shakes her head. "That"—she points over my shoulder—"is one super-sized jar of man-candy. Lou, are you sure you know what you're doing?"

CHAPTER ELEVEN

I lie naked in bed, my clean clothes still downstairs in the dryer.

Old habits die hard.

"Louise?" When only stillness answers, my gaze shifts to the bedside clock.

She moved in four days ago and her jacked up schedule still confuses me. If I'm not up by the time she's home, the kitchen commotion wakes me.

I slide out of bed and walk to the staircase.

"Louise?" I descend the stairs and make my way to the laundry machine, past the hallway clock that says seven-thirty. Morning light streams in through the cutout windows of the heavy wooden front door.

Sweet Lou should be here soon.

My kitchen is a long narrow room with a stackable laundry machine behind plantation shutter doors that rest against the far wall. I rip open what looks like a pantry and reach into the dryer.

What the hell…where are my clothes?

I pull out a bunch of Sweet Lou's things. A healthy handful of cotton lace underwear, and a big fancy flowery towel decorated with a lace border spill out onto floor. I stuff them back in and look around for the load of shorts and shirts that were in here a few days ago.

I pause as the sound of city noise becomes louder, and then distant again as the front door shuts.

Sweet Lou is home.

She usually heads straight for the kitchen. Famished after her twelve-hour graveyard shift, she offers to share her food with me if I'm here. Hanging around in the buff, given our fragile circumstances, might leave give her the impression she's been ambushed.

Shit.

I pull out her fancy towel again and knot it around my naked waist, then lean over the counter, hoping she won't notice my improvised pink paisley man-skirt. My lungs breathe in and out, slow and deep, awaiting her appearance.

Only…it doesn't happen.

A few moments pass. Then the glass liquor cabinet doors resonate as they shut, followed by the *glug, glug* of liquid being poured. Lots of it, accompanied by muffled sobs.

Something's wrong.

I tighten my towel around me and venture out into the living room.

Sweet Lou's lithe frame is stretched out on the charcoal colored couch under the bay window that overlooks the street. A large tumbler of amber liquid rests on her thigh, cradled between her palms.

A single tear runs down her cheek as she looks out the window in stony silence.

"Are you okay?" I ask.

She startles at my voice, then fixates on the flowery towel. I look down and notice the paisley bouquet perfectly accentuates the package. Perfectly, as in fuck, I hope she doesn't think it was deliberate.

"I had to borrow your towel." I explain. "Couldn't find my clothes...have you seen them?"

She shoots me a puzzled look. "I left them outside your bathroom door in my wicker basket. I couldn't find any of your laundry baskets. You didn't see it?"

"Laundry basket? I wondered what that was. Probably should get one instead of leaving things in the dryer?"

She nods, detached, then wipes the tear from her cheek.

"Hey, what is it?" I ask.

"It's been a shit day." She looks out the window.

"That I can see."

She takes a gulp of her drink. "I lost a patient."

"Lost as in—"

"Yeah."

"Oh." I hadn't considered what life at her day job was like.

"The woman-child looked the wrong way down a one-way street and got hit by a commuter bus. Forever Nineteen at six forty-two a.m." She raises her glass, then takes a gulp of amber liquid.

"Fuck. I'm...sorry."

"Me too." Sweet Lou swallows another gulp.

"Does this sort of thing happen a lot?"

"Sure does." She gives me a defensive shrug. "We lose about half our patients in trauma-ICU."

"That many?" Damn. That's a lot of dead people.

"The patients we treat are in dire straits when they arrive. It's the nature of the work." Her voice sounds regretful. "But I'd be lying if I said some didn't touch me more than others."

I approach her and pause to pick up a bottle of whiskey next to the couch. Bushmills. She drains the tumbler in her hand and I refill it before she makes space for me to sit down next to her.

"Is there something I can do?" I squeeze her knee gently.

"Not really. The old timers tell me that as I age,

the shock of losing someone younger erodes. Until then, bottoms up." She raises the glass to her lips.

"You do this a lot?" I nod toward the glass.

"It's five o'clock somewhere," she answers. "Don't you ever have a drink after work?"

"Once in a while. But not fifty percent of the time."

"Me neither," she huffs. "What I really need is to go for a run, but I've got another shift tonight." She leans back and the nape of her neck hits my arm where it rests.

Louise's caramel curls brush my forearm as she tucks one leg beneath her. I gaze down at her other leg stretched out on the coffee table. As it brushes against mine, I admire the lean, dense muscle through the thin fabric of her scrubs.

"None of this is your fault." Her face is draped across my arm. "You know that, right?"

"I know that. Here." She slaps her temple. "But here and here"—she strikes her stomach and heart —"it takes a while. She was just so goddamn young."

Distress clouds those amber colored eyes, and I pull her body close to me. Tears stream down my naked chest like a trail of hot lava. I stroke the skin of her smooth creamy cheek to wipe them away, but their heat burns my fingers and I resist the urge to suck them.

When her sobs subside, Sweet Lou uncurls

herself and pours another scotch. This time, she offers the glass to me.

"Fuck it." My fingers graze hers as I take the glass and drain it in a single gulp.

She looks surprised, then takes it back, refilling the tumbler and draining the bottle of Bushmills.

"Right before he died, my dad said that he knew I'd be okay, that he was really proud of how I'd turned out. And that he'd miss me." She rests her forehead against my shoulder as the whiskey catches up with her. "I wonder what he'd say if he could see me now."

"I'm sure he'd feel the same. You're an extraordinary woman," I assure her. "What happened to your dad?" This is the second time he's come up while she's stressed out.

Louise takes another gulp, and closes her eyes while her body shudders. "A RAM 2500 t-boned my dad's door on the double yellow of an s-shaped curve." She squeezes my waist. "We didn't stand a chance in our Forester."

"We?" I repeat. "Were you in the accident too?"

"Dislocated my shoulder." Her voice cracks. "Just as well. It was right after my first year of college, and my knowledge of nursing could fit in a thimble. I would have been an even bigger mess if I'd tried to treat him and failed."

"It's not your fault." My lips whisper soft kisses into her hair.

"I hugged him with my good arm, and talked to him until help arrived." Hot tears trickle down my abdomen as she chokes the words out. "In the end it didn't matter. The other driver died of his heart attack and Dad died from internal hemorrhaging."

I tuck her under my shoulder. "When was this?"

"About seven years ago now."

It makes sense now. "So you were the same age as the girl that died today?" I smooth tear soaked strands of curly hair away from her face.

Sweet Lou's eyes widen. "Yeah."

"When did you decide to become a nurse?" I ask.

"My mom's a nurse too. I've wanted to be one since I was a kid." A faraway look enters her eyes. "But it wasn't until after...after Dad that I decided to be a trauma nurse."

"Then maybe this is more about a bad memory instead of a bad day?" I hug her head close to me. "Just saying..."

"Maybe." Her expression is thoughtful and distant.

Against my torso, her shoulders relax. She lies across me with her temple pressed against my heart. A few minutes later, the still air rings with the sound of her steady breathing, a deep forceful wheeze fueled by a mixture of exhaustion and alcohol.

I blow out a breath and hesitate before laying my

cramped arm in the cradle of Sweet Lou's hip. She's got me pinned in more ways than one.

What the fuck have I done?

My phone roars to life as "Professional Griefers" by Deadmaus5 blasts from the console table in the foyer. The clock by the fireplace says nine-twenty. It's probably Drew, wondering what the hell happened to our nine o'clock work out.

When I decided to be late today, it wasn't supposed to be *this* late.

Another minute with Louise curled up on top of me isn't going to be good for anyone. I inch my arms around the back of her knees and shoulders, lift us both off the couch and head down the hall.

"What are you doing?" Her voice is groggy against my shoulder.

"Putting you to bed." My back pushes against her bedroom door.

She sits up in my arms with her eyes wide open. "What?"

"Relax." My voice is calm. "I'm putting you to bed, not taking you to bed."

Since the night we first met, I haven't been out with anyone, let alone had sex.

Her head shoots off my chest. "Oh... Just so we're clear...what's the difference?"

"I'd never take any woman to bed in your condition." As soon as the words are spoken, I know that the next woman I'm with will be Louise, wide awake and willing.

"Damn," she replies.

I freeze. "Excuse me?"

"Nothing." Her speech slurs. "It just means you're a good guy," she explains. "And that I'm not getting special treatment. Which is good. Only it's not." She pauses then settles herself back against my chest. "Am I making sense?"

"Tell me, when you're drunk, how much of what you say do you recall?"

"Zippo. Alcohol tends to hit me fast, because of my athletic metabolism. Me-ta-ob-lism," she repeats. "But it also wears off fast. Especially if I can sleep it off. So basically, conversations don't really stick."

"Good to know."

Sweet Lou's bedroom lies adjacent to the kitchen behind the stairs. Back in the day, it was probably used for a nanny or elderly parent. It's long and narrow, about eight by twelve. Her daybed is wedged between the shorter walls with a small side table.

Unextended, it's about the same width as a twin bed. Thank God, because the urge to crawl in there with her is way too strong, despite the ass-chewing I'm due from Drew when we meet up.

"Ride's over. Sleep it off, beautiful." I lay her down on top of the lilac comforter. With my knee next to her, I reach across the bed to remove several small pillows to make more room.

I draw a sharp breath as her hand inches up my leg. Louise's eyes are shut tight, her brows lined with troubled furrows. Her hand slides to the top of the towel, then burrows under the fold and against the skin of my hip.

"Louise...don't." My voice sounds hollow and lacks conviction.

"Usalv," she rasps.

"What is it?"

When she doesn't answer, I pull her hand away from my hip, dislodging the towel. I kneel to try and catch it, which brings my face inches from hers.

"I'm sorry...for being such a pain in the ass... and...and—thank you." She lifts her lips to mine.

Her soft kiss lingers like a gentle temptation. My body swells, and I force myself to focus on the taste of whiskey rather than the caress of her lips on my mouth and tongue.

"Goodnight." Her tired voice is abrupt. All at once her lips and hands release me and she rolls away. Several seconds pass while I listen to her steady breathing.

"Goodnight." I whisper and leave the rumpled towel on the bedroom floor and close the door on my way out.

CHAPTER TWELVE

I pull the brim of my baseball cap down until it hits the frames of my copper-mirrored Clubmaster sunglasses. I hesitate at the gym's main doors, reluctant to enter.

"Hey, Louise." Two men call as they exit through the front.

"Hey, guys." One of them holds the door for me as he leaves. "Thanks."

At the door of the main gym, I pull up my hoodie and scope out the scene. Not far from the entryway, one of the MMA guys paces up and down the path in front of the free weights.

"Hey, Drew." I rest my Clubmasters on the brim of my cap. "Have you seen Usalv?"

Drew stops and looks up at me. His brown eyes soften and his full lips suppress a smile. "He's in the cage." Drew nods toward the back of the gym. "Probably be there a while."

"No worries." I shrug. "Wasn't planning to tap him on the shoulder while he sparred."

Far from it.

I left home early in an attempt to avoid an awkward afternoon encounter, but hoped it was still late enough that he'd left the gym already. Now I've got to parade past the cage to get to the group activity rooms upstairs.

Drew chuckles. "Probably not a good idea right now."

"Thanks." I decide to go beat the crap out of the human workout dummy and set up for the taek-wondo and kickboxing classes. At least it's a lame-ass excuse to avoid him.

"Take it easy." Drew calls as I head across the main gym toward the stairs.

When I woke up this evening, my bath towel was in a crumpled heap on the floor next to my bed. My scrubs were still on, along with my shoes and socks. None of it made sense at all. Then I remembered...

The whiskey. The bed. The touch. The towel. The kiss.

What the fuck is wrong with me? Did I really get drunk and reach inside his towel?

I've been around ultra-fit athletic types my whole life, but I'd learned in my late teens that most are best admired from afar. Slick sculpted muscle alone stopped doing it for me a long time ago.

But what if Usalv is more than that?

It's doubtful. On Tuesday, I found a four pack of diet pink raspberry-pomegranate martinis in his fridge. Diet fruity martinis? Total chick drink. It screamed *girlfriend* and darkened my mood for the night.

What if Usalv has a girlfriend?

I haven't encountered glassware with lipstick that's not mine or any mysterious female clothes, but then I've lived there less than a week. Of course, the real evidence would be in his bedroom and bathroom, where I dare not venture.

It never occurred to me what it might be like to meet one of Usalv's dates at the coffee pot in the morning, or discover forgotten jewelry on an end table. What about walking in on the loud hoo-ha of hot monkey sex after work?

A shiver races down my spine, followed by a wave of nausea.

"Easy." Rodgers' baritone voice echoes across the gym. "Take it easy!"

I stop at the bottom of the stairs and look over in his direction. Rodgers strides with folded arms as he watches two powerfully built men spar inside the cage.

Usalv could never be mistaken for anyone else. Those wide shoulders and powerful back roam the apartment in a hasty quest for clothes each morning. He's shirtless and wearing gray fight shorts with black compression pants that peek out the bottom hems as he moves around like a cautious cat approaching his prey.

The other guy reminds me of Mike Tyson. Fast, well-coordinated, and from the *whoosh* of his strikes, a hard hitter. He seems small at first, but when I gauge the height of his shoulders against the poles inside the cage, he's at least six feet tall with a compact, densely muscled frame. He's also a skilled Muay Thai boxer.

Guttural grunts, fast steps, and Rodgers' curt two and three word commands occur in a regular tempo. Hard muscular bodies glisten with sweat while gloved hands bob up and down like serpents ready to strike.

"Watch that contact." Rodgers voice contains a note of uneasy warning.

Around the gym, others take note. Some steal quick glances from where they are, while others stop what they're doing to watch. Curiosity gets the better of me and I come around the stairs to check out the action.

It doesn't take long to realize this isn't a typical sparring session. Both men wear mouth guards as their only face protection. Each man moves around the other, feinting, testing, striking, counterstriking, devoid of repetitive moves or sets of moves.

This is live free sparring, as close to the real deal as it gets.

Shit.

Usalv's face is a granite mask of concentration as he avoids several strikes with an incredible display of speed for a man his size. Retaining his composure and biding his time, he springs forward and takes his opponent to the mat with a loud painful thud.

"Goddamn it!" the opponent yells as he snaps to his feet.

That voice sounds familiar, but I can't put a face to it. He's corralled into a corner with his back to me. Curious, I come around and get closer to the cage.

That's when I hear the profanity-laden trash talking contest.

Usalv's heated curses scorch like a blow torch, while the opponent gives as good he gets. I'm impressed. Some of their words are new to me, and being a big city nurse leaves me well-acquainted with vulgarity, to put it politely.

Sweet Jesus, these guys are pissed at each other.

Now I need to know who the hell was stupid enough to get on Usalv's bad side and into the ring with him.

"Oof." Usalv grunts as his opponent's kick takes aim at his liver. It's normally a match ending blow, but Usalv's monster reach ensures that his elbows guard his lower abdomen, and the opponent's foot connects with Usalv's muscular arm rather than his abdomen.

The opponent, frustrated that the liver shot failed, decides to give it another try. He telegraphs his intention—it's obvious even to me. But this time, Usalv is well prepared and the opponent gets planted on the mat. Again.

"Not when he's ready!" Rodgers barks.

When the other guy looks over after Rodgers' outburst, I gasp in surprise.

Michael? Mike Daughtry? What the hell is going on?

I come even closer and stand about ten feet behind Rodgers, careful not to crowd him.

Mike squares off against Usalv, his expression furious, while Usalv returns a menacing glare of his own.

"Coozehound," Mike spits out. Over Usalv's shoulder, he glances at Rodgers and does a double take at me.

What happens next is nothing short of a slow-motion train wreck.

Mike's glare of fury morphs into one of stunned surprise, just before he drops his guard and Usalv's nasty right cross does the rest.

I wince. *Fuck.*

"Fuck!" Mike bellows.

"Fuck!" Rodgers curses, slapping his hand against the fence of the cage.

Usalv raises his hands in the air as Mike writhes on the floor. When Mike sits up, Usalv places a gentle hand between Mike's shoulders just under his neck, as he waits for Rodgers to enter the cage. When Rodgers kneels beside Mike, Usalv moves away and crouches to watch.

Mike cups his eye as Rodgers peels his fingers away to study it.

"What a goddamned mess," he growls, removing the towel from his waist to press it against Mike's face. "Madman, what the hell were you doing?"

That's all I need to hear as the nurse in me takes over.

"Me?" Usalv explodes as I enter the cage. "He just fucking checked out in the middle of it. How the hell am I supposed to work with that?"

Usalv gives me a heated glare as I approach them. *Get out of here. Now*, he telegraphs to me. I disregard his unspoken command. *Sorry, can't do that*, I telegraph back.

"It's my bad, Coach," Mike interjects.

"Well that's fucking fantastic," Rodgers spits out.

"Mike?" I interrupt. "Why don't you let me have a look?"

An uncomfortable silence ensues. Rodgers and Usalv exchange heated glances before looking at Mike's face.

"Louise? Yeah. Please. It's fucked up."

"I've got this, Louise," Rodgers tells us.

"No." Mike is firm. "Let her look. Sweet Lou's got a magic touch."

"I'm a trauma nurse." I pull my hoodie off and spin the brim of my hat around to keep my hair out of the way as I kneel beside Mike.

"Really?" Rodgers looks up from the towel pressed against Mike's face. "Is that the physically demanding day job you wanted to keep?"

"Yeah." My hands brush Rodgers fingers as I touch the towel against Mike's face.

Rodgers nods. "A set of skills like that could come in handy around here."

"So would some head gear." I share a pointed look with all three of them before my focus shifts back the towel. "Why aren't you wearing any?"

An uncomfortable silence ensues. Glances are exchanged, feet shift, arms are crossed. It's clear that whatever's going on will not be discussed in front of me.

"Get the kit," Rodgers tells Usalv, who disappears through the cage door.

I roll the towel pressed against Mike's face into layers and increase the pressure. When Usalv returns, he places a royal blue first aid kit on the floor next to me.

"Gloves please."

Usalv unwraps a pair of blue poly vinyl gloves and hands them to me, avoiding eye contact.

Rodgers applies pressure to Mike's face in silence while I don the gloves.

"The light really sucks in here." I look up at the ceiling and glance around. "Lie over there, Mike."

I point to a section of mat underneath a fluorescent light, then reach for the keychain in my pocket. When it's clicked, the carabiner releases a tiny Maglite, which I put between my teeth before leaning over Mike to remove his towel.

A nasty gash runs along the orbital rim of his frontal bone. The eyelid itself starts to swell. There's also a small tear in the eyelid corner. It looks like a clean wound, but I can't be sure.

"No doubt about it, Mike. You need to be seen."

"Goddamn," he grumbles. "Are you sure?"

"Positive. You'll want to rule out hyphena."

"Hi-what?" he asks.

"Internal bleeding of the eye. They'll probably check for fractures of the orbital bone too." I roll the towel back over his eye. "I'll close this gash up with some steri-strips, but you need to get moving." I look up at Rodgers. "Can you get him a cold pack? Keep on it there until he gets to the hospital. It'll help with the swelling."

Rodgers reaches inside the medical kit and pulls out the steri-strips. He shuffles through the plastic kit and a few seconds later pulls out an ice blue colored pack.

"Take those," I tell Usalv, pointing to the steri-strips. "Peel them open at one end and hold them out. Thanks."

At this point, I'm on auto pilot. Three well placed strips later, I ask for gauze then place the ice pack on top of Mike's orbital bone.

"It's done," I announce. "Get moving."

"Put some clothes on," Rodgers tells Mike. "I'll go with you."

Mike nods. "Thanks, Louise."

"You're welcome. Now go take care of yourself, okay?"

Mike heads toward the locker room. One hand holds the ice pack on his face while Rodgers follows behind. When they're out of sight, I turn to look for Usalv, but he's left the cage.

I emerge to check on Usalv and find him pacing back and forth between the cage and the far wall. When he turns back toward me, I wave to him.

"Are you okay?" I ask.

He responds with an icy stare before putting his shirt back on and walking toward the far wall again.

I jerk back as if he'd given me a right cross. What the hell did I do?

Oh yeah. Right.

I'd almost forgotten my clumsy drunk-ass attempt to feel him up. He probably thinks I'm a high maintenance pain in the ass and regrets his decision to help me out.

Waves of embarrassment and insecurity hit me

in an oscillating tempo. No doubt he's counting the minutes until construction on the one bedroom unit is done.

If we're going to keep things platonic, then I need to behave and apologize.

But not now, I'll wait until we've both calmed down a bit. As Usalv turns in my direction again, I give him a dismissive wave, then beeline for the ladies locker room.

But it isn't long before the sound of heavy footsteps catch up with me.

"Louise," Usalv rasps from behind me. "I need to speak with you. Right now."

CHAPTER THIRTEEN

"Usalv…now's not a really good time." Louise slows down but doesn't stop. "I've got to get ready for my classes."

"Bullshit. You've got over an hour." I lower my voice as we pass others. "Please?"

"Okay." She stops and folds her arms. "What is it?"

"Not here." I steer her past the women's locker room. "This way." A rush of heat ignites my fingertips as they nudge the small of her back. Sweet Lou makes no move to escape my touch, but right now I'm not sure if that's a good thing.

We turn down a narrow corridor that runs along the caged equipment room next to the maintenance closet. We stop when we reach the dusty gray circuit box that hangs on the wall where the corridor dead ends.

"That's far enough." She twists away from my hand and turns to face me. "Tell me what this is about."

My hand feels...bereft without the flesh of her lower back pressed against it, so I grasp the fence wall of the equipment room.

"Louise." I reach back and pull on the tiny clipped hairs growing on the nape of my neck. "We need to stay away from each other in the gym. And when I spar, you need to leave."

"Are you serious?" Her head shoots up and smashes against the circuit box. "Oww!"

"Shit." I cradle the back of her head. "Are you okay?"

"Yes...no!" She covers my hand where it clutches a curly mass of hair. "How can you say that?"

No matter how this comes out, it's going to suck. "MMA fighters train with members of their own club." I sigh. "At this rate, there won't be anyone left to train with."

"Are you blaming that mess"—she points to the main gym—"on me? How did I manage to draw that winning lottery ticket?"

"Because you're a damned distraction. Here and at home. One I can handle. The other I can't."

"A damned distraction? Excuse me? I am nothing but low key and professional around here." She steps away from the circuit box and brings her hip inches from mine.

"You're a drop dead gorgeous woman in a gym full of rutting rams." Her irritation and proximity only stoke my anger. "Are you that clueless about what goes on around you?"

"You've got to be kidding me." She looks down at her faded black running shorts and dingy gray T-shirt. "I'm not exactly into porn star couture."

"Jesus Christ, Lou. No one around here is tight and twisted over your clothes." I try and check myself but fail. "If I'd known that a head shot would land me in your lap with *that* rack thrust in my face for five full minutes, I'd have punched myself."

Her face shoots up and flashes me a shocked expression before it connects with the circuit box again. She hisses in response, and I reach out to cradle her head. This time she catches my hand and pulls it down away from her, without letting go.

"You need to get over it, Usalv," she says with finality. "All of you. I need this job. I won't quit, or slack-off and end up curbside."

"And what about Mike?" My voice fills with contempt.

"Mike?" She sounds confused. "Mike Daughtry?"

"Yeah. That Mike." My breathing stops while I wait for her answer.

"I know him through Macy's husband." She shakes her head. "We're polite to each other. That's it. What does this have to do with him?"

"He's nursing a thing for you." I blow out a breath. "And it's a bad one."

She blinks at me, stunned. "Are you saying what happened in there had something to do with me?"

"Sweetheart, it was all about you."

My words are followed by stunned silence. I watch as Louise's perfect mouth forms an oval.

"No way." She crosses her arms and shakes back and forth.

"Let me ask you this. Have you ever dated Mike?"

"Um, no."

"Ever agreed to go out with him but never got around to it?"

"No. I've made it very clear that I'm not interested in him."

"Mmm. Ever get drunk and have sex with him?"

"Did he tell you that?" She takes an indrawn breath and pushes my arm away.

"No. But like you, he wouldn't say either way."

"Then I'll answer for both us. Never. Now you can go get bent." Her voice is filled with disgust.

This whole thing is killing me. I need to put my cards on the table.

"Wait." My hand flies to her hip, holding her in place. "Remember the day I ran into the two of you outside, and he walked you to the EL? The day after that, he told me to back off and leave you alone."

"What?" she explodes. "He had no right to do that."

"That's a relief."

"Really? And what was your response to his request?" She gives me an expectant glare.

"He saw you first." Embarrassment makes me squirm. "What could I say?"

"So the two of you got together and decided who had dibs on me?" She squeezes my forearms, then pushes me away. "Damn it, I'm not the last six-pack at the mini-mart." She shakes her head. "What a bunch of numb-nuts."

"Louise." She tries to push past me and I release her hip and grasp the metal cage wall beside us. "Mike tried to kick my ass today because he found out you moved into my place last weekend. I sure as hell didn't tell him. If you didn't, then who did?" I raise my hand in a questioning gesture before I let her pass.

She doesn't move. "Oh my God." She gasps. "Macy."

"Your roommate?" I never thought about it.

She nods and stares off into space. "Macy's always pushed the idea of me and Mike as a couple. And every time I think we've moved past it, she starts back up with a wave of subtle hints."

"Well, she hasn't given up." I'm relieved but feel bad for Louise.

"Clearly not." She sounds disappointed. "I'm

sorry Mike did that to you in there. He had no right. Are you hurt?" She rubs my elbow and lower arm where Mike's kick made contact.

"Nah." She saw the whole thing. I smile. "We were pissed off, not out of control. Neither of us hit at full throttle."

"Thank God for that."

"Still though, I shouldn't have hit him that hard." Regret washes over me. "Goddamn that guy. He's got the attention span of a gnat."

"But you don't, do you? You tend to be like, laser focused, right?"

"Have to be. Too easy to get distracted, especially doing this for a living."

Louise nods, then gives me a puzzled look. "Then why did you offer to let me stay with you? You're clearly not a fly-by-the-seat-of-your-pants kind of guy."

I flush, making me grateful for not shaving today. "Because I didn't want you to owe Mike."

She tilts her head. "You wanted me to owe you instead?"

"Not exactly." I take a deep breath. "I had a feeling that the two of you weren't on the same wavelength. Especially after overhearing that argument you had with Macy at your apartment. I didn't want to see you blindsided."

"Why do you care?" she asks.

"I don't know." I fold my arms defensively. "Why did you shove your hand up my towel and kiss me?"

Louise cringes and now it's her turn to flush. "Listen, about that—"

"Let me guess. You were drunk?"

"I was drunk," she admits. "That's not normal for me. I am sorry."

"You've never given me a hell of a lot of encouragement." I feel myself glare at her. "Now the only play I get is struck down with drunken deniability? Thanks."

"You've been really nice to me." She tucks back into the corner between the circuit box and cage wall with her arms folded. "Thank you for everything. I mean that."

"Nice?" I repeat, frustration filling my voice. "Nice? In a place like this, what the hell do you think that means?"

"I don't know." Sweet Lou gives me a pleading, troubled look. "It's not right for me to read into that just because you don't act like a Neanderthal. God knows I hate it when that happens to me."

I blow out a long, slow breath and scratch my beard so hard that there are going to be visible marks. My eyes meet hers and she looks away.

Fuck it.

One of my hands grasps the cage wall, while the other finds the curve of her hip, gripping and releasing it gently as I work up the nerve to speak.

"What are you doing?" she rasps.

"There's a lot of kicking in taekwondo, right?" I ask.

"Um...yeah," she answers in a tentative voice.

"So as long you're standing, you can defend yourself, right?"

Her eyebrows bend in confusion. "Pretty much."

"Good." My frame lines up in front of hers against the wall as I inch closer. "You don't ever need to defend yourself against me, Sweet Lou," I whisper into her ear. "Don't kick me."

"Kick you?" she repeats.

I release her hip and place my hand on the other side of her head against the wall, caging her in. Lou's gaze follows my hand before she turns to look at me.

"What are you doing?" she asks.

"Changing my tactics." Her mouth parts, just a little and I bring my lips down on hers.

It takes every bit of my self-control not to own that mouth. My kiss is slow and gentle as it's ever been, and I'm as patient as I know how to be.

I...*need.*

Need to know this isn't all in my head, that the physical signals she puts out aren't all about her being drunk or stressed or even celibate for way too long. I...*need* her to want me, too. And moments later, pieces of the puzzle slide slowly into place.

Sweet Lou's lips press against mine, stunned and

unmoving. I feel her palms spread open against my chest. My breathing stops as they still there, hesitant and undecided. I pause, expecting her to push me away, but the opposite happens.

She exhales and groans while her hands grasp my shirt, pulling me close as those perfect lips part and she kisses me back.

Her hands inch up my shoulders, stroking them through my sweat soaked shirt, until they slide around the back of my neck and pull me down as her breasts crush against my chest.

"Christ, Louise." My fingertips explore the curve of her hip, its ultra-smooth skin a stimulating contrast to the rough calluses that cover my hands.

As the pad of my thumb traces along the smooth muscles of her pelvis, she shudders and gasps aloud. Sweet Lou's back arches against the wall and those endless legs coil themselves around my waist, drawing me in, the skin of our stomachs now flesh to flesh.

Damn. It's on. And so am I.

One of my hands secures the leg coiled around me, while the other grips the flesh underneath her fine ass. Sweet Lou's hold tightens around my neck as I lift her out of the tiny corner and lean her against the fenced wall of the equipment cage.

My hands reach around her arched back and unclasp two different sports bras. As my fingers twist the freed nipples, my mouth makes its way to the tips of her breasts, delivering licks and gentle bites.

"Oh God," she rasps. She tugs the hem of my shirt, lifting it over my head. She devours my naked torso with a scorching gaze from her heated amber eyes. That smoldering mouth descends on my hardened nipple and licks it before tracing circles around it with her taut one, still wet from the exploration of my tongue.

"Louise." My voice quivers. Bolts of pure heat shoot from my nipple straight to my groin. I swell harder and larger against the cup in my compression shorts until it's tight and painful.

I release my grip on her other breast and put my hand down between us, halting the friction between those sleek thighs and my groin. I gasp for breath, but not before she starts riding the hand I've put between us.

"Louise, wait." I plead, but she misunderstands.

"How do we take this off?" Her fingers tap against my cup before they explore the waistband of my shorts.

I contemplate it myself, but this won't work. I've been dying to bury myself inside her for weeks. But between me being super torqued and her being unaware of my...my...size issues, there's a serious chance I'll hammer her insides. And damn it, I refuse hurt any woman like that, especially Sweet Lou.

"Just lean back and enjoy the ride, sweetheart."

'But—oh…" She gasps as my fingers slide beneath her clothes. Her folds are slick and sticky as I slide my hand down their center crease. As I push my hip against her inner thigh, Sweet Lou's stance widens, giving us both more room to move.

My hand moves in perfect rhythm as Sweet Lou's pelvis grinds up and down against it, both becoming wetter and faster with every stroke, her rapid breathing punctuated with grunts and tiny gasps.

She digs her elbows hard into my upper arms, bracing herself for better leverage against my hand. I'm solely focused on giving her the king of all hand jobs when our two-person cocoon shatters.

"Where the hell is Usalv?" Rodgers explodes from the main entrance to the gym.

"Oh fuck!" The sound of Rodgers voice clouds the hazy pleasure in Louise's eyes. She freezes, then tries to dismount.

"Shh," I whisper without stopping my strokes. "He won't look here. Just keep quiet."

"Are you sure?" she asks.

I cover her mouth with mine and increase the speed and pressure of my hand inside her pants.

"He's probably cooling off, Coach. He sure was pissed off."

"Well, that makes two of us."

Her eyes fly open, but I shake my head and she closes them a final time and concentrates.

"You're close. Come for me, sweetheart," I beg. I need to be able to do this for her, to make her feel satisfied.

The speed of her hips increases then stops while her entire body shudders. Louise bursts into loud panting gasps, and I cover her mouth with mine to stifle the noise.

My hand remains buried in her folds as they pulse with pleasure, and a deep feeling of male pride mixed with relief wash over me as the sound of Sweet Lou screaming penetrates deep into my throat.

"I'll go check the men's room. If you see him, let him know to come find me."

"Sure, Coach."

Our bodies heave a mutual sigh of relief. As Sweet Lou's leg buckles and her grasp slackens around my neck, I gently lower us to the floor and kneel next to her.

"Didn't they go to the hospital?" I glance over my shoulder then turn around, shaking my head.

"The nearest one isn't far." She pulls her ponytail and twists it hard around her fingers. "If they took a cab, maybe he's gone and come back."

I nod in agreement then let my eyes skate over her. Sweet Lou's tongue glides across swollen lips and her face is covered with a thin sheet of sweat.

Red scrape marks from my beard dot along her breasts, throat, and neck while the flesh starts to bruise from the marks left by my lips, teeth, and tongue.

She'll probably be pissed about that later, but right now, I'll just enjoy the view.

She looks like she just got fucked—in a good way.

"You good, Lou?" I don't even try to hide my smug smile.

She flushes deep red and rolls those gorgeous amber eyes. "Yeah, I'll do."

"Glad to hear it," I let her know.

"Good to know." She shoots me a look of distress. "But what about you? You never—"

"Don't worry about it. Everything's good." I take her hands in mine and kiss them.

I release her hands and stand to put my shirt on. "We should get out of here before someone does find us." When my clothes are back on, I offer Lou my hand and pull her up.

"Yeah. There's not much to conclude besides the obvious," she replies, then leans over to fasten her bras.

I nod, distracted by the massive, painful erection that's not going anywhere without an ice-cold shower or something that's not going happen soon enough.

"Let me go first. I want to find him instead of the other way around."

"Sure." She nods.

I plant a quick kiss on her forehead. "See you at home?"

She nods again. "I'll be there."

"Good. Gotta go now."

With a final backward glance, I turn the corner and hurry away.

CHAPTER FOURTEEN

The distant sound of a door closing startles me awake. "Usalv?"

After our gym encounter yesterday, I rushed home, hoping he'd be here. Since he wasn't,

I grabbed my class notes and headed out to the neighborhood café and hit the books, determined to avoid the appearance of waiting around to get naked.

It wasn't only for appearances, I admit to myself. After his spontaneous handiwork, Usalv left in a big preoccupied hurry. If all he's after is someone to get him off in a quiet corner when the mood strikes, then he needs to know that I'm not his go-to girl.

Because that's not...not who I am.

Truth be told, my eager participation shocked but didn't surprise me. What heterosexual female could deny Usalv's appeal?

Martial arts keep me in close proximity to fit, hot athletic guys. Before moving in to Usalv's house, I told myself that he was just another hotshot jock that I'd get used to being around.

Damn if that wasn't my biggest screw-up in recent memory.

I sit up on the daybed in my bedroom behind the kitchen. Piles of class notes and textbooks that were my only companions last night are arranged around me on the bed. As my legs swing down, stacks of study materials fly off the bedside and crash to the floor. Cursing silently, I arrange them in a makeshift pile then head out to the hallway.

"Hey, are you here?" I yell up the stairs.

The high-pitched vibration of the water pipes from the shower in Usalv's bathroom are the only audible sound. I shrug, then head into the kitchen to make coffee as usual.

But not only is the coffee made, it's half gone. On a normal day, Usalv showers, then comes down to eat before he leaves. But now I remember the sound of the front door waking me. Did he come home last night?

My hands still on the coconut creamer carton when the creak of the stairs straining under the weight of his heavy frame comes closer. Usalv hurries through the kitchen door and a look of surprised alarm flashes across his face when he sees me by the counter.

"Morning, Sweet Lou." His voice is calm and controlled, the surprised look long gone. "Didn't think you'd be up this late. Or early, I guess."

"I went to sleep about one last night. That's early for me." I stir the creamer until the contents of my cup is tawny brown. "You've already had yours?" I look up and gesture toward the coffee pot as the spoon clanks against my cup.

"Yeah. I got home late. Or early, depending how you look at it. Anyway, I couldn't wait." Usalv nods toward the hallway. "Saw your door was open this morning. I know you don't get too much sleep, so sorry if I woke you."

"You didn't come home last night?" I blurt out, ignoring his small talk.

"No, I didn't" He gives me a curious smile. "Why? Is that a problem?"

"Not at all." I backtrack quickly. "I don't...really have the right to ask that, do I? I...just hope everything's okay, that's all."

I take my coffee cup and attempt to exit the kitchen, but somehow that big body ends up in my way. Usalv's large hand reaches down and cradles the side of my hip, a gesture that's becoming all too familiar, all too welcomed.

"I spent the night at my uncle's." He plants a chaste kiss on my forehead. "Talking business. It got late. Happens once in a while."

"You don't have to tell me that." I bring my coffee

cup between us and cradle it with both hands, willing myself not to touch him.

"Maybe I want you to know." He snaps the embroidered waistband of my gray silky pajamas. "I like these, by the way."

"Yeah. Listen..." I pull out of his grasp and retreat behind the island counter. "About yesterday. You're...um, really good at...you know. You know that, right?" I stammer. "But maybe we should just keep it at a one-off. Okay?"

His response is pin-drop silence, a raised eyebrow the only indication he heard me. Usalv slowly removes the phone and keys from his hoodie pocket, then throws them on the kitchen table before he approaches me.

"A one-off?" An edge creeps into the controlled calm of his voice. "Really?"

"I think that's best right now." I'm resigned. "We both have a lot going on at the moment." I pause while he grabs the counter on each side of my waist. "And we never talked about it before I moved in."

He nods, his face inches from mine. "Okay. Let's talk about it."

"All right." If he wants honesty, I'll give it to him. "I can't do friends-with-benefits." My eyes meet his without flinching. "It works for some people, I get that. But it's not for me." I shake my head.

"You sure about that? Sometimes we just have to take things how we find them."

"I know. But not this time." I try and scoot sideways, but that arm is as strong as a steel girder. "I'm a nurse. I spend a lot of time imposing emotional distance between me and my patients and their families. I can't do that with someone I'm sleeping with." My voice sounds defeated, even to me. "I'm sorry."

"Mmm." Usalv nods, his face a stoic mask before his eyes skate down my body. I feel my temperature start to rise and hope like hell he doesn't notice.

After an intense few moments, I start to squirm. "Um, I should go." I have no idea where, so here's hoping he doesn't ask.

"You know what I think we should do?" he asks, toying with the slinky strap of my cami.

"Not really." I look around for a way to escape the human cage he's trapped me in.

"Here it is…" Usalv pulls the strap and releases it, causing an audible snap. "We'll take this slow."

"Slow?" I repeat as my throat becomes dry.

"Very, very slow." Usalv's hand leaves the strap of my cami and grasps my chin, tilting it upward for me to look at him. "And anytime we go too fast, or it feels like too much, you tell me to stop."

"Tell you to stop?" I ask in disbelief.

"Tell me to stop and I will." His eyes radiate sincerity. "Promise."

"I'll think about it, okay?" I pat his hand softly before I try and slide out of his reach.

He sighs, exasperated with my attempts to get away. Then without another word, he lifts me up onto the counter like a tiresome child. Those strong hands gently part my legs and he crowds me until there's nowhere to go.

"You do that, okay Sweet Lou?" He places a possessive kiss on my lips, trapping me in his erotic web.

That strong hand travels to the strap of my cami and yanks it off my shoulder. When I feel my arm lift to hasten its removal, a primal part of me admits defeat in this ongoing battle of wills between us.

Usalv tugs the cami down my torso until it rests on my waist, exposing my breasts. He gives a primal grunt as his face descends on them, his beard making my flesh quiver, tickle, and burn as he nips and licks the tender skin.

"Look out, sweetheart." Usalv wraps one arm around my back while he pushes an empty colander and a set of wooden salt and pepper shakers onto the tile floor. Then he lays me down with one hand, while the other pulls off my bikini underwear and PJ bottoms in a quick single motion.

"Careful," I beg as my body shivers against the uncomfortable cold of the stone counter top. "Please."

"Always."

Flat on my back, I shudder as his arm lies across my torso, resting on my breast to keep me in place. I try to shift, but he has me pinned. God, he's strong. I'm ready to protest, but then his tongue touches my abdomen, and licks a tender trail down to the space between my thighs.

He's careful without being timid. At all. Our previous encounter has stamped a possessive familiarity into his demeanor. Fingers. Tongue. Teeth. Lips. Chin. Whiskers. Groping. Tasting. Grazing. Kissing. Pushing. Quilling. It goes on, and on, and on until I lose track of time.

"Usalv, please." I beg as my pelvis starts to pulse in waves of heat up and down my core.

His lips make a smacking sound before he answers. "Please what? Tell me, Louise." His voice is calm and certain, like he's got all the time in the world.

I know what he wants me to say. I know he wants me to beg. But something inside me refuses. "Oh, for Christ sake," I mutter before reaching down to soothe myself in the absence of his touch.

"No way," he growls. Usalv pins my arm to one side and goes back down on me, his mouth filling and creating a void at the same time. His relentless tongue plunges in and out with all the force and speed that I crave at the moment, but will no doubt punish me later. He goes faster and faster, until my insides pulse at the same speed and rhythm on their own.

I cry out a loud and guttural wail that's impossible to suppress or control. As my orgasm explodes, Usalv's mouth clamps down on my most sensitive part, pressing and releasing in perfect tempo.

When it stops, he lets go of me, allowing my parted legs back together. I fold my knees and bring them up to my chest and cradle myself in a fetal position on top of the counter.

Usalv runs a possessive hand over the curve of my hip as he watches me. I close my eyes, wishing him away but not wanting him to go.

He bends down over me, and his lips find my neck and cheek before they rest alongside my ear.

"Hey," he whispers. "Sweet Lou?"

"Mmm?" My exhausted, wordless response sounds distant even to me.

He places a soft kiss on my lips. I can smell and taste myself on his whiskers and tongue. "You forgot to say stop."

Then he slaps the fleshy part of my butt, just enough to make it sting.

My eyes fly open just in time to see his back retreat. I lift my head off the counter and watch as he takes his keys and phone from the table, and pockets them without a backward glance. He exits the kitchen and a few seconds later, the front door closes with a deliberate, controlled thud.

Oh *fuck.*

CHAPTER FIFTEEN

"Hey, girl!" Macy steps away from the brick façade by the bar entrance and waves to me.

"Hey, you!" I bend down for a hug, careful to avoid the smoke and flick of ash from her cigarette. "Watch that damn thing, would you?" My words are harsh, but my tone is gentle.

"Sorry. I know you hate these things. So do I. Or so I should."

Macy's been through hell, and we all have different ways to cope, but I hate watching her self-destruct right in front me.

I shake my head. "Does Paul know you've started back up again?"

"We haven't had a conversation about it, but he probably suspects." She pulls one hand out of her pocket and studies a half-empty pack of cigarettes.

"Hmm...should I stretch these out until he arrives? Or smoke myself silly until the last possible moment?"

"Whichever." I smile at her despite myself. "But please quit again."

"Trying. But...I think I'm waiting for Paul to come home now. I just don't feel that stressed out when he's around." She gives me a strained smile." I never did."

"When he's back?" I ask.

"Early next week. A month, just like they said." She takes a long drag, burning the cigarette down to the butt. "I'm planning his welcome home party at O'Shea's. It's a week from next Saturday." Macy pauses to grind it out in a large metal ashtray. "You should bring someone."

"Thanks, Macy." I glance up at the door. "Looks like the place is filling up. Want to go in?"

"Lead the way."

The small bar occupies a prime location on this trendy street. Macy and I wanted to check it out a while ago, but then life happened. When I texted her for a meet-up this morning, she'd immediately suggested here.

The atmosphere reminds me of our usual favorite places. A pleasant buzz of chatter hangs in the air, neither too loud nor too quiet, while a familiar song that I can't name plays in the background.

"Quick! Grab it, Macy." By a stroke of pure luck, a couple pawing each other abruptly desert a tiny bar table hidden behind the entrance rail.

"Good call." Macy's tiny frame inches between the rail and table. It's a Friday night free for all, but Macy scrunches her way to the far side of the table, making it impossible to tell how long she's been sitting there to others hunting for a seat in the crowded bar.

"What I can bring you tonight?" a waitress in a white shirt and black pants asks when she appears.

"Kirschwasser?" I reply.

"Yeah, we got that."

Macy shoots me a surprised look. Most nights we split a pitcher of some exotic beer she chooses.

"Neat, please."

The waitress nods and looks at Macy.

"Irish cream," she replies.

"Kilkenny, right?"

"Yeah."

"Didn't know you were such a big brandy fan," Macy remarks after the waitress leaves.

"I've always preferred hard-A when I drink," I reply.

She shoots me a stunned look. "Well, why the hell didn't you ever say so?"

"I've never minded your choices before." I give her a pointed look. "At least when it came to beer."

"Oh?" Macy raises her eyebrows in response.

"What's on your mind, Louise?" She folds her hands on the table.

"My dear, dear friend…" My voice is gently tinged with cynicism. "How the hell did Mike find out that I was staying at Usalv's? Because he sure the hell didn't get it from me."

"Guilty." She raises her hand. "Well, fuck, Louise I had to tell him something when I called to cancel the day Usalv came over and you gave us the ditch. Which wasn't very nice, by the way."

"You heard what happened to Mike, right?"

"About his eye? Yeah, he told me he got hurt at the gym. So what?"

I lean forward. "Mike got his ass kicked in a quasi-professional brawl that he started with Usalv."

"Usalv?" A red flush creeps across her pale face.

"Yeah."

"Oh my God." Her hand flies to her mouth.

She gives a grateful smile as our drinks are deposited onto the table. The waitress looks at our faces and leaves quickly.

"Macy, I'm not interested in Mike. Please stop trying to get us together." My voice is calm and firm.

She takes a sip of ale, and her features transform into a stoic mask. People in healthcare who deliver life-changing bad news learn how to school their expressions.

It's a skill that comes in handy for other occasions, too.

"We're not destined to balance each other out," I insist. "I'm not going to make him less indecisive; he's not going to make me less intense." I pause and look her straight in the eye. "We'd drive each other bat shit crazy."

Macy's stoic mask dissolves into a look of deep resignation. It's a rare moment in our relationship.

"After Tim, you were in a world of hurt," she reminds me. "You said no to dating, not no to Mike. We'd all hoped that when you were ready, you'd give him a chance."

My stomach feels like it just got kicked. Hard.

"You were all so close," I explain. "Mike was everywhere we went. Every time. I was trying to keep things casual and polite." My temples throb gently, but the pain is manageable. "I thought you of all people knew my true feelings."

Macy exhales slowly. "Deep down, I probably did. But we'd all love to have you as part of the family. I guess that got in the way."

"We?"

"Paul, Mike, and me," she admits in a sad voice.

"Thank you." I swallow hard and feel tears well up in my eyes. "That's one of the nicest things anyone has ever said to me."

"God, Lou, please stop," Macy gushes. "I'm so sorry. To you. To Mike." Her teary eyes meet mine.

"I really was trying to help you both be happy. Please believe me."

"I have no objections to happiness, and you meant well, that's who you are. But no more. Please."

"Well, you could do worse," she jokes.

"Macy..." I warn her.

"Mike's easy on the eyes, and he's got more money than God. There's still time... Are you sure?"

"Absolutely positive."

Macy snorts. "Girl, you're only positive when you're off the market." She gives me a curious stare. "Are you?"

It's a bit unsteady but I manage to laugh. "That's a good question."

"You know, you have to own some of this Mike shit. You never gave me a heads up about Usalv. I had no fucking clue."

"I wanted to, believe me," I insist. "But with Paul's injuries and all my new stuff, it just didn't happen. Never the right time, or enough of it."

"Tell me now," she presses. "What's going on with you?"

I give her an assessing look. If I can't confide in her, who can I tell?

"In the last week"—I lean my head in—"I've been bumped, pumped and humped. Licked, flicked and wicked. Plucked, sucked, and—"

"I knew it!" Macy shoots her fist into the air.

"The way he looked at you, like he wanted to swallow you whole and didn't give a tinker's damn that I was right there. I knew he'd have you flat on your back the first week you moved in there."

I give her a silent nod of acknowledgement but say nothing.

"Is everything okay?" Macy's glee evaporates.

"I don't know."

"My God, Louise, you don't look happy. You should be happy... Why aren't you?"

"In girl code?" It's our shorthand for discussing personal topics in public places.

Macy looks around the bar. "Yeah, sure."

"Because..." I lower my voice and lean toward her. "The boys have yet to bat."

"What?" Macy's high-pitched response draws sharp glances from a nearby table.

"It's the God-awful truth," I mutter.

"Are you saying"—she looks around the bar and ducks her head—"that he hasn't taken out the toolkit?"

"Not even a glimpse of the batter's box."

"Hmm..." Macy throws an arm over the back of her stool and stares up at the light fixture for a moment. "So what happens?"

"I don't know," I reply in my best clinic professional voice. "After I...come, we're done."

She nods. "Does he get lift off?"

"I'm pretty sure he does. Whenever I've had

contact with his bullpen, he seems rock solid. But every time I try to take his pants off, he tells me later. Then he gets me off, and later never comes. No pun intended."

"But does he finish himself?"

"I don't know. This morning he made me come twice, and after—"

"Twice? Without using any heavy equipment? Jesus Christ, Louise."

"I know, right?" My frustration returns at the memory. "But I'm barely done and he's off like a shot to the bathroom. And, then—"

"Yeah?"

"He takes a shower with the door locked." I pause. "Today I asked if we could shower together, but he said he needed to hurry."

Macy throws me a thoughtful look. "So he knows his way around your powder puff, he gets lift-off, but the final act is a cliffhanger?" She pauses and shrugs her shoulders. "Maybe he's saving it up."

"Oh my God. You really think...?"

"It certainly possible. Maybe Usalv's still on the V-team."

"A virgin?" I sit back stunned "That's not funny, Macy."

"I ain't laughing, Lou."

"It's possible, I suppose." It's a moment before the shock passes. "But I don't think so. He would have said something, right? I mean, does he really think I don't notice we never arrive at home plate?"

"Well…" Macy crosses her legs and folds her hands across one knee. "Maybe if you're…satisfied, he thinks you don't mind."

"So I don't care if things are *that* one sided as long as I'm getting mine? How flattering is that." I coil a strand of hair around my finger and pull until it hurts. "Of course, maybe it's just me. Maybe I'm the problem."

"How are you the problem?" Macy asks.

"We never talked about any kind of sexual relationship before I moved in. It started in a weak moment for both of us. Maybe now that it's happened, he's just passing the time until I get my own place."

"It's possible." Macy renders a blunt assessment. "Does he ever refuse when you initiate things?"

"I don't initiate. He does. Well, not exactly." I sigh in frustration. "If we're both home and neither one of us need to leave, it…just happens." I shrug, confused.

"I remember those days." Macy smiles off in the distance before her focus returns. "Maybe things have caught him off guard too. Cut him some slack. And talk to him."

"Don't you think I've tried? Every time I do, he puts me on my back and goes to town."

"Ahh, the avoidance orgasm. A very effective

tactic." Macy's sage tone bristles. "If you want answers, then it's time for you take control."

"Take control?"

"Yes. Insist that he give you what you want. On your terms."

"And how do I do that? Get out the whips and chains? 'Cause I gotta say, that's not really my thing." I'm equal parts joking and serious.

"It doesn't have to be." Macy gives a short laugh. "Just let him know that if he wants to continue, that are some things you'd like to try, too."

"And what if he says no?"

She rolls her eyes. "If you're doing it as much as you say, it won't be that easy for him. But if you think he might try to go there, then you've got have a seduction plan prepared."

"Seduction? As in thongs and see-through negligees?"

"Hell, yes." Macy whips out her phone and does a search. "That stuff really amps things up in the bedroom. Or wherever. Oh look!" She holds up her phone. "Vic's is still having a sale! You need to get down there."

"Hold on a sec," I put out my hand in front of her phone. "Say I do this, say it works. What does this tell me? Other than he likes sex, long legs, and a nice rack?"

"Let's break this down." Macy bangs a pensive rhythm on her chin with her finger. "You need to know if this…preference…he's got is something he's willing to compromise on or if it's a serious hang up that you need to deal with. Or walk away from."

"Walk away?" My stomach sours.

'You two got all down and dirty before either of you came clean about what you wanted out of this. It's too soon to say how it'll end up. But sometimes you start off not knowing. It happens."

"It sure does." Reality sinks in, slow and painful. "I never thought I'd find myself in a situation like this."

"Like I said, it does happen. Not all relationships start with candy and flowers or romantic weekends at quaint B&Bs." She covers my hand with hers on the table. "But now that you're in it, don't fall for him and then find out later you're not compatible that way."

I nod in agreement. "So…seduction?"

"Seduction."

CHAPTER SIXTEEN

"Louise? It's me." My duffel bag hits the floor and I take the stairs two at a time before she can stop me. "I'm going up to have a shower."

We haven't spent much time together since last Friday morning, right before I left town for my weekend fight. When I got home Sunday night, she'd already left for work and begun the grueling rhythm of twelve-hour shifts for the week.

I've worked hard to avoid her since, leaving before she arrived home or coming back after I thought she'd be gone. It's killing me to be away from her, but it's the only way to give my self-control a break. Since we met in the locker room, I haven't had straight-up sex, or even wanted it with anyone but her.

So I take what I can get.

She's frustrated, even worried, and I'll need to explain soon. But my physical issues and sex drive are not a discovery best made in the heat of the moment. But no matter how I go about it, it never goes well for me.

The upside is the further that conversation gets kicked down the road, the longer Sweet Lou will be in my life. And that's a trade-off I'm willing to make for as a long as it works.

I hurry through the bedroom door, tossing my keys and phone on the dresser. As I pull my black T-shirt overhead, a low husky voice startles me.

"So how'd it go?"

Holy *Christ.*

The T-shirt I'm holding floats to the floor, while my jaw drops like a broken drawbridge. My feet are planted in place and I feel myself staring, but it's impossible to pretend otherwise or look away.

Sweet Lou the sex kitten lies on her stomach in the middle of my king-sized bed. Standing at the door gives me a clear view of her pert, perfect, thong-adorned ass and those endless lithe and lean legs. That super-short slinky nightie is completely sheer, tied together around the back by an oversized black bow, while her breasts jut out of a sheer, lacy push-up bra.

"Louise?" I rasp, while my tongue and throat take on a sandpaper-like consistency. "Wha-at are you doing?"

"I've missed you," she explains as she swings her legs onto the floor and sits up, giving me a full view of her naked front through the sheer nightie. "It's been a long week. For both of us I think."

My downstairs, semi-torqued since finding her purse hanging from the banister, roars to life, heavy as lead, and hot as a volcano. I glance sideways and measure the ten paces to the bathroom door. Close, but nowhere close enough.

"It's nice to see you too, sweetheart. What're you wearing?" Fuck it, I can't help myself.

"Let me show you." She saunters over to me, wearing sky-high silver stiletto heels. Louise is a tall woman, but with those shoes, she's over six-foot tall and almost eye-level with me.

She stops in front of me and spins around slowly. "Do you like it?" The sex kitten smiles at me over her shoulder.

"You know I do." My eyes never leave the cutout lace waistband of her thong.

"Good." Sweet Lou turns back around, tilts her head up, and kisses me. Those X-rated lips are slick with deep coral gloss, but it smears off in no time, leaving the naked taste of Louise on my mouth and tongue.

Her taut nipples strain against their sheer lace cups. As she rubs her breasts against my bare chest, their movement scrapes my naked skin, making me shiver with waves of arousal.

The next thing I know, my hands are exploring her naked curves, pulling them close. One of Sweet Lou's hands clasps the nape of my neck, holding me to her mouth, while the other skates down to the belt buckle of my jeans.

I draw a sharp breath when she grabs the top of the buckle and leads me over to the bed. She pushes me down and focuses on the waist of my pants.

"What's this?" she asks when her futile attempts to remove it become a distraction.

"A belt buckle." I sound simple and stupid, but the sight of her propped up between my thighs grappling with my hardware distracts me.

"Gee, thanks." Sweet Lou's fingers run over the exotic engraved letters. "What does it say?"

"ΜΟΛΩΝ ΛΑΒΕ." I stroke her hair.

"Ma-lone-la-bay?" She repeats like a curious child doing tongue twisters. "Is that Macedonian?"

"Greek."

"What does it mean?"

Her question makes me flush. "It means 'Come and take it.'"

"Really?" She giggles, a sound that makes me think of pink bubble gum. Unrestrained. Undaunted. Unapologetic. "You believe in putting it out there, don't you? There's even a welcome sign on it."

"I'm a fighter," I explain calmly. "And it is a famous battle cry."

"Oh..." That final piece of information transforms her giggles into full blown laughter. "I'll bet it is." She tumbles on the bed beside me, her arms curled around her stomach.

"Hey." I'm on top of her in a heartbeat. "Stop laughing."

"Okay." Just like that, she stops. She studies my face a moment, and her expression softens. My lips lower onto hers, and we kiss while she's pinned under me.

It feels good to be up on her like this. Good as in *finally*. Good as in *right*. Good as in the *Real Deal*.

I reach around her back and untie the bow of that slinky nightgown. It's done its job—now it's time to get it out of the way. To my delight, the bra and gown are all one piece, and with the bow untied, the whole thing comes off.

"Nice," I tell her, sliding it down and off her body.

As I straddle her, the belt buckle's weight causes a gap in my waistband. Louise snakes one hand down and inside, while mine chases after to slow her exploration.

Her fingernails scratch up and down my thigh impatiently, and I cover them when they stroke back up to my waist. Louise stills as she discovers my cup.

"Why...are you still wearing this?" She sounds confused.

"Planned on showering when I got home, so I left it on."

"Really? That must be uncomfortable. How do we get it off?"

I knew this moment would come and envisioned a quiet night out where I'd explain everything over drinks. Lots of drinks, with our clothes still on. Never in my wildest dreams did the thought of her ambushing me in the bedroom occur to me.

Now dread makes me nauseous.

And then, for some inexplicable reason, Sweet Lou places a gentle kiss just above my navel. How did she know? Those soft lips are a soothing balm and my arms close around her as she blazes a trail of soft kisses up to my throat.

For a moment, I'm caught up in the sheer thrill of wanting and being wanted. The sex kitten's bold advances leave me confident of her desires, which for an eternal moment, allow mine to flourish without self-censure.

It's like being eighteen again.

"We need to get you out of these clothes," Louise whispers.

Eighteen?

"Please," she begs. "I can't get this stupid belt off." Her fingers twist the back of the buckle so she can study the snaps.

I remember eighteen.

"Louise, stop." I grab her wrists.

My desperation sounds harsh, and under me, Louise stiffens and recoils. Her palms open in a placating gesture.

"Sorry," she rasps after an awkward, unbroken pause.

My body shudders and I struggle to control my breathing.

"You can let go now." Her voice soothes me. "I won't touch you again."

I release her wrists immediately. She props herself up on her elbows and twists sideways.

"Please get off me." Her sober words hang like dark cloud over my bed.

I lift my leg off the bed, and Sweet Lou slides under it. She scoots to the headboard and covers her naked front with a pillow, bending her knees to hold it in place.

"Louise... I didn't mean... I didn't say that right." I kneel on the mattress in front of her.

She leans back against the headboard and stares at the ceiling.

"Louise, goddamn it, I'm sorry."

"Are you a virgin?" she blurts out with exasperation.

I huff in disbelief, then sit back on my heels and stare at her distressed face. "You think I'm...a virgin?"

"It was the only explanation we could come up with for why you never... Well, you know." She assesses me, her eyes filled with confusion and hurt.

"We?" I repeat, unable to suppress a flash of angry curiosity. "Who's *we*?"

"Macy and me," she confesses. "I told her about us, but never would've gotten into so much detail if I knew why this keeps happening."

"Macy told you that I was a virgin? Where'd she cook that up? Her fucking cousin Mike? It sounds like something that douche would say."

"Forget where I got the idea." Louise hits me with her pillow. "It doesn't matter." She chokes up and her eyes well with tears.

"Oh goddamn it. Louise, please don't do that."

"Oh, shut it," she cries, hitting my thigh with the pillow again. "All I know is that I'm here in your bed, wearing two hundred dollars' worth of lingerie, and you won't let me anywhere near second base." Her tortured voice breaks. "And you won't say why. Why?"

If she finds out now, without any warning, it's game over. Maybe not tonight, but soon. That's if she doesn't reject me on the spot. Or we go through with it and it's awful for her. Either way, I lose.

"Louise, sweetheart, just calm down—"

"If you're virgin, that's fine. I can respect that and we can talk about needs and limits, okay?"

"Louise." I grab her shoulders, and shake them

gently until she looks at me. "I am *not* a virgin." Fuck, I can't believe she even thought that.

She responds to the news with a confused expression. "But if it's not that, then what is it? Tell me something. Tell me anything."

"There's nothing wrong," I lie. "It's...it's just been a long week with all the traveling. We haven't seen each other, and there was something I wanted to tell you tonight. I was preoccupied when you... surprised me. That's all."

"You wanted to tell me something?" Her tone shifts to hopeful, while she turns her body toward me. "What is it?"

I hesitate a moment, then reach into the front pocket of my pants. My fingers grasp the familiar worn out leather of my spare keychain. I've been carrying it for ten days, hoping like hell she wouldn't ask or notice the work crew had stopped showing up.

"The new one-bedroom unit is ready." If I handle this right, it can buy me some time.

"Oh." Her head jerks back like she's been struck. "I see."

"Sorry it took so long." I place the keychain on the bed between us. Her feet recoil from it as she shifts away.

"Louise... I didn't mean to upset you." That's the fucking truth. "I thought you'd be pleased."

My awkward attempt to break the silence backfires.

"Did you?" She blinks hard, unable to suppress the tears that stream down her cheeks. "So you raced back here from the gym, without showering or taking your cup off to tell me it's time to move out?"

Oh fuck.

"Of course not," I stammer.

"Then why?" She wipes the tears away. "Why didn't you shower, change, and get takeout on the way home?"

"I don't know," I reply after a damning pause.

"Liar!" She takes her pillow and hits me across my arm. "This conversation is over." Fury replaces sadness, drying up her tears.

"Lou, wait." Desperation returns to my voice.

"I'm done waiting." Her heated tone radiates anger. "You don't... You just don't want me," she chokes. "You won't tell me why. And I can't stay here while you keep the reason to yourself." She grabs the keychain from the bed. "I'll be out tonight." She scoops her nightie off the floor. "I'll get the rest of my things when... When you're not around."

The determined finality of her words cause me physical pain. I haven't cried since my fifteenth birthday, when my father called and said that I couldn't come home.

Couldn't. Come. Home.

After spending a year here as a friendless, freakish teenager who hardly spoke English. Eternal days incarcerated in high school hell, with evenings and weekends spent working construction for my uncle. The only thing that kept me upright during that twisted march was the belief that I'd go home soon.

Until one day, even that got taken away from me.

Familiar feelings of dread and abandonment wash over me as Louise slides her arms back into her nightie and walks to the bedroom door.

In many ways, I've never recovered.

I leap off the bed and block her exit.

"Louise. Wait."

When she shakes her head, I fall to my knees and wrap my arms around her thighs. "Don't go." I press my face against her stomach. "Please."

CHAPTER SEVENTEEN

"Damn you, Usalv." I cradle his head as it presses against my stomach.

I curse at him, but on the inside, it's directed at both of us. My pathetic inability to set limits with him both frustrates and frightens me.

"I'll tell you the truth." His cobalt eyes plead up at me. "I promise."

"You'd better," I insist. "Lies and omissions are deal breakers for me. Seriously."

"Fair enough." He stands without releasing me. "But if you want to hear it, you have to hear it all."

Usalv takes my arm and settles me back on the bed. Then he backs away and paces in long slow circles around the bedroom, pulling the curls at his nape hard enough to straighten them.

The entire room stills. I don't think either of us is breathing. His expression is a mix of determination, patience, and fear. I give him an encouraging smile, while silently bracing for what's to come.

He sighs. "You know what I do for a living."

"Of course."

"And that I'm very good at it." He strikes a calm tone, but his eyes do not meet mine and his fingernails dig into the nape of his neck. "One of the reasons I'm so good is that I'm unusually large and strong."

"I know all this." My stomach churns. "Please just tell me."

"Louise." He waits until my eyes meet his, forcing me to focus on his words. "I'm that way *everywhere*."

The word settles like cement and a hard, heavy atmosphere takes over the room.

"Everywhere...you mean?" My eyes drop below his waist.

His arms cross in front of his chest. "Yeah."

"Oh." My throat is dry and scratchy. "Well, some people consider that a desirable quality." I hadn't known what was coming, but this wasn't on the short list.

"Maybe." His frustration comes through, clear as a bell. "If you're a porn star. Or don't mind being a box to check on some nameless woman's sexual bucket list. But for a long-term monogamous relationship? That's a whole different ballgame, sweetheart."

His lonely tone makes my heart lurch, and I gesture for him to come sit beside me. He settles on the bedside, his back against my leg, with an elbow resting on his knee.

"Large, strong, healthy men have sex all the time." My voice epitomizes practiced calm. "Evolution favors it. It's the way we're all wired."

He gives a long deep sigh. "Women I've had sex with complain about the pain. Others change their minds when they see me." He pauses again. "I don't want any of those things to happen with you."

"Hold on a second. You're worried about *me* rejecting *you*?" I huff in disbelief.

"Hell yeah," he confesses. "I'm a lot of take on. Both in and out of bed."

His anguish wears a raw spot into my soul. "That won't happen." I promise. "Stop worrying."

"Louise, I ruptured a woman's cervix." The words rush out of him before his eyes shut in a tense crinkled line.

Surprise washes over me like a tsunami. The muscles in my face contract and release as my clinician mask fixes itself onto my features. "Are you sure? That's pretty hard to do."

He winces. "I'm sure."

"That must have been traumatic." I strive to be honest and sympathetic.

"Traumatic?" He snorts in disgust. "I hurt a girl I

liked a lot. She never spoke to me again. And I couldn't blame her at all."

"I know it's none of my business"—I run a tentative hand over his shoulder—"but you can tell me what happened, if you want to. I've been a nurse for a while now. It takes a lot to shock me." I give his shoulder a reassuring squeeze.

"I've never talked about it with anyone." He studies my face a moment, undecided. "Except the ER doc."

"That's okay." I give him a patient nod.

"There's not much to tell." His large body turns toward me. "It was senior year in high school. She was my first, first…"

"Your first sexual partner?" I finish for him.

"Yes." He blows out a breath. "I filled out a lot that year. It happened so fast, I really hadn't developed a good sense of my strength or size."

"It does take some time. Especially at that age."

He nods. "Well, that's all there is to it. We were having sex, she started moaning and it turned me on. I pushed too hard, and we ended up in the ER." He stares off, engrossed in the memory. "After the ER doc explained what happened to her parents, we never saw each other outside of school again."

Wow.

The shock. The guilt. The mortification of her parents finding out what had happened. It must have been horrendous. I run my hand down the smooth planes of his back.

"That was a long time ago, Usalv. You were an inexperienced kid. You're not anymore."

"I'm still strong, and still huge." His voice is bitter. "That hasn't changed."

"You *have* changed since school. Hell, we all have. Maybe...*it* isn't as bad as you think."

"It's bad enough," he insists.

"Let me the judge of that." I pause. "Show me."

He gives me a startled look. "What?"

My heart skips a beat. "I'll have to see you some time, right?"

"Right."

He stands up alongside the bed, facing away from me. I hear the pop of his belt buckle and rustle of fabric. His jeans slide down first, then his compression shorts. He steps out of the discarded clothing pile, completely naked. My eyes meet his and I give him a patient nod, before he turns to face me.

Oh. My. God.

I draw a shocked uncontrolled breath and he winces.

"You good, Louise?"

I hear the question but don't answer right away. Because I can't.

His warrior body is not the least diminished by the low evening light. My eyes skate down the front of his abdomen, fixating on the hollowed-out bones of his pelvis. The planes and proportions are as close to real life perfection as anyone could imagine.

His weight shifts from side to side as my gaze descends. Forcing my expression to be impassive, I take in that final part of him.

"Louise?" He sounds nervous. "Say something."

"Do you get any bigger?" I wonder aloud.

"Bigger?" He repeats. "Are you serious?"

"Oh. I mean, some men get larger when they…"

"I get it." He relaxes. "Not me. Not much anyway."

"That's a relief." I blurt out before checking myself.

Usalv buries his forehead in his large palm and shakes his head.

"Wait. Listen." I tell him. "It's okay. Nothing I didn't expect." My calmness impresses even me.

He stares at me in disbelief. "Now I know you're lying."

"No, I'm not. Every part of you is physically extraordinary." I explain in a matter of fact tone. "Why should this be any different?"

"So you're okay with this?" The base of his throat begins to pulse, pulling my gaze away from his groin. "With me?"

"Of course." My legs unravel and I stand next to him beside the bed, kissing the side of his shoulder.

"Sweet Christ." He studies me with cobalt eyes,

and his expression of hesitation transforms into one of heated desire. "You're all I've thought about for ages."

I slide my arms out of my nightie and it drops to the floor with a silky swish. Usalv watches me, unmoving. When I smile, his hands encircle my waist and pull me toward him.

His fingers slide underneath the elastic bands of my thong, then wraps his huge hands around my hips, and pulls me down toward him.

"It's the same for me." I straddle him on the bed, our faces close together. "I want us to try." My lips touch his, exploring their smooth wet texture. "I need you, too."

He meets my eyes and gives me a wordless shake of his head. Then his mouth descends on my left nipple, while his rough fingers twist my right one.

"Aahh." My nipple tightens into an insatiable mass of nerves. "Aa-ah!" Our hips collide, the only thing separating their scorched flesh is my filmy lace thong as I grind against him in aroused response.

In a reminder of his speed and strength, he flips me onto the bed, my head close to the footboard, and positions himself between my legs.

"Come here." Usalv pulls my legs straight into the air, and with one powerful hand, rips the skimpy thong down their length. The elastic catches on my feet before he tosses the lace garment over his shoulder. Then his hands meet at my ankles, parting them before they slide up toward my inner thighs.

"You need to be wet for this, Sweet Lou." He rests his chin on my lower abdomen. "Really, really wet."

His whiskers descend to my pelvic triangle, making it difficult to speak.

"I...don't think that's going to be problem."

His feral smile makes me flush, while the powerful hands that encircle my hips pin me to the mattress. His tongue slides around and along my folds. My hips pulse in rhythm with his strokes.

Up and down.

Deeper and deeper.

Until his warm tongue finds its way inside.

I groan. And pant. And gasp.

I can't stop the writhing of my hips as his tongue creates torrid nerve pulses that drive heat through me like electric currents. But those powerful hands refuse to relent. They pin me in place, leaving me no route of escape.

"Just a little longer," he insists. "You're so close."

Mere moments later, the spasms running through me erupt in a shower of ecstasy while Usalv holds me between his lips and tongue, applying pressure in harmony with my pulsing core.

I wail aloud, the only release available to me.

When my quivering stops, he lets go, and a

strange mix of emotion overtakes me. I feel spent and energized, satiated and aroused, all at the same time.

It takes a few minutes for my breathing to normalize. When it does, I prop myself up on my elbow and study him, his expression a mixture of satisfaction and relief.

"You good?" His smug voice suggests that he already knows the answer.

I give him a pensive raise of my eyebrows. "For the moment."

"Sweet." He smiles, rolls over onto his back and scoots up next to me. He nestles alongside my outstretched frame, one hand under his head, the other on my thigh. "I wanted you to come before we...Just in case."

"Well, mission accomplished," I assure him. "Stage one, anyway."

"You're not tired?' He sounds surprised.

"Tired?" I repeat. "No. Actually, I feel great." Is this a hint? "Are you?"

"Of this?" He gives a short laugh. "Never."

"Good." I cup his face.

"You sure?" he checks again in an uncertain voice.

"Positive."

He arranges the pillows behind us before sitting up on the bed. "It'll be easier for you this way. On top." Usalv reaches over to the bedside table, pulls out a condom and a small blue bottle.

"Let me help," I tell him, reaching for the bottle.

His expression softens into tender surprise. I spill a single drop of pearly liquid onto his tip, working it in slow circles with the pad of my thumb.

"You good?" I ask, borrowing his favorite phrase. When he doesn't answer I glance up and take in his content expression and closed eyes.

"Mmm," he answers.

My hands move down, twisting around his shaft and base, which swells in response to my touch. The eager rip of a foil packet stalls my strokes while Usalv's adept fingers roll the thin sheath along the downward path of my fingers.

"Come here. Please."

I straddle him and settle my legs on each side of his hips. Those powerful hands grip the back of my thighs, amazing me again with their strength as he holds me mid-air while I position myself comfortably on top of him.

"Usalv, let me go," I plead. "I'm okay."

"You sure?"

My arms loop around his neck. "Yes." I smile.

Resting my forearms on his shoulders, I slowly start to slide down his long broad length, taking the time to adjust to his size and the overfull sensation it brings.

"Take it slow, Sweet Lou."

I nod, and begin to move up and down on him, inching farther along his length with each thrust. As my tempo increases, Usalv moves inside me.

Swelling. Stretching. Deepening.

"Oh God," I moan aloud. As sensation radiates through me, my knees go weak, sapping my strength and control.

As Usalv's entire length plunges inside me, his broad head strikes my cervix, evoking a borderline painful sensation. I draw a sharp breath, and Usalv's familiar hands lift my thighs.

As he draws himself out, his neck muscles transform into knotted cords.

"Wait, it's okay." I beg, reaching for his hand, stalling his attempts to lift me off.

Instead I lift myself off. Then ever so slowly, I ride back down on him, this time allowing him to touch my cervix gently. The borderline painful sensation returns, but it's less intense.

I explore this new sensation, fleshing out new limits for both of us. Several minutes pass until I find the right balance of pain and pleasure.

"God, it's deep this way," he remarks as his whole body shudders.

"Yeah. It's good like this for me. Are you okay?" My words come out in quick breaths.

His only response is a primal grunt, as he

burrows himself deep inside me, as another orgasm blossoms like an evening primrose at sunset.

I rock back and forth as the sensation intensifies my orgasm with a flush of heat and ecstasy I hadn't realized was possible.

"Louise!" He thrusts deep inside me, burrowing along the heated pulses radiating from my core, then surrenders himself to both of us. He cries out again, but his words aren't in English.

Our spent naked bodies remain intertwined, refusing to let go.

CHAPTER EIGHTEEN

G*ood morning, beautiful.*
I drop a gentle kiss on her curly hair while the smooth skin of her cheek rests against my chest. Sweet Lou's breathing is deep and slow as her naked body lies alongside mine. I study her peaceful face, which evokes a strange mix of satisfaction and something else.

Contentment. Exhilaration. Happiness?

Is that what this is? Damn.

I already liked Louise, can't and won't deny it. That feisty sweet, energetic kindness only amps up the sex appeal for me. But truthfully, I expected our first time together to be an awkward, disappointing disaster. Because of me, not her.

Instead it was the best sex of my life.

I stroke her bare back down to her hip, admiring the beauty of those exposed curves and the lush softness of her skin. She's a gorgeous woman, but for me this was much more than a fantasy fuck. I feel…complete. With her. Inside her. Beside her.

"Hey," she greets me when those sleepy amber eyes open.

"Hey, yourself." I reply with a quick kiss to her forehead. "You good?"

"Yeah." She smiles. "Really good. Thanks."

"Me too." I smile back. "You hungry?"

"A little." She sits up and burrows under my arm.

"Okay. You want to go out and get some breakfast?" I'm not sure what's here and I want her to feel treated well.

"I don't know." She starts tugging my forearm hairs. It tickles and stings at once. "It's Saturday, right?"

"All day," I assure her.

"That's what I thought." She hesitates. "I have shit to do this afternoon. Would you mind if we turned it into lunch instead?"

"Not at all," I reassure her. "But I thought you didn't work today."

"I don't. Macy's throwing a party for Paul next Saturday, and I have nothing but scrubs and workout clothes. I need to get something to wear."

"The military guy who got hurt? How's he doing?"

"He made it home this past week." She sighs. "I'll know more Saturday." The tugging and twisting of my forearm hair ceases, and her hands still. "Would you like to go?"

Her question surprises me. I don't really know. "Will Daughtry be there?"

She jerks her head back against my arm. "I assume so, but I'm not sure. Do you want me to ask him?"

"To go with you to the party?" I try not to sound pissed off.

She shoots me a peculiar look. "Um...no. To see if he's going, since it's such a deal breaker for you."

"It's not." I snake my hand under her arm and cup her breast.

"Then what is it?" she asks.

"If Mike has a problem with us being together, and his cousin decides to jump in on that, it won't be pretty," I warn her. "Maybe this isn't the right time."

"I don't think you need to worry about that."

"Macy's done it before." Damn. Up until this moment, it wasn't obvious to me that I was trying so hard not be down on Louise's best friend.

"Oh. I hadn't thought of it like that." Louise sits quietly for an endless moment. "You don't have to decide now. Just let me know."

"Sure." An awkward disappointment seeps into the air, and I refuse to let this moment be spoiled. "Hey, you want a bath?"

"A bath?" she asks. "You mean shower?"

"No, I mean you haven't seen my monster tub yet, have you?"

She shakes her head, apparently as eager to lose the downer mood as I am. "This place has a *real* bath tub?"

I nod. "Want to try it out?"

"Maybe…" She sounds indifferent, but the up-and-down arch of her eyebrow is playful and provocative at the same time.

"You're killing me."

She laughs. "I know."

I grab her hips and pull her close to me. "You're smart like that, huh?"

"I can hope."

"Me too." I reply. "Come on?"

She nods and I lead her from the bed.

CHAPTER NINETEEN

"Louise! It's great to see you." Paul's upbeat voice greets me as I navigate through a sea of familiar faces gathered at the back of the bar.

"Are you kidding?" I plant a sisterly kiss on his cheek. "I wouldn't miss this for the world. Welcome home, Paul."

"Thanks. It's good to be home." His tone resonates with haunted relief.

I step back and study him. He wears a faded dark tee under his open full-sleeved dress shirt. Both look too big for him. He's lost a good twenty pounds, and his muscular frame appears gaunt and way too slender. One shoulder looks slightly larger than the other, no doubt due to the dressing underneath.

My gaze shifts to the injured arm, which he holds close to his abdomen.

"Macy lied," I tease. "You don't look half as bad as she let on."

He returns my smile, and I know that underneath all the hell he's been through, Paul is back. "Macy always had a flare for the dramatic." He winks at me.

"How you holding up?"

Paul sighs, and the tension around his eyes becomes more pronounced.

"It's good to still have my arm. And it's sure good to be back home. Everything else is a day at a time."

"You know I'm around if you need anything. Both of you."

"Thanks, Lou. And that works both ways. The only thing that's changed is your address. Don't be a stranger."

"Never," I promise.

"Hey, girl. You made it." Macy approaches us and throws her arms around me, and I do the same in return. "Wow, nice dress. Have I seen that before?"

"Brand new. I had absolutely nothing suitable for a party." It was quite a find. On clearance at Nordstrom, it was half the price of my recent lingerie splurge.

"Damn girl. Hope we didn't put you out." Macy studies my sleeveless lace mini-dress with the metallic thread woven through it and nods in approval.

"Not at all." My sky high metallic pumps have been worn twice already, so I'm getting my money's worth. Thank God, because my credit card is smoking this month.

"Please tell me you didn't do all this just for us." Macy looks around. "Where's Usalv?"

"I don't think he's coming." I shrug.

"Not coming? What?"

"Well, that's my cue," Paul interrupts, sliding his good arm off Macy's waist. "If you'll excuse me, we can all catch up later."

Macy plants a quick kiss on his cheek. "I'll come find you in a minute, hon," she promises.

"I'll be waiting," Paul nods at me before leaving us on our own next to the bar.

"Not coming?" Macy's smile disappears and she gives me a worried look. "Did you ask him, or chicken out?"

"Oh, I asked. He just didn't think it was a good idea."

"Why not?"

Macy watches my face as I survey the bar. Fifty-odd people are mulling back here. Some are from the hospital, others are part of the large circle of friends and extended family that Macy and Paul enjoy as Chicago natives. Except for friends I've met through marital arts and the ICU, almost everyone I know in the city is here.

"Come on." She reads my expression perfectly. "We've got the room behind the bar. There aren't too many people there yet." She leads me into a room behind a set of double doors. "Spill."

I take a deep breath. "He was worried that Mike would be pissed if we showed up together. He didn't want to risk ruining Paul's party and being blamed for it."

"Oh." Macy sounds dejected. "Do you believe him?"

"He's not wrong, Macy. Besides..." I shake my head. "Dealing with Mike can be...exhausting for me."

"I'm sorry," Macy replies. "I did tell Mike you were coming with Usalv, and that as far as I knew, you two were together. I also warned him that there better not be any problems."

"Is Mike here?"

"I haven't seen him yet. Maybe you should text Usalv. Tell him what I said. Invite him again."

I'm about to make an excuse when a young, edgy looking woman bursts through the double doors and makes a beeline for Macy. Her light violet hair is long in the front with shaved out sides. She beams at us with a wide, perfect smile that makes me want to like her.

"Hey, there you are!" Her loud happy voice interrupts our conversation.

Macy turns in the direction of that happy voice and smiles. "Glad you could make it, Zoe." They exchange quick hugs.

"Thanks for the invite." Her voice chimes with natural cheeriness. "Hey," she calls to me. "I'm Zoe."

"Louise." I take her outstretched hand. "It's nice to meet you, Zoe."

"Louise works in trauma-ICU. And Zoe's taken over your shift in the ER," Macy explains to us.

She looks young. Really young. Like twenty-one or two, tops.

"How long have you been in the ER?" I ask.

"About a year now. It's tough, but I really like it."

"Yeah. It sure is." The memory makes me nostalgic. "They've got a good crew down there. No doubt."

"Well, I don't know about you two, but I'm thirsty." Macy puts an arm around each of us before steering out of the reserved room toward the bar.

She waves down the bartender and orders a pitcher of something Irish, while I lean in to ask for a whiskey. As the bartender moves away, Paul enters my line of sight from across the crowded bar. I wave at him, but he doesn't see me.

Instead, he gives Macy a warning glare, willing her to look at him. Paul tries to move around the bar, but he's stopped by someone. I wonder what's wrong, until I hear a familiar voice behind me.

"Hey, gorgeous," It says.

I recognize the voice, the endearment, and the soft smack of a kiss alongside the edge of a temple. Only it's not my temple, and the endearment is not directed at me.

"Tim!" Zoe's cheerful voice exclaims. "I'm so glad you made it."

It's him. The ex. From hell.

Macy tenses beside me as she turns away from the bar. Her expression is a stoic mask, but the pure fury in her eyes is unmistakable, and it confirms what I already know. When our eyes meet, it's clear that she's completely surprised, too.

"Macy," Zoe calls out. "Come meet Tim. He's one of the docs in general surgery."

"We've met," Macy informs her, stepping away from the bar, standing between me and Tim.

"Oh, that's great," Zoe replies. "I was worried he wouldn't know a lot of people."

"Don't worry." Macy's tone is icy. "Tim gets around."

"Well, it's got to go around to get around," Tim responds. "How've you been, Macy?"

"Bereft, Tim. Very bereft. There aren't any more smug pricks in my life to cut down to size."

"I always said you'd make a great surgeon, Macy. You've got so much natural cutting ability."

I'm still leaning over the bar, and while it'd be interesting to see Zoe's reaction to this debacle, there's not a snowball's chance in hell of me turning around and joining *that* conversation. When the bartender returns with our drinks, I grab my whiskey and take a long grateful gulp.

"Hey, Louise," Paul calls in an absurdly loud voice while he approaches us from the other side of the bar. I turn toward him, the displeasure in his eyes a stark contrast to his tone and expression.

A few people nod and say hello as they let him through. "Watch the arm," he warns a few in his humorous manner.

Paul keeps his back to Tim as he wedges between my ex and Macy. "Who the hell invited him?" he grumbles to Macy as he passes. Macy responds with disgusted shrug.

"Thank you for coming, Lou," Paul announces in a gracious, baritone voice. "Have a drink with me?"

"Of course," I'm grateful for the escape from the bizarre arrangement of my best friend, my ex, and his new younger girlfriend.

"It's lucky for him my good arm's messed up." Paul remarks as he leads the way to an empty table on the far side of the bar. "I can't imagine why he's here."

"He's here with Zoe, who's completely clueless. She even tried to introduce Macy and Tim."

"Oh Christ." Paul rolls his eyes. "I should go

check on her before it gets to fisticuffs. Don't let him ruin your night."

"I'll be fine."

"You sure?"

"He's a jerk, that's very clear. And trust me, I'm not nursing a broken heart."

He nods. "Enjoy the party. Don't let him piss on your parade."

"No worries there."

Paul raises his half empty beer mug in the air, and I clank my shot glass against it before bringing it to my lips and draining it.

"Well, look at us," he tells me. "Out already. Can I get you another one?"

"I need to pace myself. But you go ahead. And don't worry about me. Please. A lot of people are damn glad you're home and want to see you. Go make the rounds. Enjoy. It is *your* party."

"Thanks. But I am going to send over another round. If you don't want to drink it, just sit and stare at it."

I laugh. "Will do."

Paul nods and walks away, leaving me alone with my thoughts and sins.

Tim and I had met when he'd covered the ER during his last year of surgical residency. Back then, he was funny, smart, likeable. I'd thought I'd found the One.

But then things had changed.

He came from a modest background and when he was offered a permanent job as a general surgeon, he'd become arrogant and superior at work. In no time at all, Tim had earned a reputation among the nurses as a major pain the ass, which put me in an awkward position personally and professionally.

"Hey, what's up, karate-kid Barbie?" Tim asks as he plunks his ass down on the opposite side of the slender bar table.

Fuck off. It takes all my self-control not to say the words out loud. "Tim," I manage
instead.

"Damn, Louise. You look great. I forgot how fine you were without scrubs or workout clothes. Which seemed to be all you wore when we were together."

"Still hating on people who used to like you?" I sigh. "Why don't you go do whatever it is you planned on doing when you decided to come here tonight?" Where the hell is that whiskey Paul promised to send over?

"Zoe asked me to come."

"And judging by her cluelessness, she's unaware of your popularity issues?" I shake my head. "She deserved a head's up from you."

"Zoe'll be fine." That arrogant dismissiveness rears its ugly head. "Besides, I'm doing what I came here to do. Which was talk to you."

"If you left something at my apartment, I can't

help you with that." My laughter is not pleasant. "We have nothing to say to each other. Please go away."

Tim ignores me and changes the subject. "I'm surprised that you didn't move back to Indiana after we broke up."

"Well, that's on you." Goddamn it, I shouldn't let him draw me into a conversation, but I'm too pissed off to shut up. "I always wanted to work in a big city ER. With or without you, that never changed."

"I guess not." He props his elbow onto the table and rests his chin in his hand. "You know when we met, you were the prettiest woman I'd ever seen. Still are."

"Fuck you, Tim." My voice is clear and calm. "You wanted to see other people. Go have fun."

"Wait." His voice cracks and for a moment, he sounds like the man I fell so hard for. "I underestimated you. And I regret that."

"Is that an apology? From Tim Mazure?" I shudder, remembering how many times I tried that last name on for size. "Hell must be freezing over."

"Call it whatever you want." He reaches over the table and grabs my hand. "Go ahead and bust me up if you need to. I know I've got it coming. Whatever. But I want you back, Louise."

Aside from my screech of disbelief, I'm speechless.

"Have you lost your mind?" I choke on my reply.

The thought of being with him again makes my skin crawl.

"Of course not." He seems surprised at my objection. "What's the problem?"

"For starters, what about Zoe?" I ask. "Not only is she sweet, she seems to like you."

"She'll get over it." Tim shrugs. "She's young."

"Like I was when we met?"

"You're still young enough."

"There he is again. The total asshole that now inhabits the body of Tim Mazure. You…are a first-class prick," I tell him between clenched teeth.

"What?" His eyes bulge with fury as he spits out the question.

"Goodbye, Tim." I stand to leave, but he tightens his grip on my arm.

"Calm down," he warns me.

"You need to let go. Right. Now."

"Just—"

Too late.

I twist my arm against his hand, while drawing my elbow toward me like a lever. Nobody's thumb is that strong. I free myself easily from Tim's grasp. He's not so lucky.

Once my hand is free, I grab his arm, and force his elbow to twist in the opposite direction. Since I'm standing over him, his other arm is too far away to be useful.

"Goddamn it, Louise. Let go." He tries to sound calm, but can't keep the fury from his tone.

"Kind of annoying when someone asks you let go and they don't, isn't? You know, if I twist just a little harder I can plant you flat on the floor." I torque his wrist and push his elbow to make my point. "Instead, I'm going to let go, and you're going to get the hell out of here. Got it?"

"You heard her," Usalv warns him from over my shoulder. "Get the hell out of my seat."

CHAPTER TWENTY

I wrap my fingers into a fist on the tabletop between them. At first glance, it looks like Louise is holding his hand, whispering to the guy sitting down. He looks calm, but that's only because she's got physical control of his arm.

"I'm not fucking around."

"Fine." He looks up at me, then back at Louise. "Let go."

Louise looks up at me, then slowly releases the douche's arm. As she does, I crowd into his space in case he tries anything else.

"Relax" he tells me before shaking out his shoulder. "Louise and I are old *friends*. You know?"

"Sure you are." My voice drips with disbelief, but Louise's disgusted eye roll confirms his claims.

My chest tightens, shooting a jolt of sucker punched panic and disbelief deep into my gut. He's not a bad looking guy, but not in Louise's league for sure. Besides, anyone who manhandles a woman is a first-class asshole.

And Louise just doesn't put up with assholes.

"Talk about punching above your weight." I focus on his hands and stance. Louise is on the other side of the table, so I can't get between them where I'd like to be. "Where'd you find this knobhead?"

"At the hospital." He cuts her off. "I'm a surgeon." His conceited self-assurance tells me I'm supposed to be intimidated.

No chance.

"Well, this isn't a spelling bee and I'm not the one about to get my ass kicked. You should leave," I warn him. "Now."

"Usalv, it's okay." Sweet Lou soothes me. "I've got this."

"Of course you do. But that doesn't make it okay. Last chance," I warn him "Get out of my seat, or I'll move you."

"Please," he goads. "Touch me and I'll sue the crap out of you."

My face cracks into a deep smile that drips with menace. It's the same response I give to opponents in the ring after they promise me an ass kicking.

"You're gonna threaten a guy like me...with a lawsuit?" I give a short laugh of disbelief. "After you grabbed my date? After she told you to let go? Shit, it'd probably just pump up my rep."

"Your rep?" he repeats. "What the hell is this? High school?"

"You need to get out more. All professional fighters have a rep. Good or bad."

"Professional fighter?" That gets his attention. "Are you any good?" Knobhead's tone implies I'm a poser.

"My next fight is on Pay Per View later this month. Tune in and tell me."

Knobhead leans onto the table, then vacates the chair. Even though I'm used to towering over everyone else, this guy seems short to me. Maybe that's why he wasn't in a hurry to stand.

He pauses. "Nice to see you, Louise. We'll talk later." Knobhead taunts over his shoulder while he turns away.

I lean in, and his shoulder rubs against my arm. He freezes and I whisper into his ear, "You're not together anymore. Don't touch her ever again."

Knobhead walks away and doesn't look back.

When I turn back around, Macy is standing next to Louise with a concerned look on her face. Seconds later, a tall man with gray eyes and dirty-blond hair joins them. He looks up to follow knob-head's path around the bar.

The guy looks at me and nods before leaning down between Macy and Louise to say something.

A second later, Sweet Lou looks up and gestures for me to join them.

"Louise," I greet her.

"Hey." Sweet Lou smiles. "You remember Macy?"

"Sure do." I turn look down at the petite woman next to Louise. "How's it going?"

"Hello again," Macy replies. "I didn't know you were coming."

"That's not a problem, is it?" I ask.

"Hell no," Macy insists. "The problem just left."

"Yeah," the man chimes in. "Whatever role you had in him leaving, thanks. I'm Paul, by the way."

"Usalv." I extend my hand but Paul pauses.

"Sorry man." Paul points to his injured right hand before raising his left for a fist bump.

"No problem." I bump my fist against his. "Been banged up pretty badly a few times myself."

"You guys doing okay?" Macy's gaze lingers on Sweet Lou's face.

"Yeah." Louise's eyes crinkle as their corners lift. "He just got here."

"Well, then let's get you some drinks. I know what Lou's having. What about you?" Macy asks.

"I need to watch it. Training," I explain.

"I think we'll just claim the table and hang out here for a while," Louise interjects. "You two should say hi to everyone and then come back after a bit."

"Are you sure? We—" Macy answers.

"—Okay, then." Paul's good hand squeezes

Macy's hip. "We'll come by later. Enjoy the party." He smiles and gives us a final nod before steering his wife back toward the bar. Paul leans down and says something to her, but I can't hear it.

When I turn to face Sweet Lou, she's standing beside the table with an unreadable expression directed at me.

"Hey." I sway from side to side with nervous energy. "Is that seat taken?"

"No," she answers.

"Can I sit down?"

She nods. When I'm seated, Louise settles back onto her own chair and watches me.

"What is it?" I ask.

"Thank you. For helping me out with Tim." She clears her throat. "You didn't need to do that, though."

"Jesus, Lou. I know you can handle yourself. That doesn't mean you should have to." I lace my fingers together on the table. "Besides, there was something off about him, about you being a couple. It doesn't fit."

"I can't disagree," she replies.

"You were with a guy like that. For real? I still can't believe it…"

"Like what?"

"Well, he acts like a jerk, and he grabbed you. Like *that*." I shake my head. "He doesn't know how close I came to feeding him his teeth."

"You and me both," she replies.

"Did he ever try that when you were with him?"

"Never. He had other ways of beating me down back then."

"How?"

"You know about my dad. How I was there when he died and I couldn't save him? Well, if I was the person that I am now eight years ago, he might be here today." Sweet Lou's arms fold across her body.

"Lou..." Her troubled expression makes me wince. "We can only do our best. You did the best you could. What else is there? Nothing."

"You're right. Tim got that, too. He was very sensitive about it. But after he...changed. He used it to play me, and got good at making me feel like things were my fault when they weren't."

"How did you get past that?"

"Time. A lot of support. Some royal ass kickings from my mother, Macy, and a few good friends. But literally, one day, I changed."

"You changed?"

"It's one thing to accept your own faults and the misery they cause you. It's another thing to not care whether the person you're with is happy. And if you don't care whether they're happy, well...you're with the wrong person."

"Or doing the wrong thing," I reply.

"What do you mean?" she asks.

"You remind me of me. Before I told everyone to

fuck off and dropped out of college. Everyone. My coaches, my uncle, even my parents. Being in college on a scholarship didn't make much difference to their lives, but I was miserable doing it."

"So you quit?"

"Yeah. Did what felt right. To hell with all the practical-on-paper bullshit."

"Wow." She blinks. "That must have been tough."

"Really?" I squeeze her forearm. "Tougher than dumping the dear doctor in the dumpster? I'm sure a lot of people thought you were crazy, too."

"A few," she admits, "but no one who really mattered." Sweet Lou withdraws her arm from my touch. "Why are you here?" she asks in a puzzled voice.

"Because you invited me." I attempt to be casual.

She nods. "But you said no. Why didn't you tell me you changed your mind?"

"Because. Because I like having you around... And I know that if I want you to stay that I have to show up for more than just booty calls."

She pins me with an assessing look. Then she laughs. A side splitting, gut busting SNL front row special.

"Easy, girl." I lean back in and grab the nape of my neck to stop the prickly heat sensation. "You'll crack a rib."

"I'm sorry." Her roar of laughter dims to a girlish giggle.

"Damn, what did I say? I'm trying to be sincere, and you're laughing your ass off."

"It's not you. Well, it *is* you. The things you say. Or rather the way you say them." She sighs and catches her breath. "Since meeting you I've had to install the urban dictionary on my smart phone."

"What for?"

"Well, you've taught me more descriptors for copulation and male genitalia than I ever learned in nursing school. You're a constant education."

I smile. "Glad to be of service."

She's looking pensive again and the hairs on my neck stand like needles on an agitated porcupine's tail.

"So...it's not just about the booty calls?" she hesitates.

"Not for me," I tell her without a second thought.

"Mmm. So what do I do with your key?" Her tone lacks emotion, but those smoky amber eyes focus on the rim of her empty whiskey glass.

"That's up to you. I don't plan on renting out that apartment right now." I'd figured that out right after the first time she made me orgasm.

"I don't understand."

I need to be honest about this. Or as honest as I can be.

"Louise, I don't want you to move out." My heart races as I hesitate. "But I just don't know if it's right to ask you stay. I...I don't want you to feel trapped."

"Trapped?"

"Neither one of us signed up for what's happened." I cover my hand with hers and look straight into her amber eyes. "Or can promise where it's going. I don't want you to feel like you have no choice because you don't have another place right now."

"Oh."

"Hang on to the key. As long as you want. When you're ready, give it back."

"That's very considerate. Thank you." I watch Louise's throat as she swallows hard. "I...really don't want to move out right now."

"Good." I resist the urge to fist pump the air. "Good," I repeat, low key and casual.

She takes my hand in hers on top of the table. "So you can't eat or drink anything?"

"Not here. My fight is in a few weeks."

"I'm sorry." She digs the shiny oval fingernail of her pinky into that full bottom lip before gently biting the tip. "We should go."

"Go? That's okay. I did promise to meet your friends." I'd prefer to do it over a couple of steaks after my fight, but this was important to her.

"My friends are busy." Her smile glimmers with pure seduction. Underneath the table, those endless legs brush against my inner thigh.

Just like that, I'm strung tighter than a drum.

"You sure?" It's a question with many possible answers.

"I don't work until Sunday evening. I've got a rare long weekend, and I want to make the most of it."

"I think I can handle that." I reach under the table and stroke the side of her thigh underneath that frilly short skirt of hers.

"I'm counting on it." Her thigh leaves my grasp as she stands. "Ready?" It sounds like a dare.

"Always," I promise.

I grasp her hand like a lifeline and lead her toward the door, out into the night filled with hidden promises.

CHAPTER TWENTY-ONE

"You good, Louise?" Usalv asks, his tone brimming with hopeful confidence.

He's been working me up with meticulous enthusiasm for a good fifteen minutes, and when I started to squirm, that's when things kicked into high gear.

Early last week, after a hospital shift and commute left me drenched in sweat, I went into the laundry room and stripped off right after coming home. While attempting a mad dash to my room right outside, I collided with Usalv while he was leaning on the door jamb, watching me.

Since then, it's become our favorite crazy-quirky place to have sex.

"I'm fine." He's pinned me against the stackable washer/dryer in the tiny utility room. I hold the metal bar of the industrial shelf that hangs from the ceiling next to the laundry machine. From past experience, I know it's very sturdy. "Relax."

Our sexual relationship is intense, fueled by a primal drive that's far from one sided. I'm happy, amazed and a little awestruck that things are going so well, but lately it's been hard to ignore the uncertainty taking root in the dark depths of my psyche.

Is this all there is to us? Just friends with benefits? Will it ever be more than this? Can it be? If I ask him that out loud, will everything we have right now disappear?

Beneath the pads of my fingers, I feel the cords in his neck relax before that massive arm snakes under me and reaches around the washer, leveraging us both in place.

With my back straight up against the machine, I lean onto his braced arm. My other hand holds the bar above me, steadying myself as he finds my entrance. Usalv's eagerness turns to impatience, the scorching kisses he scatters across my naked breasts turn to insistent, arousing bites. But he's a man of eerie self-control and restraint who won't go further unless I'm ready.

"Come here, Usalv." My legs wrap around his torso, drawing him inside.

He inches into me slowly, giving my body time to adjust to his considerable presence.

It becomes a little easier every time we're together.

Usalv is huge any way you look at him, but while he's above average in length, it's his girth that makes him monstrous. Over the past few weeks, my body has been adapting to it, so now, we're focused on ways to cope with his length.

"A-ah." His grunt is a strange sounding mix of relief and satisfaction.

As my body accepts his presence inside, our hips move in unison, coaxing ever deepening thrusts from him. I feel the intensity of his eyes watching me, gauging my reaction to his inevitable contact with the apex of my intimate core.

"Oh...Christ," I gasp, as his broad head drums against that deep place inside me. His thrusts stop, but he stays burrowed tight against my cervix. An eternal moment later, I'm engulfed by an indescribable contraction that radiates through my entire body, filling me with all-consuming sensation.

"Breathe, Sweet Lou. Breathe." His massive hands grab the bottoms of my thighs and hold me in place. I jerk back against the machine, and my grip on his shoulder slackens, leaving me suspended by Usalv's gentle, urgent strength.

My breathing comes in quick rasps, the way it does on the final fifty yards of a 5K run. When the sensation becomes too much, I grip the bar above and pull myself up as he pumps hard and deep, timing the movements so that Usalv's vigorous strokes only graze the sensitive apex of my inner core.

The pace of his entry slows, allowing me to adapt to the sensation of being touched there. After several eternal moments, the ache transforms into something else.

Something incredible.

My body shudders as he titillates my other intimate zones, igniting a blast of pleasure I've never experienced before. Usalv's name erupts from the back of my throat, but words abandon me as I utter a guttural cry before fading into oblivion.

He rests his chin atop my shoulder with his forehead pressed against the cool metal of the laundry machine. From his taut stance and firm grip, I can tell he's beginning to lose himself. But this time, something's different.

"Usalv?" My voice is a dry and gravelly when it returns.

Instead of the usual panting and accompanying sigh of satisfaction, his chest heaves, gasping for air. I'm starting to get worried when he cries out, a primal, uncontrolled outburst that startles me.

"Careful," I warn, as his legs buckle and he leans into me for support.

As we start sliding down the side of the machine, I reach up and grab the bar above me with both hands. Our descent halts for a moment, but he's heavy. My legs squeeze hard around his panting torso but my sweaty hands begin to lose their grip.

Usalv presses his shoulders into me, unjoins us, and falls to his knees. The floor is covered with the dirty sheets neither of us had time to wash. He catches and gently lays me down next to him.

"I'm sorry," he says after several silent moments.

"Sorry? What? Why?"

He caresses the back of my neck. "I... I..." Usalv swallows hard, "...got a little carried away. You must be wrecked." He sounds disgusted.

"I'm fine," I assure him.

"Don't lie," he insists. "Please."

"I'm not lying. And it upsets me that you think I would, especially about something like this."

He turns on one side, propping himself up on one elbow to study me. "Really? No headaches, or nausea? And your parts are...okay?"

"Everything's fine. We've spent a lot of time adjusting to each other these past few weeks." I sit up, wrap myself in the dirty sheets, and stare at him. "Maybe today felt special because our bodies have reached an understanding with each other. But nausea and headaches? No." I shake my head. "Why would you think that?"

He shrugs. "Past experience."

"What experience?" I tread with caution into the minefield of his life before me.

"Pain. Headaches. Exhaustion." He rakes a hand through his hair. "Women, you know?"

"No, I'm afraid I don't." My hands cup his face and force him to look at me. "Nothing we did should cause any of those things."

"Seriously?" His voice is tinged with disbelief.

"Absolutely not. At least not without other health issues." I pause, hesitant as snake on a busy bike path. "Did your...your last girlfriend have any?"

"She didn't have any medical problems. Besides, it wasn't just her. It's pretty common set of issues with the women I date."

"Oh. And, um what women are those?" The bottom of my stomach drops out.

Even he hesitates a bit. "Underwear models."

"Underwear models?" I repeat. "As in five-foot nine and a dollar-five wet?"

"Yeah." He winces and looks away. "From the fights. It's pretty much where I get to meet women."

"Oh, Usalv." I sigh, a mixture of self-soothing and understanding. "You do realize if they're subsisting on coffee, cigarettes, and lettuce leaves, that they might damn well be exhausted and have headaches all the time?"

"What?" He's incredulous. "For real?"

"Sure. I have an older cousin who used to model. We're all tall women on my mom's side. Anyway, senior year of high school, she tells me to try it, has me meet her agent. The guy says 'Call me when you lose fifteen pounds.' I was a state ranked cross-country runner at the time. Unbelievable. I said no thanks and never had any regrets."

"You've got to be kidding me." Usalv sits up and uses his fingers to pry mine away from the sheet wrapped around me. "You're the most beautiful woman I've ever seen."

"I'm not beautiful. Aren't we past the false flattery yet?" I ask. "I just work out a lot. Sports are my escape."

"Wait a minute. False flattery?" he repeats. "You really are clueless, aren't you?"

"Not usually. What do you mean?"

Usalv sits up against the dryer. "Lou... The ways guys look at you, the way they talk to you, and about you. Hell, we even get into fist fights over you." He pins me with a direct stare. "What do you think that's all about?"

"It's guys being guys." It's the truth. "A lot of it is just talk to see how far they can get. And of course, at our gym women are few and far between. Like ten to one, so selection is limited. In situations where there are more women, it's no big deal."

"So in school, the guys weren't chasing you?"

I laugh out loud. "No. Boyfriends have never been my major, especially in high school."

"Because you were so tall?"

"That and I had a rep."

"A rep? For what? This I got to hear."

"No, you don't." I'm suddenly uncomfortable. "It was a long time ago."

"Yeah. And it still bothers you. Why?"

"Because even though I've moved on, it still pisses me off when I think about it." I shake my head back and forth. "So I try to avoid it."

"Makes sense," he agrees. "How old were you when it happened?"

"Ninth grade." My voice becomes distant. "Robbie Shooter tried to make Mandy Hayes jealous by asking me to the school dance. Guess it was a safe bet that I didn't have any plans yet." A rush of humiliation makes me shiver.

"And then what?" he prompts me.

"When Mandy found out, she was pissed off. A few of her friends tried to jump me on the way home from school." A wave of satisfaction rolls over me. "Things didn't go the way they planned."

"I'll bet." He smirks. "They didn't know you studied martial arts?"

"Nope. My Dad enrolled me when I was small, hoping it would help with my confidence. It did. I was fourteen when Mandy and her friends jumped me. I'd earned my black belt at eleven."

"That's young."

"I guess so. Chong Kim was a former Korean Olympic coach who moved here to live with his adult children. He ran a martial arts-based after school program. I started there in kindergarten and stayed until college." Happy memories of that time bring me comfort.

"What happened at school?" Usalv asks.

"It all turned into a major shit show." I hug my knees. "Robbie Shooter was pissed off at me for Mandy's black eye. He ditched me before the dance."

"What an asshole," says Usalv.

"Yeah, it sucked. I was an awkward girl who was really excited that a boy had asked me to the dance. For an entire three days, I was on cloud nine. But it didn't last. And things got worse from there."

"Worse? How?"

"Mandy and her friends. When their parents saw their injuries, they complained to the school, and I got called out of lunch by the principal. In front of the whole school."

"Goddamn," he whispers.

"I can still remember the *oohs* of the idiots sitting at the table, and the bitchy comments made by Mandy's friends as I walked past them." I twist a loose strand of hair. "When I explained what the girls had done, the principal asked why I hadn't been hurt. That's when I told her about being a black belt."

"What did the principal do?"

"I got a week's worth of detention, but Mandy and her friends were banned from the dance. Robbie was afraid I'd beat the crap out of him for ditching me."

"I hope you did," he tells me.

"Nah. I was already unpopular enough with boys, at least in a dating kind of way. The whole Robbie Shooter mess haunted me through high school. I felt...tolerated, but never like I belonged." I squeeze my shoulders together. "The good news was that people didn't hassle me. They even stopped calling me the Ostrich. At least when I was around. But I counted the days until graduation."

Usalv rubs my back we sit in silence for a few moments.

"Well, that helps explain why you think guys' interest is nothing but bullshit." Usalv strokes my hair. "He was an asshole, Louise. So were the guys that never gave you a chance. What happened just plain sucks."

"It hurts when you don't fit in, and you're lonely and sad. But what makes it suck even more is that part of the reason you don't fit in is because you don't want to." I've never possessed the emotional clarity to realize that about me until now.

"You didn't want to?"

"No. I think I wished that things could've been different. That if I'd tried harder to join those cliques, it would've been better for me. But mean people suck and that's the last thing I ever wanted to be."

"They do." He stares at me with a pensive expression. "You are the kindest, strongest, most patient woman I've ever met. And I wouldn't want you any other way," he tells me. "Come here, my beautiful Ostrich."

Usalv draws my naked body into his, rubbing my back before he applies a gentle kiss to my forehead, a tender bandage on my old wounds.

CHAPTER TWENTY-TWO

"Goddamn it, what the hell was that?" Rodgers rants from ringside.

Lucky Mike, my hotheaded sparring partner, is fast and focused this morning. That's the second hit he's landed since we started, which wasn't long ago.

I wasn't sure what to expect from him today. He should have been at Paul and Macy's party a month ago, but he'd never turned up. The next time I see him he's here, waiting ringside, geared up and ready to go. He's been calm, collected, and capable ever since.

Fuck!

He tags me again, this time on the thigh with a round kick.

What the hell is wrong with me? My concentration is razor sharp, but my speed isn't great. As I shake off his last strike, I realize that I've probably dipped to about two-forty two on the scale.

"Okay, okay guys." Rodgers huffs. "Let's wrap it up. We all know what we need to know today."

Mike and I relax our stances, and he claps me on the shoulder. "Hey, Madman."

"Mike." I bend at the waist to catch my breath.

He hesitates for a minute. "You good, Madman?"

My laugh is flat. "I've been better."

"Damn." Mike puts his hands on his waist. "I was hoping it was all me."

"A lot of it was." I'm honest. "You definitely brought your A-game today."

He nods, then hesitates. "How's Louise?"

My breath returns and I stand straight. We stare at each other for a few seconds. But he's chill and his gloved palms hang unfurled at his sides.

"I'm not trying to piss you off, Mike. But we're really good." I meet his eyes without flinching. "I didn't steal her from you. She was never yours."

"I know." He's calm and collected, so unlike him. "And I'm sorry." He gives me a stern nod. "For real." He extends a vertical fist.

What the fuck is going on? "Thanks." Stunned, I jab my fist into his extended one.

"Usalv?" Rodgers bellows from his perch by the ring. "Come on over."

"Fuck. Here it comes. I better go," I tell Mike.

"Sure. See you, Madman."

"Yeah. Take it easy, Mike."

Mike nods to Rodgers, who returns a nod of approval. Then he exits through the ropes and heads toward the locker room.

I approach Rodgers, who leans in over the ropes with a pissed off expression.

"Well." Rodgers grunts as I stop in front of him. "That sucked major ass."

"All right, I had an off-day. It happens."

"Not with you." Rodgers replies. "You're the most consistent fighter that I've ever seen."

"Well, this diet consistently sucks," I complain. "And I don't like fighting at this weight."

"So it's the diet, eh?" Rodgers asks.

"Well, it ain't helping."

"I see." He pauses before giving me a thoughtful look. "How's Louise?"

Rodgers stares off into the distance as he waits for my answer. He's treading on dangerous ground and he knows it. I've become private and protective about our relationship, and I'll be damned before anyone holds it against us.

Even him.

"If she's not here by now, she went for a run before going home."

"Oh." Rodgers stands and crosses his arms. "So

you're not out partying all night? Boozing it up, maybe?"

I give a short laugh. "Hell no. We're both too busy. And she's busier than I am." I pull off the towel hanging from my waistband and rub the sweat from my face.

"Well, if that's the truth, then your problem can only be one thing."

"I haven't got a problem, Coach."

"Sure you do. It's too much sex."

I freeze, then peel the towel away from my face and stare at him. "What?"

Rodgers looks around the gym, then hops off the edge of the ring and gestures for me to follow. I hesitate a moment, then squeeze between the ropes and jump down beside him.

"You're having too much sex," he informs me after a quick look around. "At the wrong times. On the wrong days."

"Too much sex? Is there such a thing?" I try to turn the situation into a joke.

"Yes, there is. Especially for a pro athlete." Rodgers shakes his head. "You know, I've never done the birds and bees conversation with you. You've always been so consistent with your training. And so inconsistent with women."

"Well, that's changed," I assure him.

"Obviously."

"Really? What else is obvious?" I feel myself starting to get pissed off, which sucks because most the time Rodgers and I see eye-to-eye on everything training related.

He sighs. "You two are doing it sometime between seven thirty and eight thirty in the morning, which leaves you no stamina for sparring."

Every now and then, Rodgers checks me with a strong dose of reality and reminds me why he's a top tier trainer. Because he doesn't miss a fucking thing. He's dead right. Louise and I hook up right when she gets home, so she gets enough time to rest and I can get to the gym.

"Mike did a helluva job this morning."

"Because you were really piss-poor."

"Ground you've covered already." I wring my towel around my knuckles. "But that's the most focused he's ever come to work and it makes this look worse than it was."

"Damn it, you sure got a never-ending line of shit this morning. You also get here about fifteen minutes later than usual. You're not late for sparring, but you're not as focused either."

Rodgers is an honest man. I value his opinion. But that doesn't mean he's right.

"When I lost the first ten pounds, I felt fine. Then you told me I needed to lose another six. After another four, I felt weak."

"But you were faster."

"Maybe, but it wasn't the diet."

"Then what was it?"

"Elevated testosterone levels." I tell him after a long silence.

"Elevated...?" Rodgers looks around and ducks his head. "Are you on something?"

"For real?" I glare at him. "You can tell what time of day I'm doing it, but you can't tell if I'm juicing or not? Fuck that."

"Okay, my bad," he grunts. "Elevated testosterone levels? Do tell."

"After she moved in." My voice is calm and certain, meant to assure him as much as me. "But before we started sleeping together." I blow out a breath. "When I got torqued, I'd ice off in the shower. Miserable way to treat a case of blue balls, but that's what improved my workouts."

"Could be." Rogers tilts his head. "It is the best natural way of raising testosterone levels. But one most guys can't pull off. For obvious reasons."

"That's what improved my workouts. Not the fucking weight loss."

"Well," Rodgers' eyebrows furl. "Can you... elevate them again?"

I meet his eyes with an icy stare. "Hell, no."

"Then you know how this works. You've got to cut back on sex." He's uncompromising.

"I think that would be a mistake."

"I'll bet you do."

"I feel more focused," I complain.

"Sex can do that," Rodgers admits. "But you never had problems with focus before, so whatever's going on doesn't have anything to do with your training."

"It does for me." For the first time in my life, I have stability without drama, chaos, or loneliness. That's worth something to me, even if Rodgers can't see it.

"Except for young jocks, who sometimes have sex multiple times a day," Rodgers' expression is an unfamiliar mix of frustration, disbelief, and irritation. "Every athlete I've ever known, coached, or heard about agrees that past age twenty, too much sex impairs training and athletic performance." He folds his arms in front of him. "And you ain't twenty anymore."

"Sure, Coach. Problem is, it works in reverse too."

"Ah, and now we get down to it." His hands rest on his waist. "You have a major fight in three weeks. Are you out of your fucking mind? You should be zipped and locked until after."

"I don't know about that." I shrug. "Some guys say it helps them focus. Maybe I'm one of them."

"Nope." Rodgers' jaw clamps shut. He's biting his lip, trying to control his temper. "A pitcher, goalie, quarterback, maybe. Any job that requires strategic adjustment and rapid physical response."

"Yeah…so why not me?"

"Because," he growls, "your job also requires a helluva lot of strength and stamina. For anyone like that, lineman, power lifters, fighters, it's a fucking train wreck. Testosterone's just too damn low."

He's right and he knows I know it. But I refuse to give in.

"Fine, we can make some adjustments." I agree.

"'Some adjustments'? You've got a goddamned fight coming up."

"I've always got a fight coming up. Or a training camp. Or weights to lift or a run to do." I can't hide my irritation anymore. "Now's a good time for change. Professionally and personally."

"And how do you figure that?"

"This guy I'm fighting is a young hot head. Never fought someone ranked top five before."

"This guy you're fighting trains like a beast and hits like a pile driver." Rodgers looks worried. "Now is not the time to change your game plan."

"It's the perfect time." My voice is calm. "Against the kind of opponent I have the best chance with."

"Usalv, listen—"

"No. You listen." If I've ever yelled at Rodgers before, I don't remember. "You were wrong about this diet. But I sucked it up and went along anyway.

I'm not going along with this. Work with me." I force myself to calm down. "Please."

He looks as if he's just been bitch slapped. In a way, I guess he has. "What the hell do you expect me to do?"

"Well, I'm not going to live like a monk *and* eat like a stick insect forever," I assure him. "Come up with something else."

"Come up with something else? Stop having sex until after your match. Keep your weight at two forty-two."

"Come up with something else." I spit the words out through gritted teeth.

"Listen, if you don't like what I've got to say, find another trainer."

"I've been doing this a few years myself," I reply. "If that's the best you can do, then maybe it is time." I pause to meet his eyes and let the words sink in. "Pay me out for my share of the gym, if that's how you want it."

He's speechless, but his face is pale. I know he doesn't have the money right now. After my fight, if I win, maybe. But not now.

"You are shithouse nuts, you know that? Christ." He sounds shocked. "How much did you weigh when you were icing it off?"

"Two forty-eight."

"How much did you weigh when you started

having sex? I mean with Lou, of course. It's just her right now. Right?"

"Just her. Two forty-four."

"How much now?"

"Probably two forty."

"Take it back up to two forty-two. But no more than one per week. Let's see what that does to your energy levels."

Well, at least that's something. Truthfully, about two forty-five is the sweet spot, and it's only marginally better than two fifty in terms of speed. But with the company I keep, it's all about the marginal edge.

"As for sex..." Rodgers' tone demands my attention again. "Anything inside a week of the fight is a big hell no. Law of the jungle. You want to fight at this level, that's how it is."

"Fine. I'm not trying to kill my career here." I assure him.

"Then what the hell are you trying to do?"

"Get to a place where there's something besides a career." It's hard for me to admit and it's the last thing a coach wants to hear.

"You picked a helluva time."

My sigh sounds loud, even to me. "I didn't pick anything."

He gives me a deft nod, then continues. "No sex for forty-eight hours before major sparring. No sex for twelve hours before weight lifting, light sparring, or five mile runs. And for Christ's sake, you don't sit at a desk all day. Stop doing it right before you get here."

I nod. "I'll do the best I can with my training. And to be fair to Louise."

"Fair to Louise?" Rodgers rolls his eyes up to high heaven. "Right."

CHAPTER TWENTY-THREE

I look up at the large clock in the front of the small auditorium. The muffled sounds and muted movement of other students filing out of the exam becomes more rapid as they finish up and head toward the door.

I'm running out of time.

Which of the following drugs is associated with the reaction of Stevens-Johnson syndrome?

A. Lamotrigine

B. Nevirapine.

C. Allopurinol

D. All of the above

D. Right? Yeah. Sure? Fuck.

Usalv and I have been humping like rabbits for the last few weeks. For a while, both of us seemed to be waiting for things to get boring, tiring, inconvenient...but so far, that hasn't happened. In fact, after running out of condoms last week, we decided to change our birth control.

Now I'm paying the price in other ways.

"Just let things take us where they go," he'd told me after we christened the staircase. The memory of him running around in search of clothes wearing only a towel makes me blush even now. He'd called out to me and we headed up to his room, but never made it.

"Watch your time, please," the professor warns.

Shit.

Pantoprazole is not used in which of the following cases?

A. Gastritis

B. Peptic Ulcers

C. Zollinger-Ellison syndrome

D. Thalamus hypertrophy

C? No, D. No C. Shit! It's D, D—I hope.

But the more we're together, the more I want to be with him. How many times in your life are you with someone who's seen your scars, quirks, and bad hair days but still thinks you're the bomb?

My history is hardly vast, but Usalv is a mind-blowing lover. At first I thought it might be a fluke, the anticipation combined with long abstinence for me. The man possesses near superhuman strength, but he's hyper-aware, like a giant panda tending its Lilliputian-sized young.

I feel great, sleep better, am less stressed, even

after a shitty day. He's easy to live with and so easy to like. Besides all that, it's good being around him.

But not at this particular moment.

What of the following are chelators used to treat mercury poisoning?

A. D-penicillamine

B. DMSA, 2, 3-dimercapto-1-propanesulfonic acid

C. Dimercaprol

D. All of the above.

D…D? Again? How many Ds are on this miserable test?

"Five minutes," the professor announces.

Damn it, this is not the way I do things. My *modis operandi* is hyper-organized and super-prepped. I didn't even know there was test today. How did this happen? When did my schedule get so screwed up?

Which of the following are symptoms of drug induced photosensitivity?

A. Nausea

B. Scleroderma

C. Onycholysis

D. Hemolytic Anemia

C, maybe? Shit.

"Okay, it's time. Finish up, please."

As I make my way to the front of the class, Dr Zimmerman's eyes lock with mine. She's a no-nonsense anesthesiologist whose shifts in trauma-ICU occasionally overlap with mine. Her pointed look is a silent indication that she wants to speak with me.

My stride becomes a slow creep, as I hope in vain another student will try to monopolize her after the test.

No such luck.

"It's Louise, right?" she asks as the final student shuffles out.

"Yes, Dr. Zimmerman."

"You weren't here last week and I wanted to check in." She gets straight to the point, and my radar detects a royal ass chewing on the horizon.

"No, ma'am. I was a little run down and wanted to get some rest before my weekend shift." Which is the truth, if she doesn't ask what had worn me down so much.

Usalv and I left the gym together after my taekwondo class finished. We ended up going out for dinner afterward and having sex on Friday morning. Since I had a short shift that evening, I'd slept in and decided to ditch lecture that day.

"Are you still working a clinical schedule?" Dr. Zimmerman's eyebrows rise above her dark brown eyes in a mixture of concern and disapproval.

"Yes, ma'am. Trauma-ICU."

"Ah." She nods in recognition. "That's where I know you from." Her face twists into a scowl. "But aren't you in the DNP-anesthetist program?"

"Eventually I plan to transfer. But right now, I'm

in the MSN program, completing the required lecture classes part-time."

She pauses a moment before speaking. "So the hospital reimburses you for the course work while you're employed?"

"Yes, ma'am."

"Well, you've certainly bitten off a lot to chew, Louise." Dr. Zimmerman shakes her head. "And I totally get that you need your income. How did you do on the test?"

"Okay, I think." I shift my feet under me. "But not as well as I wanted."

"Some of the other students asked me to change it, because they wanted more time for lab work in another required class. We held a vote last Friday. You were the only one not here."

"I see." Crap.

"While this class does not have a clinical or laboratory component, attendance at lecture is expected," she informs me. "I know you have a lot of clinical experience, but the DNP-anesthetist program expects that of its candidates and adjusts the pace and coursework accordingly."

"Yes, ma'am." My voice is calm and certain, and I mentally stop myself from crossing my arms.

"Have you considered cutting back on your clinical commitments?" she asks.

"I want to hang on until after I'm admitted to the

DNP-anesthetist program and complete the required courses."

"I see." She seems disappointed as she hoists her bulky messenger bag over her shoulder. "As I'm sure you're aware, this course is a critical component of the program. If you attempt to transfer, nothing short of a top grade will be acceptable."

"Yes, ma'am."

"Ms. Becker." She hesitates. "You've got a lot of potential, but you're carrying one hell of a load. Don't let yourself get too run down." She stops moving to make pointed eye contact. "Or too far behind."

"Thank you, Dr Zimmerman."

She nods, and without another word, turns her lanky frame and descends the stairs to the exit. I watch her depart, then shuffle back toward my seat to collect my things. Instead, I collapse with a tired thud back into the chair.

Well, that sucked.

It's clear from Dr Zimmerman's warning that I need to get it together. That means toning down my relationship with Usually so that I can reprioritize my nursing studies. But now seems like the wrong time to take our relationship for granted.

Things have never been better for me. But what about for him?

He's the only man I've lived with...but is what

we're doing considered living together? Or are we just roommates who have sex?

By now it's obvious to me that I'd like it to be more. After all, friends with benefits is not a situation I ever aspired to be in. But what if that's all this is to Usalv? How do I convince him to take a chance on us while I'm pulling back from him at the same time?

I plant my forehead between the laced fingers of my hands.

Of course, there's always the possibility that he's just interested in keeping things casual. If that's all he wants, then when and how do I break away before it burns out and leaves me an emotional train wreck?

I groan. Aloud, I think, and look up to check the room again to see if anyone heard me. Instead, I find myself alone and overcome with an urgent need to get the hell out of here.

Sweat pools in the arch of my philtrum, and I rub it off my face with the pads of my fingers. The humid Chicago summer prevents the air conditioner from working well in the mat rooms, and I'm forced to stop beating my favorite human dummy senseless and drag the giant room fans out.

It's early Saturday morning, in the lull before the morning classes start. My first choice was to run in Oz Park, but an erratic summer thunderstorm tanked those plans. On a normal Saturday morning,

I'd just go back to bed, but after yesterday, I'm avoiding Usalv.

After the test, I hit the university library until it closed, then crept home and slept downstairs in my own bed. He's still confused about my short shift Fridays so I don't think he realized I'd come home, and we didn't speak before I left again this morning.

All part of my plan to try and get my head straight.

"Morning, Louise," a familiar voice calls as I wrestle with an industrial sized fan in the corner of the mat room.

"Hey, Coach. How's it going?"

"It's getting there. Got a minute?" The tips of his black athletic shoes loom into my line of sight as I push the cord into the outlet.

I stand straight and peer over his shoulder at the gray wall clock behind him. It tells me I've got about twenty minutes to finish a thirty-minute workout.

"Can it wait? I can come find you after morning classes."

"Afraid not," he tells me and shakes his head. "Things will be too busy then."

And with that, my desperately needed early morning workout goes to hell in a handbasket.

"Okay," I sigh. "What's up?" I move out from behind the fan and stand in front of him.

"Anyone else here yet?" He turns to look at the entrance.

"Not yet. Just me."

"Good." The news makes Rodgers tense rather than relax. His stance leaves me with an uneasy feeling for the second time in twenty-four hours.

"Have you seen Usalv today?" He glances around the room again.

"Not so far." I'm relieved to tell him the truth. "Was he supposed to be here today?"

"I thought so." He glances back toward the door again. "But he said he wanted to try switching his schedule around a bit."

He did? "News to me." I reply. "Maybe he went for a run?"

"Thought the weather would put him off."

"Maybe he plans to wait it out. It is Saturday, after all."

"Did he tell you that this morning? Was he there when you left today?"

I'm stunned by the question and assess his uncomfortable expression for a few moments before answering. It's clear he wants to talk about more than Usalv's schedule.

"He hadn't come downstairs before I left this morning. We haven't seen each other since yester-day." It's the absolute truth.

"Christ, Louise," Rogers grunts in frustration. "I know you're staying with him."

"That's right," I admit. "He's helping me out while I look for a new place. So what?"

"So what? So, based on his shitty morning work-outs, it's clear you're sharing more than a TV and microwave." He folds his arms and I watch his fingers clench the top of his forearms.

"That's none of your business, Terence." I've never called him that before, but here's hoping he finds my presumption intrusive. "And I don't have to stand here and discuss this with you."

"Louise, wait." I try to walk away, but his hand brushes my forearm. "We're all a little old for bed checks here."

"Thank God for that," I reply. "What do you want from me?"

Rodgers laces his fingers together and wraps them behind the nape of his neck. "I need your help. With Usalv." He focuses on the ceiling while he speaks.

"My help?" I'm stunned.

Rodgers nods. "His morning workouts are as flat as tonic water after New Year's."

My stomach sours with dread. "What do you mean, flat?"

"No energy. No stamina. No aggression." He explains in a worried voice.

"Have you talked to him about this?" I ask.

"Yep. Says it's his damn diet."

"I believe him. He complains all the time about it." It's the truth. The first time he came to the old apartment, he'd bitched about it. That seems so long ago now. "He says he's sleeker but weaker. He doesn't like feeling that way in the ring. Did he tell you that?"

"Yeah." Rodgers looks embarrassed. "That and a few other things. We've talked about it. His diet isn't the problem."

"So what is?"

"Well." Rodgers rubs the back of his neck. "I think it's a little too much polish on the brass knobs."

My head jerks back to study his face, looking for confirmation of his meaning. His crimson complexion and pointed stare tell me that I haven't misunderstood him.

"Really, Terence?" I raise my hands in the air. "You want to go there? With me? Now *that's* brass." I turn away from him and walk toward the door.

"Louise, wait." He falls in alongside me. "You're a nurse, right? I can talk to you straight up."

"No," I gasp in response, stop, and stand there staring him. I'm not one of the guys, and I refuse to discuss this with him. "You think because I'm a nurse it's okay to discuss my sex life? No. Hell no."

He sighs, looks around, then steers me down to a quiet corner of the room.

"Believe me, I don't want to talk about any of this," he says, sulking. "But he's got a big fight coming up, and he's never been this...undertrained."

"I don't know what you want from me. I can't help with his training."

"I'm not asking you for help with his training. That's my job. But even I can't help him if he won't listen to me." He pauses for moment." I need your help, Louise. Usalv needs your help. Please."

"Of course I'll help him. He can ask me for anything."

"That's just it. He won't."

"Why not?"

"Because the one thing he needs from you the most is the one thing he's afraid to ask you for." Rodgers lowers his head with a slight shake.

His solemn face makes me panic. "What? What the hell does he need from me?"

"He needs you to cut him off. Keep it zipped and locked above the knees." Rodgers folds his hands. "A change in a fighter's sex life screws up their training. A sudden drought messes up the sleep cycle. A rapid uptick depletes their stamina." He looks at me. "Sound familiar?"

I'd wondered about that. Just this morning, when my head cleared enough to assess the cost to my own career, I'd become curious about what it was doing to Usalv's. Now I know.

"And what am I supposed to say? Rodgers told us to cut it out? We're not teenagers you caught screwing around in the backseat."

"Don't do that. It would cause more harm than good."

"Then what? Tell him I'm not interested anymore?" I shake my head. "I can't do that to him."

Rodgers looked flustered. "Headache, Backache. Too tired. Time of the month," he suggests.

"For how long?"

"Until the fight is over."

"Three weeks? Are you insane?"

"What?" He seems honestly confused. "My ex-wife had headaches that lasted for months."

"I can see why," I tell him through gritted teeth.

"Louise." He takes a deep breath. "Do you have any idea what's at stake here? If he wins, he stands to make over a million dollars in payouts, endorsements, sponsorships. Do you want that to be on you?"

"This is not on me. He knows what's at stake, too." But even I don't believe what I'm saying.

"You know, I'm just a gym rat who trains guys to fight. Sometimes I have to look out for their best interests. When they won't. When they...can't. I hoped that maybe a nurse could understand that."

A pang of guilt courses through me. I never meant to mess up Usalv's life, just like he'd never meant to mess up mine.

"This sucks. You know that, right?"

"Thanks, Louise."

CHAPTER TWENTY-FOUR

The clock on the mantle chimes out twelve-fifteen as I pace in front of the fireplace. It's Saturday night and I'm trying to ease off in the bedroom to keep my fighting from going to hell in a handbasket. Since we need to cut back, I've prepared a special evening for Louise tonight.

Only problem is, she's not here.

By seven, the sheets were changed, the bathroom was cleaned. Hell, I even bought a new bottle of Bushmills along with some candles and that fancy bath stuff she likes.

By nine, she still wasn't home, so I thought I'd screwed up her schedule again, but then noticed her Dansko clogs on the foyer doormat. Sweet Lou always wears those when she works.

At ten, I risked castration for being over-possessive and texted her. Ten minutes later, she replied. I needed to relax, everything was fine and she'd be home soon.

"Louise?"

The front door eases open with a loud creak. I strain to hear Sweet Lou's footsteps from the darkened living room. She shuffles to the stairway and peers up at my bedroom door.

"I'm here, Louise."

She startles at my voice. "What are you doing still up?"

"Waiting for you."

"Oh." Her response is an unenthusiastic mumble.

"I thought you'd be home sooner." My voice remains calm but questioning.

"I'm sorry. I didn't realize we had plans."

WTF?

"Oh." I struggle to stay calm. "Well, we've been spending every evening off together, together. A text would have been nice."

She nods, speechless before pulling the light jacket off her shoulders and tossing it onto the banister with tired robotic movements. A long silky forest green sweater held shut by a slender silver zipper clings to her curves over tight skinny jeans.

"You look pretty tonight." It's true. Hopefully by saying it aloud I can get this night back on track.

"Thank you." Her tepid smile encourages me.

"Come join me." I gesture toward the chaise

lounge near the window. As I step out of the darkness into the lamp light of the foyer, Sweet Lou's lips part as she stares, and I struggle to suppress a surge of pure pride.

I'm shirtless with wet hair from an earlier shower. Black and blue striped pajamas ride low on my hips, exposing fifteen years of punishing workouts.

Saying *no* will not be easy for her.

She hesitates a moment, then sinks down into the sofa and curls those endless legs up under her. Long, unpolished fingernails rake through thick heavy curls as she wraps them in a tight bun with an elastic band around her wrist. Lines etched near the corners of her mouth give her a stressed out, tired appearance.

I know just the way to sort her out.

"There's a new bottle of Bushmills." I walk over to the table next and stand close, making it hard not look at me. A bottle of amber liquid and a clean tumbler rests next to her favorite chair.

"Would you like a drink?" I brush against her nearby elbow as I reach for the glass.

"No, no thank you. I've already had a lot tonight."

Her words stop me cold, and a rush of irritation rises up my neck like the pummeled puck of a high striker. "You went out for drinks? With who?"

"Macy. We caught up a bit after I pulled a late

night at the library." She rubs my forearm in a soothing gesture. "I needed someplace to be that wasn't work, school, or here, you know?"

Really?

"Surely being here isn't all that bad for you?" I kneel down in front of her to study those unguarded, expressive eyes.

"Being home is very...distracting for me." She unfurls those long legs onto the floor where her knee brushes against mine.

Sweet Lou's gaze wanders down to where we're touching and then slowly skates upward over me where she fixates on my abs, biting her lower lip as she stares.

"I think a good distraction is exactly what you need right now."

I touch her knees, then gently part them. I graze my mouth against her in an eager kiss. She stills a moment before those tender lips move against mine and her tired body shudders back to life.

I fumble with the slender zipper of her sweater. The metallic buzz of tiny teeth working fills the air.

"Ah-h." A strangled groan erupts from her throat.

My heart races at the sight of her flesh colored bra with tiny flowers along the top of see-through fabric. I trace the flower stems up from the bottom ruffle to the tiny nipple that serves as the bud. Perfect.

Her thighs brush against my hips as she shifts into me. Moments later, Louise cries out again, and she wraps her long legs tight around my waist.

Fuck, I love when she does that.

An urgent heat scorches through me. I get to my feet, lifting her with me. But as we turn to head for the stairs and up to my bedroom, she shifts to an uncomfortable angle in my arms.

"Oh, God," she begs. "Don't. Stop."

"Don't worry, I won't," I whisper into the nape of her neck.

"That's not what I mean. Let me go please." She squirms underneath me and struggles to place her feet on the ground.

"What?" I rasp in her ear, shocked and confused.

"We…we shouldn't do this." She sounds firm and resigned.

The room stills until all I can hear is the sound of our tortured breaths and the quick beating of our hearts pressed together through the filmy lace of her bra.

"Why the hell not?"

"I'm sorry. I guess I'm a little…"

"A little…?"

"Tired." She glances down at the floor.

"Tired?" Something's wrong.

She's never said anything like this before, never acted this way before. Have we both been sore or tired after a long week or bad day? Sure. But we're always glad to see each other, no matter how we end up spending the evening.

And neither of us ever starts something we don't want to finish.

"Didn't you sleep this afternoon?"

"Not so much. Had a lot on my mind."

"Like what?" Something tells me I'm not going to like this.

She turns toward the lounger and settles back where she was, then brings her knees up to her chest and hugs them. "I've had a shit week."

I rest my hands on the waist of my pajamas and stare down at the floor. "We all have them, sweetheart."

"I know, but you don't understand..." she pleads.

"Bet I do." Images of getting my ass handed to me by Lucky Mike Daughtry followed by Rodgers clergyesque pep-talk flash through my mind.

"I'm sure you do. I didn't mean it that way." She breaks eye contact and shakes her head. "But I really fucked up my class this week."

"Okay..." I raise my open palms to the ceiling. "But you've put in extra time tonight instead. It'll be fine."

"I hope so." She nods. "There are just so many hours in a day though."

"Don't worry so much, sweetheart. We all get a little overwhelmed and tired." I kiss her shoulder before pulling the fuzzy sweater back over it. I run my hand down her shoulder and grasp her fingers. "Things will be better in the morning. Come on... let's just go to bed."

I pull her gently up from the couch, but she resists.

"Um, I think I'll have a shower then crash in my room tonight." She pulls away. "I've got to get up early tomorrow."

"Why? It's the one day of the week you do sleep in." I meet her eyes and she turns away from me.

"I've got to study." Her gravel voice cracks.

"But I thought that's what you did tonight?" Concealing my irritation becomes more difficult by the minute.

"I need to study some more. I'm way behind."

"Don't you think you're being a bit ridiculous?"

"I knew you wouldn't understand."

"Well, then you should have also realized that I know you're a shit liar. Anyone who knows you would say the same. And I know you better than anyone." I let my words hang in the air.

"I'm not lying," she explodes.

"Then what the hell are you doing?" I ask.

"I'm trying to focus on what's important."

"I thought we were important."

Louise springs off the couch and walks to the far side of the coffee table, putting distance between us before she turns to face me.

"We are. It's just that I've been planning this

career move for a while." She hugs her knees. "I've switched jobs to get ICU experience, taken extra shifts, lived with roommates, moonlighted to make this work. It's all turning to shit before my eyes and I can't let that happen."

"Your career? This is about *your* career?" I retreat to the living room entrance. "I don't fucking believe this. Where does that leave us?"

"I'm not sure. Exactly." She sighs. "I just think that we both need to breathe a little and let the rest of our lives catch up."

"I thought you didn't do friends with benefits? Or am I misunderstanding?"

"I don't." She's firm. "But you told me once that if I thought we were going too fast, or if it felt like too much, I could ask you to stop. Do you remember saying that?"

"Yes."

"Well...I'm asking."

"Fine." I feel my blood pressure surge. "But don't you think we're both old enough to make room in our lives for someone else? Haven't we both worked hard enough for that to happen?" Questions I've been wrestling with alone come pouring out of me now.

"I don't know how to do that." She sounds hopeless.

"Neither do I. But guess what? I can be as detached and distant as you want me to be." My lie is an act of self-preservation. "What I can't do is turn it on and off like a switch, depending on how you're feeling about the rest of your life at any given moment. I deserve that level of consideration and respect from you."

"Yes, you do." Tears well in her eyes. "I just can't give it to you right now." She appears defeated, out of arguments, out of fire. "I can't promise not to be distant if I'm stressed out. And I can't deny my feelings when we're together."

"Well that's fucking fantastic." All I want to do is take her in my arms and tell both of us that everything will be okay.

"I'm doing the best I can, okay?"

"So am I."

"But I'm being immature for not wanting to flush my training down the tubes? Thanks a lot."

"Immature?" What brand of bizarro is this? "I never fucking said that."

"Sure you did. You just said I was old enough to figure out how to make this work."

"Aren't you?"

"Yes! No! I don't know..."

"You know something, Lou? This is batshit craziness." I've lost my patience along with my temper. I stomp out of the living room to the laundry, and grab a pair of pants out of the basket and a shirt from the dryer. I get dressed. Fast.

"What?" she cries from the living room.

"You're pissed off at me, because I won't give you what you want. The problem is, you don't know what you want. Or you're just not brave enough to say it out loud. So here's where I get off the merry-go-around."

"What are you doing?" she asks.

"I'm trying to be honest with you." I stop in front of her on my way to the front door. My soul fills with remorse as I stare into her tearful eyes. "I'm trying to tell you that I give a fuck. And I think you want to hear it. So now that you've heard it, the rest is up to you."

"Up to me? What do you mean?" Panic erupts from her expression.

"The next time I touch you, it will be because you're begging for it," I whisper into the hair at her crown. "You want me? Come get me."

I grab my phone and keys from the foyer entry table. My chest tightens as I open the front door and walk out into the crisp air of the Chicago night.

CHAPTER TWENTY-FIVE

"Welcome to tonight's Friday Night Fight. I'm Toby Green here with Miguel Lopez. We'll be calling the action for you this evening."

"Good to be here Toby. Tonight's main match is shaping up to be a must-see event. For this heavyweight match-up we've got Chris 'the Raptor' Manning fighting against Usalv 'Madman' Markovski in a three-five-minute round match up."

"Manning's had a lightning rise through the ranks. He's known for his devastating combination strikes which have earned him some major upsets early in his career. But he's got his work cut out for him tonight."

"Agreed, Toby. Markovski is a seasoned veteran, former heavy weight title holder and top contender who's incredibly fast for a man his size. Plus, he's got an unrivaled ground game."

"And that sums up the contest we'll see tonight. Whether Manning's style of striking will keep this fight vertical or if Markovski can take it to the mat. Manning does not want to find himself grappling with Markovski on the ground."

"Very true. But don't forget that both men have the strength and speed to deliver a one and done punch. Anything can happen here."

"Let's head down to the prep point where the fighters will check in to the octagon..."

"Macy, over here!" I yell from my table in the corner of O'Shea's. She's at the hostess station when our eyes meet. Macy waves back and then hurries over to my corner table, closest to the big flat screen by the bar.

"Hey, Lou." She shifts a nearby chair over so she can see me and the flat screen at the same time. "Thanks for the invite."

"I couldn't not watch this, but seeing it alone? No way." We exchange a quick hug. "Thanks for coming. Seriously."

"Oh, you know us Irish. We love a good drink and we love a good fight. Turning down a twofer is heresy." She nods at the full pitcher of Killkenny I've ordered for the table. "Pass me a cup. Actually, pass me two. Nobody should drink alone and I'm drinking. So you're on duty."

She pours out two beers and slides one over to me.

"It is good to see you, Macy."

"It's good to see you too, Lou."

We clink our glasses together and I take a slow, thoughtful gulp of beer.

Both our lives are big hot messes right now, but neither of us wants to discuss our problems or wallow alone. We just want some company and a little distraction. So we sit in comfortable silence for a few minutes and watch the Friday night crowd file into the bar.

Last Sunday, Usalv packed up and headed to Pittsburgh for his Pay-Per-View fight. Leading into tonight, he needed to get through a week of sponsor promos, interviews, weigh-in, and fan events.

I was both sad and glad to see him leave. Things had been tense after our disagreement the week before he left. Every time I'd tried talking to him, he was distant. Pleasant but distant. And whenever I tried to talk about...*that*, he'd shut down and find an excuse to leave the house.

It's nice to have a break from the tension, but somehow, it still sucks that he's away.

"Is Paul coming?" I ask.

"He's here." She scopes around the bar and points him out. "Looks like he's catching up with somebody." Macy nods in approval. "Good."

"I'm glad he came. The more the merrier for me tonight."

Macy sighs. "Getting him out can be hard sometimes. Part of the healing process, I suppose. But right now, he wouldn't come out for too many people. So in a bass-ackwards kind of way, it's all good."

"Small steps," I tell her.

"Mmm. Hmm. Very small."

I'm not sure whether we're talking about her and Paul or me and Usalv. Then it dawns on me that it doesn't really matter.

We turn our attention to the flat screen, where a man in a dark hoodie makes his way through the crowded arena up to the octagon. He stops at the prep point, hugs his corner men before stripping down to his shorts, then stands in front of his cutman and a referee.

Macy gasps. "My God, Lou. Usalv is fighting...*that?*"

"That is Chris Manning. The Raptor."

"Jesus, he looks bigger than Usalv."

"He is." And suddenly I have a very bad feeling about this.

Uneasiness makes me squirm and I shift my legs forward to focus on the screen. I watch the cutman reach up to spread a layer of petroleum jelly over the hard, jagged features of Manning's face.

His elbows and forearms are tattooed with

feathers and talons, and when he bends them, he looks like an eagle attacking its prey. Manning turns to enter the octagon, providing the TV audience a glimpse of the enormous inked eagle's wings spread out over his massive back. The image of a grotesque human spinal column holds the wings together, giving the illusion of lifting him into the ring.

"Hey, did I miss anything?" Paul asks as he plants himself in the chair next to Macy and takes a drink of her beer.

"No. He's coming out now." My eyes refuse to leave the screen.

Soundgarden's "Rusty Cage" blasts into the arena as Usalv begins his walk to the octagon. The camera follows his face while he moves toward the ring, escorted by a sea of corner men and security guards. He stares into the camera for a second, then looks away to focus on the path ahead.

His gray and red T-shirt contain his name in wide white letters up the side seam, with the name of the gym, DeadFall MMA, in red across the front hem, and a few sponsor logos on the chest and sleeves. Usalv stops at the prep point and hugs each of his corner men before removing his shirt.

He pauses a moment to scan the nearby crowd, then stands in front of his cutman. Wearing only compression shorts, Usalv closes his eyes while petroleum jelly is applied to the angles of his face.

Moments later, the referee inspects his head, hands, and body before waving him into the octagon.

"Usalv looks good," Paul says.

"He sure does," says Macy.

Usalv enters the cage and I watch him pace from side to side. There's no swagger or playing to the crowd. His hands are on his hips as he focuses on the floor, occasionally looking up at his opponent, who's waving at the crowd to get them to cheer louder for him.

"I don't know. He looks a little too lean." You can see every ripple of every muscle in his body, but he's very gaunt, like a patient who's been ill and lost too much weight. But that was Rodgers' plan, wasn't it?

Coach Rodgers... When this is over, I'm going to kill that SOB.

"Ladies and gentlemen, live from Paints Arena in Pittsburgh is tonight's Final Friday Night Fight. This is a three-round contest in the heavyweight division between two giants of the octagon. Now it's time for the main match up on our card tonight!

"Introducing first, fighting out of the blue corner, a Muay Thai fighter with a professional record of seven wins, two losses. He stands six foot eight inches tall and weighs in at two-hundred fifty-five pounds. Fighting out of Oakland, California the twelfth ranked contender in the world, Chris 'the Raptor' Manning!

"And fighting out the red corner, an MMA fighter with a professional record of seventeen wins, three losses.

Standing six foot five inches tall and weighing in at two hundred forty-two pounds, and fighting out of Chicago, Illinois, the former heavyweight champion and the third ranked contender in the world, Usalv 'the Madman' Markovski!"

Macy and Paul's conversations, along with the movements of people in the bar trickle into background noise as I watch the referee point at both men before bringing his hands together to start the fight.

Manning rushes across the octagon to meet Usalv. It takes just a few moments to understand the style differences between these two men. Manning's style consists of high energy movements that include bobbing, weaving, and test strikes. It's a stark contrast to Usalv's calm and calculating style.

Grudgingly, I understand why Rodgers wanted Usalv lean for this fight. Manning can't possibly keep this up for three rounds.

Both fighters circle each other, looking for an opening. Manning stings Usalv with a low hard kick to the calf before barely missing his face with an overhand punch. Usalv rushes in and tries to take him down, but Manning's a big guy who's able to free his leg from Usalv's grasp with a sharp elbow to the shoulder blades, followed by a vicious knee to Usalv's ribcage.

"That's great take down defense by Manning, Miguel!"

"Toby, Markovski just doesn't miss too many opportunities like that."

"It's very rare. Markovski is a tactical striker. When he makes a big move, he's usually very effective."

"He's too lean, damn it. And Manning's not tired enough." I slap my hand on the table, causing a puddle of beer to slosh out of my glass.

Next to me, Macy shifts and places her hand on my arm. "Take it easy, hon. It's not over yet. And this isn't Usalv's first fight. He knows what he's doing."

"I know he does." My index finger swirls around the puddle of beer. "And I know it's part of his job. But it's so hard to watch him be hurt."

"He's lucky he's got you to worry about him," Paul says.

I nod in silent thanks. It's a sympathetic compliment, but right now it doesn't make me feel better. I *am* worried. Watching Usalv fight is like watching a car wreck. I can't bear to see him hurt, but turning away is next to impossible.

The men circle each other a few more times before Manning tries another combination strike. This time, an upper cut tags Usalv's chin before he can entirely move out of its way. He responds with a kick that Manning checks.

"Nice one by Manning!"

"Manning will rack up some points for that."

"Absolutely, Toby. Unless Markovski makes some-

thing major happen in the next forty-five seconds, this round is going to Manning."

"Don't count him out yet, Miguel. We know from Markovski's past fights that a lot of submission finishes we've seen from him are due to earlier leg kicks."

"Louise, is Usalv...okay?" Macy asks. "I thought he was the favorite to win."

"He's been better. It's true." My eyes never leave the screen.

I've watched him in person and on film, even sparred with him myself. He's one of the most deliberate, decisive, devastating fighters I've ever seen. Usalv tends to conserve his energy by not attempting high numbers of rapid strikes. But when he does strike, he rarely misses and usually does lots of damage.

This round, his strikes and takedown attempts have been minimally effective. The man I'm watching is not Usalv at his best. It makes me start to wonder what toll these last few weeks have taken on him.

Rodgers convinced me that Usalv needed a break he was unwilling to take to prepare for this fight. But what if it's turned him into a hot mess like it's done to me? I can't sleep, my appetite is shot, and my normal daily routine has become overwhelming.

"Ow! Shit!" Macy's outburst focuses my attention back on the fight.

Manning attempted a takedown and Usalv managed to keep on his feet. But now Usalv's back is pinned against the cage and he's taking lots of knee strikes to the inside legs as he grapples with Manning.

"Now they've taken it into the clinch. This is where Markovski is the most dangerous."

"But Manning took him there, which seemed to surprise Markovski a bit. Not the strategy anyone expected to see from Manning."

"Well, so far, Markovski's holding his own and is refusing to give up his back."

"Yes, but he's sure paying the price for it. Those knee jabs that Manning is delivering are brutal strikes that are chewing up the fleshy parts of Markovski's legs."

Suddenly Manning manages to get free of Usalv's grip and strikes him twice in the face with solid blows. I watch in horror as blood streams down Usalv's face and splatters onto Manning's back as Usalv struggles to defend himself.

"Oh Christ!" I watch, horrified as Usalv tries to wipe the blood away from his eye to clear his vision in between blows from Manning. Thank God he manages to tear himself away just before the bell rings.

The camera pans in on Usalv's face as he returns to the red corner with a hand over his eye and a vacant expression on his face. I've lived with him long enough to recognize that look. He's checked out. His mind isn't on this fight.

Good God, what have I done?

"Fuck, that's nasty." Paul winces. "It's a good thing he lives with a nurse."

"Shut up, Paul," Macy hisses.

"Just sayin'."

"Paul!" Macy smacks his shoulder.

"Sorry, Louise." He reaches across Macy and pats my arm.

"It's okay, Paul." Hot tears stream down my face. "It's not your fault. It's just really hard to watch someone you love be hurt like that."

I love him.

There's pin-drop silence around the table as we all process what I just said. But there it is, the truth I refused to see for months. And it hurts down deep that anything I said or did is contributing to the beat down Usalv's taking right now.

"It sure does. It hurts like hell." Macy replies. "Makes you want to strip those chicken feathers off the other guys back with your fingernails."

"Exactly." I erupt with nervous laughter and wipe my tears away.

"Well." Paul clears his throat. "I think…we need another pitcher for the table. I'll go get one."

"Thanks, hon," Macy replies. "Looks like it's gonna be a long night."

CHAPTER TWENTY-SIX

F uck, that hurt.

The cut feels like it's right below my eyebrow, although it's hard to tell with all this blood running down my face.

Bruce, my long time cutman, slams me onto a stool and begins to work his magic. Damn it, I don't like sitting between rounds. It makes me stiff, but it can't be helped right now.

After wiping the blood off my face and mouth, he grabs the back of my head as he holds an ice cold enswell across the cut. I feel more than see two of my corner men slap freezer bags full of ice against my chest, back, and biceps.

"Put an ice pack on my leg." I point to a large throbbing welt on my thigh.

"What happened to our plan?" Rodgers' voice is calm but frustrated. "You are much faster than this, and much faster than him. Watch his front leg, Madman. A heavy front leg means it's coming from the hands. If his weight is back, get ready for a kick and take him to the ground. You've got good control of the octagon. You need to use it better."

I nod as Bruce takes the enswell away to look at my eye and finish his work. When he does, I turn my head to the crowd and scan the first few rows.

No Sweet Lou anywhere. Damn.

Well, things had sucked after Lou had told me that we should cool off for a while. It made me scared shitless to tell her how much it meant to me for her to be at this fight. Since I couldn't stomach another big hell no from her, I'd told Rodgers to get her to come.

Guess that hadn't worked out.

"What the fuck are you looking at?" Rodgers explodes.

"She didn't come?" My impaired gaze scans the crowd.

"No, she didn't come." He's impatient. Too bad.

"What did she say?" I snap my head around to face him.

"I didn't ask her."

"You didn't ask her?" I feel my anger rise to match his, and my corner man's arm stiffens against my chest. "Why the hell not?"

Rodgers glances at the ringside TV camera, then shifts his back, obstructing the televised view of our conversation. He leans in close and blows out a slow, controlled breath.

"This fight is already a disaster without her here," he growls with quiet fury. "The whole training camp has been piss-poor. She's a complication you don't need right now."

"Stop treating me like some numb-nutted teenager," I growl through gritted teeth.

"Would look at yourself? Jesus fucking Christ. Get your fucking head back in this goddamned fight before this poser chicken hawk hands you your ass. We'll talk about this later."

I stand up and tower over him, never breaking eye contact. "I'm going to visualize your head on that guy's shoulders, right before I kick his ass into next week. And when this is over, we're having words." I rip the ice bag against my chest out of my corner man's hand and thrust it into Rodgers midsection.

"*Hmm, there seems to be some tension over in the red corner, Toby.*"

"*Well, Terence Rodgers, Markovski's long-time coach, is the man with a plan. And things clearly aren't going according to plan at the moment.*"

"*Markovski's a very tactical fighter and his tactics aren't working well right now. Let's see how this second round goes.*"

All I can see is red. All I can feel is rage. My

hands are up, and my weight shifts from one leg to another as I nod to the ref my readiness to fight.

Hurry, goddamn it. Hurry.

Whatever Bruce did to my eye won't last long, which puts me in one helluva bind. I can't take this fight to the ground and risk being blinded by blood pouring into my eyes with that monster pounding away on me.

I'm hell on wheels down on the mat, but not when I'm choking on my own blood or being blinded by it. Which means I need to keep this fight vertical, right where Manning wants it to be.

The round starts and I hurry out to the center, vying for control of the octagon. Manning gets there late and he's forced to circle me, instead of the other way around. Since the radius of his circle is longer, he has more steps to take, which will tire him out faster.

"How's the eye?" Manning wears a shit-eating grin.

I smile and say nothing. He knows I'm hurt, so it's no surprise that he tries to strike my damaged eye again.

Only problem is, he's kinda tired now. He got some good shots in the first round, but they came at full retail price. He's breathing a little heavy so soon after the break.

I recall Rodgers' ringside advice and watch for Manning's heavy front leg. When he shoots an over-handed right at my eye, I'm ready. As soon he opens up, I'm right there with hard punch to the side of his left ribs. From the brutal loud thud of my hand against his trunk, I know it's a solid blow.

"Wow! I could hear that all the way over here."

"Yeah, Manning's hurt, Toby. Look at him. He can't catch his breath."

I take a quick look at Manning's face. It's twisted up with pain, and his shit-eating grin is long gone. He's hurt. Good, but he's not where I need him yet.

As Manning tries to catch his breath, he backs away. He's got to be tired, and right now he's not tired enough.

"Don't let him rest!" Rodgers shouts at me. "Go after him!"

The cut across my eye starts to bleed again. The blood trickles down my face and I wipe it away to prevent it from blinding and choking me. As the wound swells, it's getting hard to see.

I charge at him fast, launching a barrage of strikes at his head. They land mostly on his forearms, which shield his face. My strikes aren't doing too much damage, but I'm hoping to goad him into a tired, sloppy mistake.

It works.

Manning throws a spinning back kick, but it's too high and his stance isn't solid. I grab the kicking leg and upend him. He lands flat on his ass, stunned.

But he's too far from the wall for me to pin him against it.

"A big move for Markovski... but what's this? He's not going after Manning on the ground?"

"Looks like he wants to keep the fight standing. Not his usual style."

"Not at all. This fight just got a lot more interesting."

"And now look at this. Manning doesn't want to get off the ground!"

"I'm confused here. I thought Markovski was the wrestler and Manning was the striker?"

"So did I, Toby."

"Get the fuck up." I gesture toward him, then back away so he's got to chase me down.

Manning sits there a few moments, his legs facing me defensively. That son of a bitch is having a rest. I shrug at the ref to complain.

"Get up," the ref orders him. "Fight."

Fuck.

We're both tired, our bodies are chewed up, and my vision sucks. Manning looks up at the clock and I follow his gaze. Ninety seconds until the round ends. Unless the TKO comes first.

Manning and I exchange looks. Both of us sense that the end of this fight is near. He tries to end it first by going for the takedown, only he ends up grappling with me in the clinch while I'm back against the wall.

Big mistake. There is where he didn't want to

find himself. And I'm not nearly as tired as he needs me to be for this to work.

Manning frees a hand and launches a few head shots in the direction of my bad eye. But he's opened up now and I respond with a few hard knee shots to his inner legs before I get control of his hand.

Then I see it. Clear as day. As he tries to line up a shot, his right elbow drifts away from his rib cage. My leg shoots out and my shin connects, delivering a textbook liver shot.

"And Markovski delivers a huge switch kick to his right obliques!"

"Oh, I think he hit the liver, Toby. That's a huge shot."

"Manning's in trouble! Big trouble!"

Given the choice between a solid well-placed kick to the balls and a liver shot, it's a kick to the balls for me, no contest. Manning staggers back, trying to catch his breath, trying not to collapse, unable to protect himself.

I've got this and rush forward.

By the time I reach him, he's down on one knee. I put him on his back and take him to school on ground and pound. He covers his face and head with his arms as my fists pummel him. He turns away from me and gives up his back, but his hands don't move to protect the exposed side of his face. I feel the nitrile gloved hands of the referee push me off Manning and it's over.

"Markovski takes it! Four minutes, thirty-eight seconds into the second round, and this fight is over by TKO."

"And that, ladies and gentlemen, is what makes this such a crazy sport. Anything can happen and fairly often it does."

"Fuck, that hurts. I'd rather be punched." I complain to the doctor, as the contents of the syringe he's injecting into my eyebrow causes a burning sensation.

"This is the worst part. Once the lidocaine takes effect you won't feel anything."

"You've done this before, right?" Needles scare me.

He laughs. "Since back when you thought a ring was nothing but a piece of jewelry. Hold still." Another stream of liquid flows into my body, much less painful than the first. When the syringe is empty, he pulls the needle out from the side of my head.

"How's he doing, Doc?" Rodgers calls from the door of the improvised treatment room in the Paint Center.

"Pretty well." The doctor, an African-American in his late fifties, leans over my eye and feels the cut with careful, practiced hands. "It's not such a bad cut as it is in a bad place." He smoothes my flesh and presses on it. "This is down to the muscle, not to the bone."

"That's good news, right?"

"Very good news."

"How long will you need, Doctor?" Rodgers asks.

'He's needs four, maybe five sutures." The doctor replies. "Twenty minutes, tops."

"You want me to stay or come back later, Usalv?" It's a loaded question and we both know it.

"Will it bother you if we talk while you're working?" I ask the doctor. I'm less likely to go ballistic if someone else is around.

"Not at all. Just pretend I'm not here."

Rodgers shuffles into the room and pulls a chair near the exam table I'm lying on.

"Great job today, Usalv. This was an important win for us. A lot of people were hoping for an upset, expecting Manning to beat you, like he has a lot of top heavyweights."

I say nothing. Right now, I don't give a damn about the fight or what it does or doesn't do to my ranking.

"You'll definitely be on the next big international card. And if things go well, they'll have no choice but to give you a title fight."

My response is to adjust the ACE bandage holding the ice packs on my chewed-up thighs. The only audible sound is the ice sloshing and the plastic bag crinkling.

"Congratulations on the win today." Rodgers attempts to end the uncomfortable silence.

"You put this all on her, didn't you?" The quiet explosive tone of my voice fills the room. "The fight, the title, even the bonuses. It was going to be your fault if I won and her fault if I lost, right?"

Rodgers shifts in his chair. "I did talk to her. About how you needed to keep focused."

"Focused? Focused on what?"

"The fight. This fight. Your career."

Anger makes me shift and the doctor scolds me. "Easy, son. Hold still."

"Sorry." I mutter then take a long slow breath to get control of myself. "Just so you know, your back alley approach to *fixing* this has fucked my mood, motivation, appetite, and sleep cycle for the last two weeks. I won this damn fight in spite of you, not because of you, so thanks for fuck all."

There's pin drop silence in the room. Even the doctor's hands stop working. Maybe he's antici-pating me moving again. I wish like hell that I could see Rodgers' face.

"I'm sorry, Usalv." Rodgers' tone is brisk. "I underestimated your feelings for Louise and how important she is to you."

I admit nothing. "You underestimated me. Fuck that." The doctor's hands haven't started moving again, so I sit up and face Rodgers. "Get used to Louise Becker being around. If you can't handle that, I'll understand." I shrug. "Take the rest of the trip to think about it."

"The rest of the trip? And where are you going be?" Rodgers is stunned.

"As soon as the doctor finishes sewing me up, I'm getting the hell out of here."

"But what about the parties, promos, and sponsor meet ups?"

"Handle it. That's the one thing I do trust you with." I lay back down on the table.

"Thanks, but it's you they'll want to talk to, get pics of."

"Tell them my eye's messed up and I need to see a specialist." I turn on my side to glare at him. "I've got a lot of shit to sort out at home."

CHAPTER TWENTY-SEVEN

Holy *shit.*

An uneasy feeling hits my stomach when the traffic jam outside Usalv's house confronts me. Usalv's not supposed to be here. Perhaps one of the neighbors is responsible for this party pandemonium? No chance. By the time my journey to the front door ends, it's clear from the loud music and raised voices within that this is party central.

Christ, so much for ramen noodles, ibuprofen, and an early night.

I take a deep breath, push the door open and step inside. A pile of unfamiliar bags and shoes occupy the space where my Dansko clogs normally sit by the door. Cautiously, I step out of the foyer and peer into the living room.

Thirty or so reasonably well-dressed people

mingle while drinking bottled beer and cocktails. The music is too loud to hear the conversations of the unfamiliar guests around me.

"Hey!" someone shouts from the lounger underneath the window. She's wearing a tight sleeveless dress with unnatural looking cleavage spilling out a slit in the front.

"What?" I reply after realizing she's speaking to me.

"I think you've got the wrong place." Her gaze shifts to my mud splattered scrubs and a mixture of irritation overcomes me.

'Um, no I don't." My tone is deliberately dismissive as I look for Usalv.

"It's not Halloween," she shouts, then laughs aloud. Too loud. It's hard to tell if she's drunk, naturally bitchy, or both. It never pays to argue with someone like her, but I'm a little too pissed off to stop myself.

"And some of us aren't wearing a costume," I reply, raising an eyebrow at her outfit before shaking my head.

"What did you say?" Instead of Queen Bee realizing that she shouldn't mess with me right now, she hops off the couch and gets all confrontational.

Oh, please. Go away.

"You've clearly had too much to drink." I tower over her. "Maybe you should go outside and get some fresh air." My nurse voice speaks, reasonable and calmly authoritative.

"Oh, hell no," she stammers and her breath reeks of alcohol. "You don't get to tell me what to do. *You* should go. Now."

Damn it. Where is the man I love? I need to find him. Right now. He needs to know. I need to explain. And dealing with this drunk Barbie doll is not on my to-do list.

"See this?" I dangle my keychain in front of her bloodshot eyes. "This is my key. To this house. Where I live. So if anyone's ass is going to be dodging the door knob on their way out, it's yours. Now calm down, sober up, and go away." My annoyance hits her full throttle.

The look of shock on her face is replaced quickly by distraction, then excitement. "Usalv!" she calls and pushes past me to the foyer entrance.

Pangs of disbelief and rage rattle through me as she drapes both her hands around his muscular forearm. But his only acknowledgment comes when he pulls free of her grasp.

When I look up at his face, his eyes follow me with a predatory fixation.

"Louise." His voice is a hypnotizing rasp.

"Hey, Usalv." I'm nervous, relieved. And excited. He looks every inch the fit warrior that keeps me coming back. There's so much we need to discuss.

But will he even listen? And how does he feel about things between us?

"I thought you were working." His voice is calm and certain, devoid of obvious emotion.

"I was." I changed shifts to take last night off and watch his fight. "Home now." I fold my arms. "Thought you were in Pittsburgh?"

"I was. Home now."

"Good," I reply.

"Yeah?" He steps toward me and extends his hand. "Come with me."

"Where?" I ask.

"Your room." His shoulder turns towards the hallway.

"Okay."

He takes my hand and leads me down the hall to my bedroom, indifferent to the curious looks we receive.

"Nice party." I tell him.

Usalv says nothing, just shuts the door and clicks the bolt into the locked position. Then he turns toward me, hands on his waist, his expression a strange mix of pain and fury. But before I can respond, he retreats behind a stoic mass and slowly starts to unfasten his belt.

"Congratulations. On the fight." My voice fails to drown out the metal clinking of his belt buckle.

Usalv's only reply is silence. Then with excruciating slowness, he untucks his shirt, pulls it over his head, then slides his pants and shorts off in a single motion before kicking them away.

"Oh my God," I gasp.

He stands naked in front of me, silently commanding my undivided attention. His eyebrow is stitched where Manning punched him. His ribs are swollen where Manning kneed him. His thighs are purple and black where Manning kicked him.

And his protruding erection looks robust and eager as he approaches me across the long length of the narrow room and backs us toward the bed.

"I don't want to talk, Lou." His hoarse voice brims with urgency and need. "Just take off your clothes."

"But…doesn't it hurt?"

"Yes." Usalv pushes my hand away as I reach for his bruised ribs. "But not any place that's important right now."

"But—"

"I'm going be a total dick here, Louise. I want one thing from you right now. Just one. You gonna give it to me, or not?"

"But—"

"Yes or no." He shakes his head at my protest. "Yes… or no?"

"Yes." Whatever else needs to be fixed, it's been way too long for both of us.

"Good." There's an edgy, explosive quiet in his tone. "Now take your clothes off."

I reach down and pull my shirt up, but before it's off, Usalv's impatient fingers tug urgently on my drawstring pants. When they're loose, he bends me over my mission dresser and strips me naked from behind.

One of his hands grips the dresser next to my head, while the other reaches down between my legs and pushes them apart. His frenzied fingers fumble inside my folds as he guides his shaft toward my entrance. With a single jarring thrust, he fills me entirely.

"Oh, God." He doesn't ask if I'm okay. And there's no point. I'd rather feel all the raw sensation being with him gives me than feel any less. He shut me down so hard after we argued about taking a break that I wasn't sure we'd ever be together like this again.

As he strokes faster and deeper into me, I feel the tension leave his body. The arm bracing itself against the dresser wraps around my breasts, crushing the ribs underneath as he cradles his forehead in the arch between my shoulder blades.

The speed of his strokes slows and he brings his lips close to my ear. "Don't...*ever* do that again," he growls, then stills inside me.

"I won't. I promise." Although I'm not sure exactly what *that* is, it's clear what he means.

He grunts in response and then starts again, his strokes a startling mixture of punishment and forgiveness. This isn't about pleasure or passion or bliss. It's about fear and need, regret and release.

For both of us.

Rodgers was able to convince me that my relationship with Usalv was damaging his career because I'd fallen in love without admitting it to myself. Because of that, it made sense to deal with things the way I usually do—prioritizing career over personal life. But that wasn't my choice to make alone. It was Usalv's, too.

He leans against the wall and tries to reposition himself before he stops. When I look back at him over my shoulder, his forearm is pulled up against the side of his badly bruised ribs.

"Stop this, you're hurting yourself." I try and pull away, but his free arm holds me in place.

"No! No. Wait, just give me a second." He catches his breath. "My ribs will hurt for a while, and I'm not going to stay in park." A few more seconds pass, and he hurries to push himself away from the wall.

"Hold on a minute," I insist, then start sliding up and down, pushing my hips back into him.

Usalv's whole body shudders in response. "Wait… Louise, what are you…doing?"

"You think because I said yes that you get to make all the decisions?" My back arches as I move up and down. "Think again."

"Sweetheart, you don't need to go so fast," he

replies, although it doesn't sound much like a complaint.

"That's what you think. You're not the only one whose been tied up in knots for the last few weeks."

He starts to speak but ends up stammering out an incomprehensible moan. I lose myself in the sensation of being in complete control, and the happiness of this single moment. Caught between the pain of the recent past and our uncertain path forward, this moment, the space between those two points, is one I'm determined to stretch out for as long for as possible.

"Oh, Christ...Louise," he pants, a mix of pain and release. He leans his shoulder against the wall and presses his hand onto the small of my back.

I'm so focused on reveling in our moment together that my own climax surprises me. Usalv cradles my hips while he braces himself against the wall. When we're done, he leans over me and kisses the nape of my neck.

The only audible noise is the sound of our rapid breathing in unison. Once we've both recovered a bit, Usalv ushers me gently toward my daybed, which lies parallel against the narrow back wall.

My exhausted body collapses onto the bed. Leaning against the wall, I draw my knees up to my chest and watch him stagger over, lowering himself gingerly onto the bed. But Usalv is too tall and physically damaged to sit up like me. After a moment, he lies down on his side. Drawing his knees together, he rests alongside me, with my shins brushing against the top of his thighs.

"This bed is ridiculous. How the hell do you get comfortable on this?"

"Well, it does fold out."

His large body looks extremely cramped. "If I'd time for that, we wouldn't have done it standing up."

"Sorry for not being sorry." It's the truth.

He snorts with laughter and scratches the beard along his jawline.

"I'm glad you're back," I tell him.

"Are you?" he asks. His voice sounds casual, even teasing, but his breathing stops while he waits for me to answer.

"Yeah. I am."

"Good." He nods. "Good. It's nice to be back." He rubs his hand along my shin.

We sit in silence, finding comfort in our closeness. After a moment, the strength and will to speak returns to me. "A little while ago you told me to never do *that* again. What *that* did you mean?"

Usalv's hand stills on my leg. "You made me a promise, too. Remember?" He kisses my knee and then removes his hand. "What did you promise me, Sweet Lou?"

I twirl my fingers around a dark patch of curly hair on his thigh. "Did Rodgers talk to you?" I ask.

"He did."

"Mmm. And what did he tell you?"

"That he didn't get you a seat to the fight like I'd asked. Among other things."

"That's true. I had to switch shifts to be able to see the fight at the bar with Macy."

"You saw?" He seems surprised.

"Of course. I couldn't not watch." I smile. He *had* wanted me to come.

"What'd you think?"

"It sucked. Watching you get beat up like that. It was awful."

He rolls over on his back, forcing me to rest my legs on top of his and drape them over the bedside. He stares at the ceiling with an unreadable expression.

"Rodgers told me I was screwing up your training and your career. I didn't want to do that," I explain. "When I watched the first round and saw how badly you were getting your ass kicked, it made me feel responsible."

"You weren't responsible," he replies. "You did what he asked."

"It doesn't matter." I take a deep breath. "It sucks watching someone you love get hurt. Even when they do it for a living." I hesitate then repeat myself for clarity. "I love you, Usalv."

Usalv freezes on the bed next to me. Literally, he looks like a fucking zombie. He's motionless for what seems like an eternity. Okay, so I didn't know what to expect.

But it sure the hell wasn't this.

I'm about to ask him to say something, anything, when someone knocks on the bedroom door. He turns over and sits up, putting distance between us in the process.

"Fuck off!" Usalv shouts at the door.

The interloper responds by twisting the knob impatiently.

"Hey!" Usalv shouts. "Go the fuck away!" He picks up my college mug from the bedside table and hurls it at the door.

The plastic handle sheers off and flies across the room. It hits my dresser then skates across the floor and stops next to the daybed at his feet. The loud fast clicking of stiletto heels retreating across the tile floor fills the air. Something tells me they belong to that drunk bitch from the living room.

He picks up the broken mug and studies it in silence.

"I'm sorry, Louise." His tone is so odd that I don't know if he's talking about the mug or something else.

"It's okay." I hop off the bed and retrieve the handle from the floor. "I can fix it."

"Listen." He stands and starts gathering his clothes. "Get dressed and come out to the party for a while. I'd like you to meet some of my friends."

Is this good or bad?

"Um, thanks, but it's late." I'm feeling shitty at the lack of acknowledgment of my feelings, never mind the lack of reciprocity. "But I'm kind of tired and really don't feel much like partying right now."

"Believe it or not, neither do I." He tries to laugh, but the pain in his ribs cuts it short. "But it is what it is, and you can't stay in here hiding all night. Besides, they've seen you... You should come out."

I delay my response to watch him dress in record time. His shorts and pants go on all at once. Then everything gets smoothed out and down, and he's ready to go.

Damn, who knew a man could get dressed that fast?

"Um, yeah. Sure," I tell him.

"Good." He plants a chaste kiss on the top of my head. "See you in a bit."

I nod in response, and he's off like a prom dress.

Damn. So much for my candid bravery. Just...*oww*.

CHAPTER TWENTY-EIGHT

By the time Louise's bedroom door slams behind me, I'm already in the kitchen headed for my secret stash of vodka in the freezer. The frosty cold bottle hides behind a wall of ice packs and some frozen shot glasses. I pull out the bottle and set one of the glasses on the counter.

I fill the glass too full, then knock back the bracing ice cold shot in a single gulp.

Louise *loves* me? What the fuck does that mean? And what the hell am I supposed to do about it?

"I love you Usalv," my mother had told me. "Don't make trouble for your Uncle Paskal while you stay with them. And when everything's okay again, you'll come back."

And then she'd sent me to the US and I never lived with them again.

"We love you Usalv," my sisters Marija and Milena

had told me before I moved to Chicago. "Don't cry. We'll all be back together soon."

But then we never were.

"Don't be afraid, Usalv. *I love you,*" Emily had told me before we had sex for the first time.

Then I'd taken her to the hospital and she'd never spoke to me again.

I take a few deep breaths, then knock back another shot. Does this mean Louise will leave me, too? That's not the way it's supposed to work, but that's how things usually turn out for me.

Does she expect me to tell her that I love her, too? Because I can't. It's not that I don't. But those words change things superfast and I'm not ready for that. Aside from some recent bullshit about my training, things between us are good. Really good. There's no need to change things up.

Damn, it's hot and loud in here, and I won't be alone for long. I'm trying to figure out my next move when a very unwelcome voice calls my name.

"Oh, Usalv. There you are." The click-clack of stiletto heels marches into the kitchen, invading my space.

"Kylie." I take a deep breath and fold my arms. "What the hell are you doing here?"

"I heard you won." She approaches me and I tuck myself behind the corner of the counter. "And that there was victory party was at your house."

"Kylie..." I shake my head. "You should have known not to come here."

"Why? Because of that tall woman with the long curly hair?"

"Because you and I are done."

"Okay, but that doesn't mean we still can't be friends, does it?"

Oh, for Chrissake. "Wouldn't we need to be friends in the first place for that to happen?"

She huffs and rolls her eyes before ignoring my question. "So...is she just a hook up or are the two of you hooked up?"

"Kylie, she lives with me."

Her eyes widen in surprise, but instead of accepting the obvious reality of the situation, she gears up to screw with me. "Yeah, she said something like that before. Funny thing though, none of the guys mentioned you were with anyone when they told me about the party."

Typical Kylie, ignoring everything she doesn't want to hear. It's one of many reasons that I'd decided to slam the brakes on our dysfunctional relationship.

"Because they didn't know," I explain.

"Exactly!" She pounces. "You moved in with someone, and those guys didn't know?" Kylie shakes her head. "Come on. That's bullshit."

"My plan was to introduce her tonight. And you

being here makes it very awkward." I gesture toward the door. "I really wish you'd leave."

"Why? How come I can't meet her?" Her familiar combative tone sends a heated rush of anger to my face.

"Why are you hell bent on making this painful, difficult, and shitty for everyone?"

There's strained silence between us as Kylie processes my request. We've always had an on-and-off relationship. It's funny, but looking back now, I'd ended things with Kylie the same night I met Louise.

The fucking merry-go-round that my personal life had turned into was a disorientating ride that I wanted to get off. At least that's what I'd told myself at the time. But now I realize the truth. It was because of Louise. I wanted her in my life, there and then. No one else.

"Is this one of your friends that you wanted me to meet?" Sweet Lou calls from the doorway.

Holy shit.

Louise isn't wearing nursing scrubs and a tired ponytail anymore. Nope. She leans up against the door jamb wearing tight skinny jeans and black ankle boots, with a smoke colored sheer shirt and vest that has see-thru cut outs.

Damn, Sweet Lou looks good.

I can tell Kylie's intimidated. She should be.

"Yes," Kylie replies. "I'm Kylie." She comes around the corner and stands straight.

"Louise." Sweet Lou replies. She hesitates a moment, then enters the kitchen.

"Do you want a drink, Louise?" Kylie asks, grabbing the blender. "Looks like a frozen margarita."

"I'm not a fan," Louise replies.

"Too bad," Kylie tells her.

"Any scotch in here?" Louise ignores Kylie and asks me.

"It's on the table," I answer. "Out there."

Louise shrugs. "Never mind then. I'll get it later."

Kylie puts the blender back and opens the refrigerator. She's trying to give Louise the impression that this is her space, that Kylie knows her way around. I know, because she's done this before, causing major cat fights in the process. But so far, Louise is keeping her cool.

"Do you have any pomegranate martinis, Usalv?" Kylie asks.

"Not any cold ones," Louise answers. Her voice is clinically calm, but her mouth is set in a hard line. Kylie has finally set her off, but I'm not sure how.

Just kill me now.

Kylie shuts the refrigerator doors, leans back against it and gives Louise a bitchy smile. "So how long have you been living with Usalv?" she asks.

Louise shrugs. "About three months."

"Oh." Kylie gives her a bitchy pout. "Was that

before or after we stopped sleeping together, Usalv?"

Enraged, I try and speak, but my throat is parched and no words can escape. Instead, a half wheeze, half choking sounds escapes. Louise looks over at me for a second then turns back to Kylie.

"After," Louise assures her in a calm, collected voice. "It was after."

"I'm not so sure about that," Kylie taunts.

"I am." Louise walks past her to the pantry alongside the fridge. "When I moved in, your pomegranate martinis were in the fridge. About two weeks later, it was obvious Usalv wasn't drinking them, so I put them in the pantry." Louise opens the folding door and pulls out three warm bottled cocktails and sets them on the counter. "They've been here ever since."

"Sweet Lou." Fuck. I hadn't even thought about that before she moved in. "I—"

"He hasn't asked about them or touched them. Neither has anyone else." Louise takes a warm bottle from the counter, twists the top off, and sets it down in front of Kylie. "Help yourself, Kylie. Cheers."

The heels of Louise's boots strike a slow confident rhythm as she heads for the door. She stops before turning around to stare at me. "I'll see you later." Then she's gone, without so much as a backward glance.

Goddamn it.

"What the fuck is your problem?" I explode at Kylie. "Then you wonder why we can't be friends?"

"I was only—"

"No, no, no. I'm not listening to another goddamn word. Get the fuck out of my house and don't ever come back."

Before Kylie can say anything, I haul ass after Sweet Lou. Her bedroom is empty, which sends me racing down the hall to the living room. I try to navigate through the sea of friends and other familiar faces quickly, but it takes time. Too much time.

When the hellos, the selfies, the jokes, the promises to be right back are finished, I'm just in time to see Sweet Lou pouring the last shot from a whiskey bottle into her glass. She glances around the room and our eyes lock for a moment. Then Louise shakes her head at me before downing the contents of the glass and heading out the front door.

I run out after her, chasing her down the cement walkway to the street.

"Louise? Louise! Wait." To anyone watching it must look like she put my balls in her purse before she left, but it takes me less than a second to realize I don't give a fuck how whipped this makes me look.

"Let me go, Usalv. Please." She tells me without

stopping and continues at a rapid pace down the street.

I hurry to stand in front of her, forcing her to stop and look up. Tears stream down her face and she rubs them away with angry ferocity.

"Oh Christ. Please don't cry, Louise." I smooth her hair down. "I never stepped out on you with Kylie or anyone else. Never ever."

"I don't think you did." Fresh tears fall again. "But it bothers me that you invited her here on a night when you thought I'd be gone." She shakes her head in disbelief.

"No, no I didn't invite her." My voice pleads. "Hell, the party wasn't even my idea. When some of the guys heard I'd come home today, they spread the word and showed up."

"And yet here she is," Sweet Lou mumbles and brushes past me.

"Don't take her seriously. I'm begging you." I take hold of Sweet Lou's arm. "Please. Kylie doesn't want to be with me, but she doesn't want to let me go until she finds someone first. I know it's fucked up. Kylie just turns into a bitch when she's scared."

"Really?" Louise asks. "And what about you?"

"Me?" I'm defensive. "What about me?"

"Is this how you act when you're scared? Or is it something else?"

"Scared?" I shift from one leg to the other. "I'm not scared."

"Whatever," she mumbles and resumes walking.

"Wait," I explode. "What the fuck, Louise?" My pace matches her as I walk alongside her. "I have no idea what you want me to say."

"You want sex." She throws her hands in the air and shrugs. "And that's pretty much it, right?"

"Goddamn it." I pause and collect myself. "I can't imagine any way to answer you that's not going to get me in a shitload of trouble."

"Why did you let me sofa surf at your place?" she asks.

"Because you were in a tight spot and needed help." I push my hands down into the front pockets of my jeans.

"And that's it? Just being a good guardian angel?"

"Something like that." Her question makes me squirm. "Back then, I just wanted you to be okay, whether you slept with me or not."

"Why?"

"The truth is, I liked you." It's honest. "I liked spending time with you. You made me feel like I wasn't alone, like I belonged somewhere when we were both home."

"Okay, so you and I get along well enough when we're not flat on our backs. But that doesn't mean it's any different than how it was between you and Kylie."

"Look, you're talking crazy right now." This conversation is way too upsetting. "Kylie and I got together because we were both lonely but didn't want to be alone." I grasp her shoulders. "But being with her never stopped the loneliness. It stopped with you."

"Well, thank you for that. But no matter how things started, I think you're happy with the way things are between us right now."

"What the hell's wrong with that?" I explode.

Tears well up in her eyes. "I'm not."

A cold wave of pure, primal fear rushes through me. "Why not?" I sound hoarse.

She wipes a single tear away with the back of her hand. "I have a harder time living in limbo than you do. Maybe it's a character flaw, but I can't help it."

"You know what?" Panic swells inside me. "This is crazy, having a conversation like this out here on the street. Let's go back home and we can talk it out. Please."

"Talk? About this? At party central?" She gives a short laugh. "I don't think so."

"So that's it? You don't want to talk? What the hell do you expect me to do?"

"Not a thing. There's not anything more to say. In fact, I should probably move out." Louise hugs her shoulders, dislodging my hands from them, breaking our physical connection.

"Move out?" My world grinds to a halt. After a long, stunned silence, she continues her soul crushing edict.

"Thank you for letting me stay. You did me a huge favor, and I'll always be grateful. But you need your space and distance, and I need to move on with my life."

No. No, no, no. *No.*

"It's been a stressful few weeks for both of us." The calm certainty of my voice cracks. "I think we need to just, just chill out a bit and not make any decisions in the heat of the moment. Let's go back to the house. We don't need to say anything." I've broken out into a cold sweat. "Besides it's a little chilly, and you shouldn't be walking around without a jacket. Come on," I plead like I'm talking to a wounded animal.

"I'll be fine. I need some fresh air to clear my head." She starts to walk away then turns around one more time. "Usalv?"

"What?"

"You can just forget about what I said it earlier. I didn't really mean it. It was just…afterglow."

"Afterglow?"

She nods. "Just forget it."

In another moment, she fades into the darkness.

CHAPTER TWENTY-NINE

"How could I be so fucking stupid?"

A couple casts alarmed looks in my direction, then quickly hurries past me.

Stop acting like a lunatic, I admonish myself for speaking aloud while hurrying down the street. The instinct to run six minute miles and quell my rocket-high stress levels is tanked by these idiotic high heel boots.

I wipe fresh tears away as I'm forced to admit this evening appears to be an unfixable disaster. What the hell possessed me to tell Usalv that I loved him?

It's the God's-honest truth, my inner voice tells me. I needed to be honest, to let him know my feelings. Truthfully though, the hopelessly unrealistic optimist in me believed he felt the same way.

But what happens instead? Disaster, that's what. Usalv got up and dressed so fast it had made me wonder if the smoke alarm went off. Then when I go look for him, he's chatting it up with his ex. The one with the porn star boobs three times too large for her size two frame.

Why can't I fall in love with a good man who loves me back?

The cold stillness of the night distracts me from my distress. It's late summer in Chicago and the nights get cool now. My thin filmy shirt provides zero warmth against this cold, damp breeze. The weather forces me to admit it's time to return home, and I look up to study my surroundings for the first time in a half hour.

That's when reality hits me. I'm kind of lost.

My route began where it does when Usalv takes me running, but somewhere along the way I've missed a turn. When my path runs across a street that's vaguely familiar, I veer down it, hoping to run across a recognizable landmark or intersection.

Shit.

It's after one a.m. in Chicago, I'm cold, lost, and my feet are aching from these damn high heels. There isn't a cab in sight, and my phone is charging back home. As I stand in front of a row of closed shops looking lost, the sound of footsteps creeping cautiously toward me become audible.

When my head turns, no one's there. The skin on my forearm puckers as the hairs stand straight up, and I hurry toward the corner streetlight, hoping to find people, a passing car, or a cab.

There's no one here.

No people, no traffic. And why would there be? The only things here are stores that closed up hours ago. My instincts urge me to bolt, but these damn boots prevent me. I don't want to run and risk falling, and now isn't the time to stop and fiddle with their metallic heel zippers.

Behind me, the sound of footsteps gets faster and closer.

With no one else around, I race out into the middle of the street. If I'm attacked, there's a better chance of being seen, rather than being dragged behind a car or building. Besides, being attacked from behind is about the worse way it could happen.

At the center of the intersection, I turn to face whoever's there.

A young guy in his twenties invades the glow of the street light on the corner. He's wearing a gray hoodie, with red basketball shorts and high top sneakers. Tall and gangly, he slows down but doesn't stop when our eyes meet.

"Hey," he tries to sound casual, like he's just passing by, except he stops at the corner and watches me. After a few seconds, he decides to cross the street and walk toward me, like he just happened to be going that way.

"What's your problem, babe?" He looks me up and down. "Scared?" He smiles like he's turned on.

"Leave me the hell alone." My voice resonates with stilted calm as my feet snap into a fighting stance.

He snorts in disgust before he charges at me, grabbing my throat. I pin his wrist to my chest and hyper-extend his elbow with my left hand, forcing his head toward the ground. His head and neck get treated to several knee jabs, but my footing isn't solid and my strikes lack their usual knock out force and precision.

When the guy gets his hand between my knee and his jaw, it's clear that knocking him out with a blow to the head isn't going to work. Some people can take hits to their head and stay upright. It's my bad luck I ran into one. He'll be bruised tomorrow, but not knocked out tonight.

I torque his hyperextended elbow, forcing him onto his knees, then deliver a solid kick to his ribs before running like hell for a block and a half. Thank God! A familiar building looms ahead, and only when I pass it do the physical effects of my adrenaline rush catch up with me.

"Fuck." I bend at the waist and take big

controlled breaths. My heart races and ears ring from a massive headache. The stress of fight or flight leaves me gasping for air much more than any physical exertion.

I've never been in a street fight before and the experience freaks me out. Pads, rules, and referees are just fine with me. I stand there, hunched over, gasping and praying something like this never happens to me again.

"Goddamn." I lean up against the brick façade of the familiar building to take off my heels. My calves are cramped, my arches are killing me, and the balls of my feet are covered with heat blisters.

I collapse onto the concrete and stroke my feet, applying pressure to cramped tendons and muscles. Sensation stirs slowly back into lower limbs and ankles until they feel ready to function again. When I finally stand up, I feel more than see the full throttle charge that knocks me over onto the sidewalk. My body turns to minimize his target, but my head hits the concrete. Hard.

It leaves me dazed and seeing stars.

The hoodie-clad douche has caught up with me and he's really pissed off. I'd assumed he'd given up for the evening, but a street fight isn't over just because someone quits. Another hard lesson learned tonight.

He sits on top of me, swearing and cursing while

he punches my face and torso. He tags my mouth and chin pretty hard, and I'm startled by the sound of my own pain-laden scream. It sends a surge of adrenaline through me, igniting my survival instincts.

I ball my fists hard and place them over my temples while protecting my face with locked forearms staggered at the elbows. My defensive posture prevents further damage, but I can't stay here forever. The thing is, once you're pinned on the ground, most fighting styles are pretty useless in circumstances like these.

"You've got dangerous kicks. Seductive even. But if you run into someone who knows what they're doing, they can hurt you, Sweet Lou." Usalv's words come back to haunt me.

If you can't move, you can't fight. And right now I can't do either.

This is a bad place for me to be, and I've got to change it up fast. I jam my knee hard into his kidney and attempt to buck him off.

"Damn bitch." He growls in surprise and pain, then turns sideways to control my strikes to his back.

That's all it takes.

As he leans forward to give himself room to turn around, I hook my ankle around his leg and buck again. This time, he loses his balance, landing a hand on the ground beside my head. I push his elbow out while my foot stays locked around his ankle, then buck for dear life one more time.

He lands on his back next to me with a loud thud that forces the air from his lungs.

I scramble to stand, and a wave of nausea hits me. Thankfully, I'm still barefoot, which makes it easier for me to keep upright. I've got a better chance now than I do on the ground, but my vision is blurry.

We're both breathing heavily as he stands up and squares off in front of me. He's not speaking anymore, which makes him even harder to follow in the darkness. There isn't much I can do except take a defensive posture and wait for him to come at me. Trying to attack someone you can't see only works in the movies.

What the hell?

A dark blur streaks into the light of the street lamp. Its powerful arm wraps itself around my attacker's throat before dragging him back into darkness.

"Who's there?" I ask.

"It's me, Louise," Usalv replies. "Be careful!"

You're kidding right? I approach the blurry images and the sound of scraping shoes on pavement being drowned out by the grunts of men fighting.

From behind, Usalv rips my attacker off the ground. He tries to fight back, gripping Usalv's arm, punching over and behind his own head, trying in vain to dislodge two hundred fifty pounds of well-conditioned muscle coiled around him like a giant python.

Usalv carries him like a spasming ragdoll to the side of the brick building. Then he slams the guy, hard, into the brick wall. One. Two. Three times. All with the ease of an angry child trying to break a plastic toy.

The toy breaks, gasping and grunting in pain as its solid pieces shatter with a painful crunching sound.

My attacker crumples to the ground like a wet, discarded blanket. His curses are replaced by moans of pain, and then silence, as Usalv stomps him with vicious body blows where he lies curled up on the ground. Only when the writhing stops does Usalv relent.

When it's over, Usalv turns to find me propped up against a street lamp, watching him.

"Are you okay, Lou?" He asks between labored breaths.

"I...don't know." It's difficult to think and speak at the same rate everything is happening around me.

Usalv looks down at my attacker and shakes the now still body with his foot. Satisfied that he's down for a while, Usalv rushes toward me. As he does, I take a step toward him, then stumble to my knees.

He says something in his native language before rushing toward me.

"Louise? Louise?" Usalv kneels down and shakes my body, bringing on a vicious wave of nausea. "Are you hurt?"

"Yeah," The loud ringing in my ears makes it a struggle to hear him. "I think I am."

"Where?" He's panicked. "What's wrong?"

"Hit my head. Ha-ard." It's difficult to speak. "Concussion, I-I think."

"I'm calling 9-1-1. Just hang on." Usalv speaks into his phone, the conversation sounds distant, his words difficult to understand. While he speaks, the stars in the sky become indistinguishable from the random ones popping into my field of vision.

"Usalv, Usalv!" My fear elicits a wave of panic. "I need you to keep me awake. As long as you can."

"Yeah, sure." He's calm again. "Are you cold?"

"Very." My body rests on the bare concrete. Neither one of us has jackets, so Usalv tries turning me to the side, close to him.

I vomit all over his shoes, my hair, and the sidewalk.

"Oh my God," Usalv rasps.

"Yeah. Don't. Don't do that."

"Stay with me, sweetheart." Usalv rubs his hands down the length of my body, trying to keep me warm. "Talk to me."

"When…when, the ambulance gets here, make them take me to URMC."

"Tell them yourself." He strokes my face, his

tender touch a drastic contrast to the concern in his eyes. The sound of the ambulance gets closer, but it's too far for me to do what he asks.

"I can't. Promise me." I grasp his hand. "Promise."

"I promise."

"How did you find me?" My words tumble out. Until he answers, I didn't realize that I'd spoken out loud.

"Pure luck." He strokes my hair. "When you left, it looked like you were heading off on our jogging route. I almost passed by you, but then I heard." He gulps. "Fighting."

"Oh." Why is that disappointing? "That's not what I mean."

"Well, what do you mean, Sweet Lou?"

"Why...why, why are you here? What made you look for me?"

"You were gone a long time." His voice is calm and certain. How nice. "When you didn't come home, I got worried and called your phone. It rang in your bedroom."

"Oh." The disappointment lingers. "Thank you."

"You're welcome, sweetheart."

"Do you remember what I said?"

"When?" he asks.

"In my room. I think."

He smiles a little sadly. "I remember."

"Good. I didn't mean it when I said I didn't mean

313

it." This is super important to me. "Please don't forget."

"I won't," he promises.

"Not ever," I insist, feeling more agitated.

"Not for the rest of my life." He takes a deep breath. "I swear."

"Good." Then my rush of words ceases and my world fades to black.

CHAPTER THIRTY

"Usalv?"

I stop pacing across the back of the ICU visitor's room. When others are here I sit quietly, but when the room is empty, I march like a sentry on duty.

"Macy? How is she?" I fold my arms.

"Still unconscious, but she's stable." Macy's expression is puzzled. "Hasn't anyone come to speak with you yet?"

"No." I don't hide my irritation. "Someone from the ER let me know they were moving her up here. Then they told me they'd let me know when she was settled."

Macy glances at her smart watch. "We're in the middle of shift change. I heard she was here just before the start of my shift. Come on." She steers me by the elbow. "She's settled in. I just saw her."

"Thanks, Macy."

"Sure." She opens the door and we exit the patient waiting area.

It's pin-drop silent in here as we approach a cluster of desks where several men and women in sky blue scrubs congregate. A few make eye contact with Macy as we pass and nod wordlessly at her.

"This way," she whispers as we turn left down another corridor. As Macy slows in front of a door, the sound of medical equipment humming and buzzing becomes audible. She stops in front of the entrance and takes a deep breath.

"Macy?" When I look down at her face, she wipes a tear away quickly.

"This is might be a little…shocking for you." Her voice is crisp. "Hell, it was for me, and this is my day job."

"Take your time." I wrap an arm around her shoulders and hold my breath while she chokes back sobs. "And we'll both get through this."

Macy takes a minute to collect herself, then goes rigid before speaking. "We will. And so will Lou." She pauses again. "Her face is banged up. The right eye is swollen, and her mouth is bruised along the lower jaw. The bottom lip is split."

"From where he punched her?" My jaw clenches.

"Mmm. They'll probably have a facial plastic surgeon look at her, just to be safe." Macy attempts to reassure me, "This is her department, you know. They'll take good care of her."

"How is that son of a bitch?" Funny, I can't remember his face, but the thought of him haunts me like a monster from a bad nightmare.

"From what I hear, he's messed up. Broken ribs, nose, cheek. Dislocated shoulder. Fractured tibia. He won't be attacking anyone for a while."

"Well that's good news, at least."

She grunts with contempt. "On behalf of women everywhere, thank you." Then Macy wraps her arms around my waist and squeezes me. "And thank you for saving my friend."

"It was an act of selfish desperation." I feel tears well up in my eyes. "I can't imagine my world without her."

"Yeah." Her voice wavers. "Ready?"

Fear and anticipation churn in my stomach like a bad booze combination. "Yeah."

"Okay then. Here we go." Macy slides a large glass door open and we enter a narrow, dimly lit room with a single patient bed.

It freaks me out that the only thing I recognize about her is that curly caramel hair. It's pulled away from her face with a fabric headband. My Sweet Lou sits up at an angle in her hospital bed. The purple swollen flesh around her mouth distorts the once delicate line of her jaw. Her round amber eyes are shut tight, and there's something troubled about them. She doesn't look like she's sleeping, but the fact that she's so still scares me.

I study the tubes coming in and out of her body and listen to the beeps and whirrs of the machines attached to her.

"Can you tell me anything?" My eyes never leave Sweet Lou's face.

"I'll go find her ICU nurse. They can walk you through this."

"I'd rather hear it from you. Whatever you can tell me."

"She's not an ER patient anymore." The sound of her footsteps comes closer as she re-enters the room. "I can only tell you what I know from when she was there. Things might have changed. You must speak with the care team here."

"I promise. But it's been one hell of a long night and I'd appreciate hearing something from someone."

"The ER sent her for an MRI. There's no skull fracture, or bleeding in the brain. That's really good news. She has a moderate head injury."

"What is that? Like a concussion?"

"Yes."

"I've had a concussion before. A few of them. But I've never passed out from one. Well, not for more than a few seconds anyway." I swallow hard. "Why is she still out cold?"

"Everybody's different," Macy explains. "And

while she hasn't woken up, she has displayed elevated responses to stimuli. They're just not consistent. They'll monitor those responses here in ICU to make sure they keep improving until she wakes up."

"When will that be?" I ask, knowing she probably can't answer.

Macy shakes her head. "No one knows. If you want a best guess, you should talk to the ICU medical staff. A nurse I know here said that Dr. Cooper was attending today. She's top notch. Try and be here when she makes her rounds."

"When is that?"

"I don't know. This isn't my department. I'll ask Louise's nurse to come down and speak with you on my way out." Macy glances at her watch. "I should go. My shift started and a friend is covering for me. Be sure to ask about Dr. Cooper's schedule."

"Can I talk to her?" I blurt before Macy leaves. "Can she hear me?"

"It's very likely." Macy pauses next to me and looks down at Louise. "In the ER, she opened her eyes when our doctor said her name. But so far, only once. Louise also asked one of the ICU nurses treating her if she was there for change-of-shift report. When the nurse said no, that Louise was an ICU patient, she passed out again."

"And that's good?" These stories scare the hell out of me.

"Yes. It means she's responding to external stimuli. On some level, she can probably hear you. Although I wouldn't be shocked if she doesn't remember your conversation, or if any response she gives is nonsensical. But talk to her. Reassure her. Ask her to wake up. It's the best non-medical thing you can do for her right now."

"I'm not going anywhere," I reply. "And thanks, Macy. For everything."

"Right back at you, Usalv."

Macy pauses at the door and our eyes meet. Whatever bullshit we held against each other before this melts away in those few moments. She gives me a quick nod, then hurries down the corridor.

CHAPTER THIRTY-ONE

Oww. That...*hurt.*

What's her name again?

She's new and I've only worked with her a few times.

Damn.

Why can't I remember her name?

I'm usually good with names, especially at work.

Oww! My eyes fly open.

"Hey, rookie, watch the line would you please?" The sound of my own voice startles me. Not because I didn't intend to speak, but because I haven't heard it. Not in a very long time.

"Louise?" What's-her-name stops what she's doing and turns toward me.

"Your pen is catching on my IV line," I complain. "You're yanking on the needle every time you move."

"Sorry," she mutters and dislodges her pen from my line. "Can you keep your eyes open while you speak? Can you stay awake?"

"My eyes?" Why are they shut? I concentrate, hard, and open them. "Why is it so bright in here?"

"Let me dim the lights," what's-her-name tells me. "Is that better?" she asks after a minute.

"Ye-es." My eyes open slowly, and I look around. I'm at the hospital, in my department, but I'm not working. "Why am I lying down? What's happened?"

"Take it easy, Louise. You're in the ICU. You've had a concussion and you're just coming out of it."

"A concussion?"

"Yes, do you remember what happened?"

"No." Of this I'm certain. "Not a thing."

"That's okay, Louise. It's normal." She consoles me with a gentle pat to my arm. The arm with the IV in it. "I'm going get your stats really quick and let one of the docs know you're up."

"Pra...Pre-yah..." I mutter with miserable success.

"Priyanka. I'm Priyanka."

"Right." That's not a hard name to say. What the hell's wrong with me? "Thank you, Priyanka."

There's a clinical pause while she examines me and the machines monitoring my condition. When my numbers are collected, she starts to leave, but turns around at the door.

"Oh, and your...boyfriend? He went to get a coffee. He said he'd be right back. Can you say his name for me? I'm having trouble with it."

"Uew-sa-lav," I say it perfectly.

"Great. Thanks. You know, he's been here since you arrived," she tells me in a cheerful voice.

"Oh." Is that good? I don't remember. Priyanka's news fills me with uncertainty. She shoots me a puzzled look, then gives me a quick smile before leaving.

Usalv is here? Yeah, he's here. My memory is messed up, but somehow I already knew before she told me. The sensation of my brain being offline and suddenly functioning in overdrive to catch up with life in real time jars me like a bolt of electricity. My temples start to pulse as I focus on my memories of what happened.

The party. The...sex. My declaration of love. Usalv's fast exit.

Pain floods my temples. But is it real or a memory? My thumbs press hard into my skull as I force myself to push through the excruciating fog.

That bitch in Usalv's kitchen... Too many whiskey shots... My exit from the house...

Sadness. Fear. Confusion. Terror.

I scream. It's not a glass shattering tirade, but everything around me stills in anticipation before it reacts.

"Louise?" A large hand strokes my forehead. "Are you okay, sweetheart? Can you open your eyes?"

I open my eyes to see large cobalt ones studying me with intense concern.

"Hey, Sweet Lou." Usalv sits in a gray chair next to the bed and smiles at me.

"Hi-i." It's good to see him, even though deep down something seems off. "What happened to me?"

His expression becomes a mix of anger and concern that he's quick to mask. "You had a concussion."

"I'm aware. Priyanka, my nurse, told me. How did I get a concussion? Do you know?"

"Yes," he says then pauses. "But maybe we should wait until your nurse gets back." Usalv looks over his shoulder at the door.

"Well if you don't want to tell me, then call her please. Trying to remember what happened makes my head feel like someone's splitting it in two with a hand axe." I lean forward to clutch both sides of my head.

"All right, I'll tell you." He reaches for the call button next to my bed and presses it. "The night of the party, after you left the house and went for a walk, you were attacked." His voice is calm and certain as his eyes study my expression.

My eyes shift away from the intensity of his gaze

and focus on the far wall, trying to take in what he told me.

"That explains why the last thing I remember is hellish terror," I reply. I look down at my lower body. "Was it...sexual?"

"No. No." He plants a chaste kiss on my forehead and rubs my cheek so hard it almost hurts. "I would never let that happen." He presses his forehead into mine. "As it is, I damn near killed him."

"You were there." It's a fact. I don't remember, but somehow, I know.

"Not for all of it." His voice is remorseful. "When you didn't come back, I got worried and went looking for you. I'd almost given up." His face looks strained at the memory. "But then I heard...fighting."

My brain processes his words. They force me to wonder if I'll ever remember what happened. Part of me isn't sure that I'd want to. But some things about that night come back to me.

"What about you? You were in bad shape after your Pay-Per-View. Did...*he* hurt you?"

"No. The guy had you on the ground, but he took one hell of a beating for trying to keep you there." Usalv's voice is distant. "The broken nose, the dislocated jaw"—he shakes his head—"that wasn't me, Louise."

"You mean...I did those things to him?" My

memory fails me. "But he still kept coming? Why would he do that?"

"Someone broke my nose in a fight before," Usalv tone is almost casual. "If there's not much blood flowing down your throat, you can keep going. I won that match. This guy was either in a fit of rage or amped up on something or both."

"Are you sure it was me who did that?"

"Positive. I broke his ribs and ankle. Was trying to avoid his head because I didn't want him to pass out." He pauses. "I wanted him to hurt for a while after what he did to you."

"Oh my God." A long time passes while the weight of his words sinks in. They feel like an anchor around my neck. "Thank you. For coming after me." My throat swallows hard before I continue. "But why did you come? And how did you know I wasn't okay?"

"I didn't know." He breaks eye contact and stares past me. "I wanted to talk to you and got sick of waiting for you to get back."

"You...wanted to talk to me?" My mood turns optimistic. "About what?"

His hand stills on my forehead, then withdraws. "I wanted to apologize."

"Apologize?" I grasp his hand. "For what?"

"Everything." He shrugs. "The argument we had before I left for Pittsburgh. The party. Kylie. Lots of things."

"Oh," I reply. "That. Don't worry about it. I've forgotten it. Literally." I try to laugh but it sounds hollow.

Usalv responds with a stilted, wordless smile.

"Is there anything else you want to discuss?" I ask.

There's an awkward pause while I wait for him to mention what happened between us in my bedroom that night, to acknowledge my feelings for him, to tell me he feels the same way. But the more time passes, the more awkward it feels, until it approaches weirdness. Panic wells inside me until it bursts.

"Why are you crying, Louise? Stop that. Please." His voice becomes anxious.

"I'm sorry." I rub my eyes with balled fists, fueled by ferocious embarrassment. "I don't know what's wrong with me." It's a lie. His silence just delivered a soul crushing blow and my ability to manage emotions is extremely fucked up at the moment.

"Sudden mood changes can be expected for a while, Mr. Markovski," a voice calls from the doorway. "It might not be possible for Louise to explain her feelings."

Dr. Gayle Cooper stands in the doorway, watching us with dark ebony eyes over the maroon rims of her geometric eye glass frames. She's worked trauma ICU since before me, and she's among the best docs here.

"What should I do?" Usalv asks her in a concerned voice.

"Remain calm. And most of all, be patient," she advises. "This might go on for a while."

Usalv nods and gives me a reassuring pat. "It's going to be fine. You'll see." He smoothes the hair on my forehead then rubs away my tears with his thumb pads. "You haven't had a chance to speak to the doctor yet. Do you want me to stay?"

"No." Right now I want him far away from me. It doesn't make sense, but that's what I'm feeling. "It's all good. Give me some time with Dr. Cooper, okay?"

"Sure. If that's what you want." He seems surprised as he turns away and looks at Dr. Cooper. "I'll leave you two alone."

"Thanks, Usalv. I'll see you later." My voice is on automatic pilot.

"Of course," he replies and squeezes my hand. He releases it quickly and nods at the doctor before exiting the room.

"Hello, Louise." She approaches my bedside. "It's nice to see you up."

"Hello, Dr. Cooper."

"Gayle. Please."

"Thank you. Gayle." Though we've often worked the same shifts, we've not spoken much outside of our work. It's weird and strangely comforting to talk to her like this.

"How do you feel, Louise? Any pain?" she asks after a quick glance at my electronic chart.

It takes me a few seconds to answer. "My body is...sore. From running, fighting, getting hit. But what really sucks are the headaches that come whenever I try to concentrate or remember what happened that night."

"I'll make sure to prescribe something for pain." She nods. "But you shouldn't push it right now. You know that, right?" She tips her head and long gray dread locks frame the rims of her glasses.

I shrug in a helpless gesture. "What does that mean?"

"I like your stats. I like what I'm seeing here right now." She gives a sage, reassuring nod. "Your prognosis is good. But you need to give yourself time to heal. You know that, right?"

I know she's right, and she knows I know it. "What exactly does that look like?"

Dr. Cooper pauses, then pulls up a chair next to me and settles into it. "I'm going to recommend a month of full-time, outpatient treatment. Your treatment will include neurocognitive evaluations and therapies for symptoms you might have that we don't know about, or that might develop after you leave. It also includes a patient support group, which no one thinks they need, but everyone ends up admitting helps."

"A whole month?" I'm stunned.

"To start with," she confirms. "We'll need to see how it goes."

"But, but..." My head starts to hurt. "What about my job? What about school?"

"Take it easy." Dr. Cooper pats my hand gently. "You'll need a medical leave of absence from both. You're probably looking at three months off from work. Your job is both physically and mentally demanding. You've got to be a hundred percent before you can come back."

"Understood." My response embodies her clinical dreariness. "What about school?"

Dr. Cooper gives me another sage nod and pats my hand before she speaks. "That will take longer." Her voice grows quiet. "As you know, we need to limit high level cognitive tasks for a while. And graduate medical studies are about as high level as it gets."

The room stills as I process the news. "How long?" My eyes well with tears.

"A guess would be at least three months, possibly longer. Again, with reevaluation and follow up. You should be able to get a full refund for the term." She reaches into her pocket and pulls out a business card. "I've taught in that program and have colleagues that do. If you run into problems, call me."

"Thank you, Gayle." My tears start to flow again.

Dr. Cooper waits a few moments, then continues, "Your prognosis is good, Louise. You've got your whole life ahead of you. Your job and a great career, and people who care about you. You've had a lot of visitors, and that doesn't include the fine-looking man who's clocked more hours in ICU than me since you've arrived." Gayle and I exchange smiles. "You've got a life worth fighting to get back to you. You've seen it happen. You can get yours back too. You know that, right?"

"Yeah. I know that." There's a lot going on that was taking a toll on me before this happened, but it looks like my brain is going to be okay. Someday. That's huge.

For the time since waking up, I feel hopeful.

CHAPTER THIRTY-TWO

I squeeze the box of the engagement ring through the fabric of my jeans as I approach the entrance to Sweet Lou's hospital room. It's a rose gold vintage ring, with a big round diamond surrounded by smaller ones along the setting and around the band. I keep picturing her expression when I give it to her, and how it will look on her long thin finger.

The thought makes me smile.

When I returned after the doctor left, she'd gone off to sleep. The nurse told me it was a good time for me to go home and rest. Confused and troubled about my future with Louise, I walked the whole way. It took me over an hour, but I wasn't it really in a hurry. As my head started to clear, I passed an old-school jewelry store, and this ring—*our* ring—was in the window.

Just like that, I knew what to do. I hope she likes it.

"Louise?" My voice is just louder than a whisper as I call her name from the doorway.

She's sound asleep, lying slightly elevated on her back. The sight fills me with disappointment and relief all at once. After entering the room, I lift one of the visitor's chairs and set it down by her bedside, then settle in and wait for her to wake up.

Over the last few days, studying her face while she sleeps has become a habit, a way to pass the endless hours in a hospital room while waiting for the slow changes you pray will take place. Her demeanor is different today. Sweet Lou's facial features are more relaxed, the tense lines around her mouth are gone, along with the deep crease between her eyes.

I rub the back of my hand along her forearm and sigh. Louise's arm bristles, and it makes me grateful, especially after all those days she didn't respond to anything.

"Hey," she says without opening her eyes.

"Hey back," I reply. "Didn't mean to wake you."

"You didn't. Not really. I was starting to get up." Her eyes open cautiously. "Ow. Can you dim the lights, please?"

"Sure." I study the numerous gauges and gadgets on the wall above her bed before giving up and walking over to the dimmer switch by the door.

"Better?" I ask as the lighting takes on a dusk-like quality.

"Perfect. Thanks." She sits up and focuses her attention on me.

I scratch my fingers against the ring box in my pocket, holding it in place through the fabric of my pants as I settle down beside her.

"You look good. Really good." It's true. "How do you feel today?"

"Much better," she confesses. "They'll probably move me out of ICU soon and send me home either tomorrow or the next day."

"That's good news." I stroke her hair and smile. "It will be good to have you home."

There's an awkward pause as she shifts away from me and tries to sit up. "Yeah. About that. I was hoping to ask you for a favor."

"Sure. Ask away."

Sweet Lou takes a deep breath and her body coils with determination. "If you haven't rented out your ground floor one bedroom apartment yet, I'd like to rent it from you. At market rate."

"My...what? Why?" I stammer.

"It's like I told you the night of the party," she explains in a stoic voice. "That I want to move out of your house. Despite all of this"—she gestures around the hospital room—"nothing's really changed."

"Nothing? Are you for real?" I release my grip on the engagement ring in my pants.

Louise sighs. "Usalv, you saved my life. I will always be grateful to you for that. And you will always hold a special place in my heart. But I was right about you in the beginning. I just let myself get carried away. We both did."

"What are you talking about?" This feels like some crazy, surreal experience.

"Remember the first time we amped things up? In the gym closest? Before we got down to it, I told you that you were a really nice man, and that it wouldn't be fair for me to read into that just because you didn't act like a Neanderthal." She shakes her head. "And then you gave me an orgasm, and that's exactly what I did. I read into things."

"That's not true." I rise from the chair, and I start pacing the small room.

"I think it is. You're an extraordinary human being, Usalv, who's been extraordinarily kind and giving. That's just who you are, and I've got to stop confusing that for...deeper feelings."

Her determination makes me bristle. It also scares the hell out of me.

"Are you telling me that you think all of this has just been altruism?" My voice is louder than usual. "Of course I have feelings for you, Louise. Deep ones. Stop talking crazy."

Louise takes a long, slow breath. "Maybe. But you don't love me."

"I never said that I didn't." Anger mixed with desperation creeps into my tone.

"You never said you did, either." Her words are followed by pin drop silence in the room.

I grip the sides of my neck while I resume pacing. How can I tell her what she wants to hear? That night, before she left the house and was attacked, I'd come very close to saying 'I love you' out loud to her. And what happened? She'd damn near died.

Those words are a curse coming from me.

"Okay, let's come back to this in a minute." I'm desperate to change the subject. "Is now even a good time for you to move? Especially given your physical condition?"

"Yes." She meets my eyes with a steady gaze. "For both mental and physical reasons. The one bedroom is much smaller, and it's on the first floor. It will be much easier for me to navigate."

"And mentally?" I prompt.

"Being able to live on my own will be a huge boost mentally." She hesitates before continuing. "And having some distance will give us both some time to adjust, to figure out what's next."

"Okay," I reply in a defeated voice. "There's no way I'm going to stand in the way of your getting better. Take the other apartment. I can have your things moved in the next day or so. You really didn't have that much."

Louise nods back at me. "Thank you, Usalv."

"You're welcome, Sweet Lou."

Just like that, my marriage proposal goes up in flames. I feel like a lost ship in the middle of the night. No engines, no lights, no direction.

Fuck.

CHAPTER THIRTY-THREE

"Tell me you've got beer in the house." Macy insists after I open the front door of my apartment.

"Sorry, girl. Not until after therapy's over. Got a ginger-ale though."

"Ugh. That's nothing but a tease." Macy steps through the doorway, her hands full of carry out and a beautiful bouquet of flowers. "I'll take one, though."

"Sure. Come in, please."

"Should I just put these with the rest of the collection?" Macy holds out a bouquet while nodding toward several others resting on a long thin table that helps separate my kitchen from the living room.

"You really didn't have to bring me flowers." I scold her a bit as I take the bouquet and give her a hug of thanks. "A Schwartzy with extra pickles and fries is more than enough."

Macy laughs. "Same old Louise." She hands me one of the plastic bags hanging from her arm. "For you, my dear."

I take the plastic carry out bag, then wrap my arms around her again. "It's so good to see you. Thanks for coming over."

"You're welcome." She hugs me back. "I miss you a lot. It's great to have Paul back, but I wish we had more time." Macy sighs. "Hopefully, when things get back to normal, we'll be able to hang out a little more."

Normal? What the hell does that even mean anymore?

"That would be great," I reply. "Do you want to eat at the table, or on the couch?"

"Couch, please. Just like old times." Macy looks at the fashionable sofa and tables. "Only a little more chic. When did you get these?"

"I'm renting them. Same with the kitchen furniture. And the TV." I'd selected them from the website of a company with really high ratings before I'd been discharged from the hospital. They had arrived here the next day. It turned out better than expected.

"This is...cozy." Macy gives the place an appraising look while I get two ginger-ales from the fridge of my tiny kitchen. "Cozy, but very nice."

"Thanks. It's working out well for me." My tiny kitchen is part of an open floor plan that includes the living room. The front door opens right into the living room, too. It's all done to maximize the use of the small space, which makes it easy for me to get around.

"How's therapy going?" she asks as we settle into the living room and dig out our food from Styrofoam containers.

"Going well, actually." Unable to resist, I take a big bite of my sandwich before continuing. "Next week is the last week full time. Then it starts to taper down over the following month. I feel a lot better. I'm more sure of myself."

"That's great." Now it's Macy's turn to dive in to her sandwich. "How do you like living alone?"

"Better than when I first moved to Chicago. But time will tell. I've had a lot more visits than I expected. But that's people looking in on me since... You know. When that stops happening, who knows how I'll feel."

"True." Macy takes another bite of her sandwich and chews slowly. After a few minutes, she speaks again. "How's Usalv?"

My blood pressure spikes at the mention of his name. "He's good. Good. Twice a day he checks in with me. Once in the morning, again in the evening after he returns from the gym."

"That is good." She reassures me. "Are you two... going to try and patch things up?"

"There's nothing to patch up really. We're just two people after two different things."

Macy shoots me a puzzled look. "Have you had sex with him since you got out of the hospital?"

"No." I admit, confused by her question.

"But he comes to check on you at least twice a day?"

"Yes."

"Lou, that doesn't sound like someone who's just looking for a no strings horizontal workout."

"I can't tell you what he wants, Macy. You'll have to ask him. I can only tell you what he doesn't want. And that's me."

"Whoa. That's really harsh."

"It is harsh. It's also very painful. Can we change the subject please?"

Macy shrugs. "Of course."

"Thanks. Because as long as you're here, I'd like your opinion on something."

"What is it, Lou?"

"I hate asking you this, especially after the big shit storm it caused the last time we discussed it." My chest heaves under the weight of a deep breath." But do you think Mike Daughtry would still be willing to help me find another place?"

Macy's mouth widens into an oval and her sandwich falls into her lap with a splat. "Really? Are you sure?"

"Yes. Provided I'm not required to date him or live next door to him. Or live in his apartment."

Macy smiles. "I don't think you'll have to worry about that. He's trying to fill that slot with someone else."

A thousand pound weight lifts from my shoulders. "Kudos to Mike and his new woman. Believe me, no one is happier to hear the news. But...you don't think my request will cause him problems on the relationship front, do you?"

"No," Macy assures me. "But why do you want to move from here?"

"Because I'm still in love with Usalv. And there's nothing worse than being in love with a man who only wants platonic sex. He keeps getting his all the while repeating his disclaimer, reminding you how great things are and that there's no need to change them. Sometimes I can hardly breathe." The admission tears through my soul.

"Back up a minute." Macy interrupts. "Where did you get the idea that he doesn't love you back?"

"The night I was attacked, I told him that I loved him. Before I was attacked."

"Really?" Macy's voices raises in shock. "What happened?"

"He got dressed in world record time and left. That's why I was walking the streets with high heels at one in the morning. I couldn't stand to be near him after that."

"That doesn't make any sense," Macy tells me after a long, stunned silence. "At the hospital, he never left your side. Every time I came up to check on you, he was there. I know he has feelings for you. I've seen it."

"Whether he does or doesn't, he sure the hell won't admit it to me." Tears flow freely from my eyes. In the last month, there have been so many tears that I just let them flow unchecked now. "It hurts being around him, knowing he doesn't feel the same way. And I've been hurt enough this year."

"Yes, you have," Macy assures me. "I'll speak to Mike for you. Don't worry. I'm sure he'll help out."

CHAPTER THIRTY-FOUR

"Madman? We need to talk." Mike Daughtry calls to me from across the gym.

As I sit up on the weight bench and reach for the towel tucked inside the waistband of my shorts, Lucky Mike beelines over to me, his expression a mask of irritation and impatience.

"What is it, Mike?" I ask when he reaches me.

"You want to do this here?" He looks around the weight training area.

It's about ten in the morning and I'm just getting started, while the amateurs and before-work crowd have all but cleared out. It's been over a month since Louise was attacked and things still aren't back to normal, at home or here.

I wonder if they ever will be.

Louise moved right into the downstairs apartment after arriving home from the hospital. A company dropped off some rental furniture, and Louise paid them extra to drag her stuff out of my house. Within an hour of being home, she was gone again.

"Sure, I guess." There's not much I give a shit about these days. "What's up?"

Mike takes a quick look around the gym and when he sees we're by ourselves, shoots me a nasty-ass glare. "You are a major fucking dumbass, Markovski. You know that?"

"Christ, Mike. Tell me what you really think." I get up from the weight bench and lean against the stacks. "Who the hell pissed in your cornflakes today?"

"You know, it took a lot for me to give up on Louise without acting like a total asshole." His hostile eyes bore into mine. "But I told myself, and so did others, that I was being a good guy, respecting both of your feelings, letting it go. Giving up on her without a fight, gentleman-like." He snorts in disgust.

"That's all true. What's your point?" I remain calm and certain while my teeth grind the tender flesh of my inner cheek into hamburger, checking the hot flash of temper that courses through me.

"My point? Here's my point. Fuck. You." Mike flips me the bird, jabbing at me in rhythm with his words. "You blew it for both of us, dumbass."

"What the hell are you talking about?" My mouth tastes like blood.

"I'm going to tell you this." Mike starts pacing in circles. "Man to man, the way you *didn't* tell me when you moved Louise into your house up the back stairs like a thief in the night."

"Tell me what?" I stand to my full height and take two steps toward him.

"Louise asked me to find her a new place." Mike's hands rest on his waist. "Like, yesterday. Sooner if possible."

"What?" My voice fills with shock as the blood drains from my face.

"Yeah. And I'm going to help her." He tells me without flinching. "Not because I still want her. Hell no. God knows that I couldn't take much more of this anyway." Mike shakes his head. "But I'm going to do it because I feel sorry for her."

It's my turn to flinch. I back off Mike and lean over the barbell and try to catch my breath.

"How the hell do you fuck something like that up?" Mike throws his hands in the air. "Fuck that, don't answer me. I'm not sure I want to know."

"The truth is, I don't myself." I shudder as a deep sigh erupts from me.

"Jesus, you had her in your house, in your bed." He spits out in a mixture of clueless exasperation. "All you had to do was keep her there."

"From the moment I saw her, not slept with her, I haven't even looked at another woman, let alone been in anyone else's bed." I shake my head in misery.

"She loves you, asshole." Mike voice becomes calm. "Or at least she did."

"And when was that? When I let her stay in my house without cashing her rent checks because she had no other place to go? How about when I dragged that sick fuck off her and beat his ass into next fucking Christmas? Or staying at the hospital until she woke up?" I glare at Mike with a helpless expression. "Don't my actions count for anything? Because if they don't, then maybe I'm not the right man for her."

"Hell, we both know how the goddamned posers get laid," Mike replies. "They whip out the I-love-yous faster than their dicks and soon they're getting all they can handle. Depending on how fast a woman wises up, they can get a lot of mileage out of it, too."

"I've never lied to a woman about loving her to get sex." It's the truth. "Louise is the first woman who's so damn obsessed with hearing the words."

"It's true that some of us don't need to work it much to get sack time. But it's a mixed blessing. Especially when you fall for a woman who insists on certain conditions. It can seem... Overwhelming? Demanding? Compared to how easy it was with others before her." Mike's words ring with truth and unfamiliar wisdom.

"I check on her twice a day, every day. Just to see if she's okay."

"So you do love her, don't you?" Mike's voice is calm and leading.

"I never kiss or touch her, or bring up sex to gauge her interest."

"Mmm." He nods. "Have you told Louise that you love her?"

"Not in those words," I admit.

"Right. That's a big hell no." Mike cracks his knuckles. "When she decided to move out, what did you say?"

"The first time Louise mentioned it, she was upset and I told her we should talk after she calmed down. Instead she took a walk and got attacked." Guilt sickens me from the inside. "In the hospital, she asked to rent my downstairs apartment. Louise insisted it would be best for her recovery, so I did what she asked."

Mike remains silent for a long time. "So you never told Louise you loved her, or that you wanted her to stay?"

"No." My mood turns somber.

"Jesus Christ. Madman, you're a good guy, but a real dumbass." Mike's words are harsh, but his voice is filled with pity.

"Fuck that. I went over to the hospital all set to

propose. But then Louise said she wanted to move out. There didn't seem to be much point after that." I shut my eyes at the devastation a *no* from Sweet Lou would have caused.

"Hold up a minute." Mike shoots me a surprised scowl. "You were going to propose? Like, with a ring on a bent knee, propose?"

My only response is a silent nod.

"Jesus fucking Christ." Mike smacks his hand against the barbell. "You can't let her leave without knowing that. You need to sort this shit out and fast. Pick up the pace already."

"I don't know. Maybe the whole thing is just isn't meant to be."

Mike sighs, then leans over the weight bar next to me. "Women need to hear the words, Madman. That's how they're wired."

"What if she says no?"

"What if she doesn't?"

CHAPTER THIRTY-FIVE

"Hey lady, there's some big guy out there who won't let us load your things," the mover with a gray goatee complains from the doorway.

"What?" It's nearly noon and Usalv should be at the gym now. What's he doing here?

"Says he needs to talk to you first." His barrel chest lifts his entire body when shrugs. "You want to take care of this, or should I call the cops?"

"No, don't do that. I'll be right down." I fumble with the tape on the moving box, smoothing it down before squeezing past the barrel-chested mover standing on the porch checking his smartphone.

Damn. I'd hoped to avoid a confrontation. Being so physically close to Usalv while remaining emotionally distant has become intolerable. Over the last month, he's brought food and picked-up prescriptions from the pharmacy. He stops in twice a day. But through it all, our interactions are brimming with a sober sterility that's killing me.

Down by the street, Usalv paces alongside the moving truck. It's a crisp fall day, but he's only wearing a black T-shirt over his dark blue denim jeans. His black leather court shoes make scuffing sounds on the pavement as he turns around to stride back in the other direction. He's so preoccupied that I'm almost run over after stopping in his path.

"Louise." He stands straight, quickly masking the nervous surprise in his eyes.

"Usalv." I take a deep breath, hold it for a few seconds, then let it go. "What are you doing?"

"What am I doing?" He makes an open-handed gesture toward the moving van. "What the hell are you doing?"

"We both knew from the start that this was only temporary." I fold my arms. "Right?"

"Did we?" Usalv's eyebrows arch so high that his scar almost touches his hairline.

"Yeah, we did."

He starts to stay something, then shakes his head and resumes pacing. At the ramp of the moving van, he turns back around and continues before stopping a few feet in front of me. "Okay, so maybe the real estate part of this was a little shady, but what about the rest of it?"

"I- I…don't know what you mean."

"Liar," he goads me with a raspy whisper. "You can't leave. Not like this."

"I can't stay." My voice starts to crack. "Not like this."

"Like how?"

"Like in an open-ended, casual relationship." God, don't cry. Please don't cry. "I can't stay here, close to you, living like this and waiting for you to remind me one day that this wasn't for real."

"Shit." He shakes his head as he looks down at the sidewalk. "This whole damn thing stopped being casual a long time ago. I think we both know that."

"No, we both don't know that," I reply. "You know how I feel. I don't know how you feel. Hell, maybe you don't even know yourself."

"Really? I know how you feel? Because you told me and that's that? 'Pay no attention to the man behind the curtain.'"

"What?" My throat goes dry as I recognize the reference.

"I wanted to talk about what happened in your room the night of the party." He shoves those huge fists down into the pockets of his dark denim jeans. "But you needed some fresh air and went for a walk instead." Usalv closes his eyes for a moment. "At the hospital, you announced your plan to move downstairs. You asked, but you didn't discuss. And now, you're moving out at a time you'd thought I'd be gone. Your feelings are as clear as mud to me."

"How did you know I was leaving today?"

"Mike." He tells me in a quiet, gentle voice. "Even he thinks I'm getting the shaft in all of this. Which says a hell of a lot, by the way."

A rush of guilty fury courses through me. "That's not fair. It wasn't his place to say anything."

"Fair? Shit, Louise. If I've been untruthful about my feelings, you've been dishonest about your desires. How fair is that?"

"That's not true." My defense sounds unconvincing even to me.

Usalv reaches out and cradles my head between his two large hands. "Do you really want to move out of here? To break up with me? To stop having sex?" His eyes bore into mine, refusing to let me look away. "Am I that shady? Is this all that unpleasant? Because if that's how you really feel, then go ahead and leave. I won't stop you."

"You know it's not," I confess.

"How do I know that?" he presses me. "The same way you know I don't love you? Fuck that."

"That's not fair. I told you when I moved in, friends with benefits didn't work for me. You said let's see how things go. When our careers started to tank, and I said we should take a step back, you stormed off. When I said that I loved you"—my voice cracks—"you set a world record for the speed-dressing sprint. You *know* how I feel. You just don't know you feel about my feelings."

"I know how I feel. It's just hard to say it the way you want me to."

"Why?"

"Because everyone in my life—my mother, sisters, even my first love—told me that they loved me just before they left for good. And when I even considered saying it the night *you* stormed off, I damn near lost you."

Oh God. "I had no idea about any of that. Why didn't you tell me?" I ask.

"Because, because, how could you not know how I felt?" His voice is filled with disbelief. "The things I did for you, what we…did together, all we've been through. Can you honestly say you had no clue about how I felt?"

"I was scared. And hurt the night of the party." I admit, turning away from him. "All I could think about was getting away. Away from the hurt of not being loved. And the fear that if I stayed things wouldn't end well for me."

"It sucks feeling pressured, doesn't it?" He wraps his arms around my waist from behind me and whispers into my ear. "You know you have to do something, but you have no fucking clue what the right thing to do is, and you're worried anything you try will blow up in your face."

"It does suck." I stroke the powerful forearm gently folded around my abdomen. "The last thing I ever wanted was for you to feel pressured into doing something you didn't want. I'm sorry, Usalv."

"I'm sorry too, Louise. For ever giving you a reason to doubt me." There's a long pause and I feel one of his hands leave my waist to dig inside his pocket. His chest heaves against my back before he holds his breath. The sound of a spring-loaded snap brings my gaze down to a velvet red jewelry box cradled in his large hand.

"Oh my God," I spin around to face him. "Oh my God." My chest tightens with shock, excitement and…hope. "What is this?"

"It's an engagement ring," he explains in his calm, matter-of-fact way. "I'd hoped to propose in a different setting, but since your stuff is out on the curb, I needed to change things up a bit." Usalv swallows hard. "I hope you like it."

"It's beautiful." I feel along the edges of tiny stones surrounding a larger oval diamond. It's unique and attractive without being too ornate. "It's perfect. Something I'd have picked out for myself. God, you really know me, don't you?"

"Don't leave, Louise. Please." Usalv pries the ring out of the box. "I don't want to be with anyone else. Or live without you. We can get married tomorrow or thirty years from now. Whatever you want. I…just need for my feelings to be clear, and if this doesn't do it then I'm all out of ideas."

"Oh, this does it." My voice cracks and tears well up in my eyes. I watch as he slides the ring onto the third finger of my left hand.

"It's a little big," he tells me, twisting it around my finger.

"It's fine," I smile. "I'm used to that."

"Then say yes, Louise."

"Yes."

EPILOGUE

Two years later...

"You got this, Louise?" Charlie looks at Usalv's bleeding nose as he shoves him onto a ringside stool.

I gently probe Usalv's face to check for a break. Fortunately, he doesn't have one. "I got this. Thanks." The MMA cutman nods but sticks close and watches me.

"Hon, is the room spinning?" I ask him.

"Yeah. But it's slowing down now," Usalv replies.

I don't like the sound of that. "Okay. We'll check on that in a few minutes."

Usalv took a hard knee shot to his nose when he went for the takedown. Thankfully, he saw it coming and protected his face. But now it's bleeding profusely and I've got another four and half minutes to get him ready for the next round.

"Does it hurt, hon?" I ask.

"Um…yeah," Usalv answers stoically. Even with all the crowd noise, the pain in his voice comes through clearly.

"Well, get in a happy place, because treating it isn't going to be a day at the spa, either."

"I could use a day at the spa," Usalv tells me.

"Couldn't we all? Hold still." I apply a cotton swab soaked in adrenaline hydrochloride to the cut, then press his nostril firmly against it.

"Oh fuck." Usalv makes a hissing sound as he draws in air between clenched teeth.

I'm an apprentice cutman, who gets cut a lot of slack. Cutmen treat fighters' wounds during fights, and my background as a trauma nurse comes in handy.

It was several months after the attack when I went back to work, but only part-time. Part-time wasn't enough, but full-time was still too much and that's when the idea of being a cutman came to us. From the start, my apprenticeship under Charlie seemed more like a partnership because we've learned so much from each other.

School took even longer. For some reason, I couldn't listen to a lecture and write notes at the same time. A cognitive impairment that eventually faded after about a year. Strangely enough it cleared up about a week after we got married. Usalv joked that if I hadn't been so particular about the wedding details, I'd have been cured much sooner.

"What's the damage, Lou?" Rodgers barks at me.

"It's not broken. He'll be ready to go in a few minutes."

"Good." Rodgers leans over the other side of Usalv and barks strategy and pointers at as I work.

Usalv and Rodgers patched things up right after he proposed to me. In its own way, their professional relationship is a lot like a marriage. Rodgers has put in as much time and effort on Usalv's career as Usalv himself. Of course, Usalv's image and reputation is now synonymous with the DeadFall MMA brand. Hell, they even have their own merchandise now.

"Terence, I need to finish up."

"Sure, Louise." Coach Rodgers steps away, and assesses the opponent and his corner.

"What's your name?" I ask Usalv.

"Oh shit. Really?" He rolls his eyes at me. "Usalv Markovski."

"What's your wife's name?" I continue undaunted.

"Louise Becker-Markovski," he replies.

"How many kids do you have?"

"One on the way."

"Where are you?"

"In Las Vegas."

"What are you doing here?"

"Getting grief from my bossy cutman."

"Hon, trust me. Concussions are not fun. Don't be a pain in the ass."

"I'm at the World Championships, defending my title," he answers in as sober voice.

"Good job. Hang in there, love." I smile. "He got lucky with this pop to the nose."

It's round three of the title match, and Usalv is defending his belt for what we've privately decided is the final time. During our perfect honeymoon on the Turks and Caicos Islands, we fleshed out a plan for our lives together. If I were ever physically capable, I wanted to finish my anesthetist training. But regardless, I wanted to be pregnant by thirty.

Usalv had ideas of his own. Being a fighter had provided him an early escape from a life he didn't want or choose for himself. Now that he'd escaped, he felt like being a pro fighter had served its purpose. There were other opportunities he wanted to pursue while he was still young.

"Two minutes," Charlie whispers to me.

"He'll be ready," I reply.

Usalv is now heavily invested in his uncle's property business, and things are going well. His uncle is ready to check out, and when Usalv retires from fighting, he'll take over.

Usalv's personal real estate investments have turned out well, too. In fact, we've rented the other large unit in the Brownstone to Macy and Paul. We love our new neighbors, who we see every day when we're home.

We're pregnant. Three and half months along, and we're both overjoyed. It's a boy. We've even picked out a name. Patrick Usalv Markovski. For my Dad. And for my son's dad.

No one knows yet. If Usalv retains his title, we'll announce it at the victory celebration. If he loses then, we'll start telling our family and friends.

"Sweet Lou, are you done yet?" Usalv asks.

"Just about." I pull the enswell off and dab the wound with some petroleum jelly mixed with adrenaline hydrochloride. "There you go."

Usalv sits up, using his final seconds to stare with determined focus into the octagon. He glances quickly over at his twenty-five-year-old opponent, who's already standing.

"Is the room still spinning?" I ask.

"No." He sits silently, assessing his opponent.

"Win or lose, we still have it all," I remind him.

"Damn right. As long as we get to go home together, that's all that matters."

"Go out there and kick that kid's ass. You got this, right?"

"Yeah, I got this." He flashes me a killer smile.

"I love you, Usalv."

"I love you, too, Louise."

The bell rings, and he's off like a shot. My warrior husband with the heart of gold.

REVIEWS HELP AUTHORS TO KEEP WRITING BOOKS. IT'S THAT SIMPLE. PLEASE SHARE YOUR THOUGHTS ON BOOKBUB AND YOUR FAVORITE BOOKSELLERS WEBSITE. THANK YOU!

THE HEARTS SO FINE SERIES:

THE CASINO PLAYERS SAGA

When an affluent former maid agrees to pay her brothers gambling debts, she gets an offer she can't refuse from a wealthy casino owner.

CASINO PLAYERS TRILOGY BOXED SET, Available now!

Please note, this is a serial and all the episodes are intended to be read in the following order:

Book One, All In

Book Two, Double or Nothing

Book Three, Ante Up

ABOUT THE AUTHOR

Annabeth writes steamy contemporary romances that explore the edges of passion and possibility. Her stories contain characters who exude emotional awareness and authentic human weakness as they journey towards their happily ever afters.

Away from the keyboard, she loves to travel, read and bike, in addition to helping with school activities. She calls creative-friendly Austin, TX home, where her family and menagerie of pets keep her company while she's at the keyboard.

BB bookbub.com/profile/annabeth-saryu
f facebook.com/authorannabethsaryu
a amazon.com/author/annabethsaryu
P pinterest.com/annabethsaryu